PRODIGAL

PRODIGAL

ZARIA GARRISON

URBAN
CHRISTIAN

www.urbanchristianonline.net

Urban Books, LLC
1199 Straight Path
West Babylon, NY 11704

ISBN- 13: 978-1-60162-937-1
ISBN- 10: 1-60162-937-0

First Printing November 2009
Printed in the United States of America

10 9 8 7 6 5 4 3 2 1

This is a work of fiction. Any references or similarities to actual events, real people, living, or dead, or to real locales are intended to give the novel a sense of reality. Any similarity in other names, characters, places, and incidents is entirely coincidental.

Distributed by Kensington Corp.
Submit Wholesale Orders to:
Kensington Publishing Corp.
C/O Penguin Group (USA) Inc.
Attention: Order Processing
405 Murray Hill Parkway
East Rutherford, NJ 07073-2316
Phone: 1-800-526-0275
Fax: 1-800-227-9604

This story is dedicated in loving memory to
my beloved mother
Mrs. Lillie Mae Williams Garrison
May 27, 1935–August 31, 2007

Acknowledgments

First, and foremost, I must thank God, who is the head of my life and the true author of this book. I thank Him for giving me the gift of writing. I thank Him for transforming Gena into Zaria, so that my writing became for Him and about Him. I thank Him for trusting me with His words and allowing me to represent Him.

To my family, thank you for your support in all that I do. Thank you for reading, critiquing, and just being there throughout. To my son, John, thank you for seeing in me something you'd want to be. I love you.

To my friends and business partners, Ebony Farashuu, Kelli Little, and Sandra Poole, thank you for being a part of the process from the beginning to end. Ebony, your voice encouraged me and helped me to make the story the best it could be. Kelli, you helped me to find my ministry in the midst of the story line. Sandra, Miss Editor Lady, thank you for being the grammar police. I couldn't have completed this story without you. Most of all, thank you all for being a part of my dreams with *EKG Literary Magazine*. You ladies keep me grounded while helping me soar.

My cover models Lililita Forbes and Ilinita Johnson-Mack also known as Jumelle, of Music Man Dre Productions, I sincerely thank you both for agreeing to be the face of *Prodigal*. You ladies are phenomenal and I'm proud to be a part of what you do.

Joylynn Jossel and the Urban Christian team, thank you for believing in me when I had stopped believing in myself.

I must also thank Kendra Norman-Bellamy and the members of The Writer's Hut. Thank you for embracing me as family and helping me learn as a writer.

To the other authors under Urban Christian imprint, I appreciate your friendship and commitment to helping each of us excel. I am honored to share a label with each and every one of you.

To my former pastor and first lady, Dr. Thomas J. Bowman and Sister Susan Kingwood Bowman, thank you for showing me the example of a strong black man, with a beautiful woman by his side, who both love the Lord. You have no idea the things you've taught me or the ways you've touched my life; just for being you. I miss you so much, but I thank you for being a part of my life and helping me to grow.

Last but certainly not least, what can I say about the members of Soul City? It can't be explained, only experienced. Thank you for being who you are, no matter what. Each of you has touched me in some way, and for that I am grateful.

Part I

Chapter One

The cab driver slowly pulled up to the curb and stopped in front of the ranch style house. Phoebe peered out of the back window at the home she grew up in, and a cold chill ran down her spine. The windows surrounded by freshly painted yellow shutters looked like eyes staring at her soul, mocking her with secrets she did not want revealed. As the cab driver put the vehicle in park and waited for her to pay the fare flashing on his meter, Phoebe tried to come to grips with the realization that she was actually back at the place she had vowed never to return.

She had never wanted to come back, and certainly never had planned to, until the night she received a phone call from her sister as she was climbing into bed. "Hello?" she had mumbled sleepily.

"Phoebe, it's me, Phylicia. Mom's had another heart attack. This one is worse. You need to come home as soon as possible."

Her heart jumped into her throat as she sat up and asked, "Is she all right? Is she . . . Is she dead?"

She heard her sister sigh before answering her. "She's alive, but barely. It was a massive heart attack this time, not mild like the last one. You just need to come as soon as possible. I don't know why, but she's been asking for you."

"She's been asking for me? Well, I was planning to come home at Christmas anyway. Tell her that and just give her my love."

"Your love? Did you hear what I just said? Mom has had a severe heart attack and she's been asking to see you. It's barely spring, and Christmas is months away. You mean to tell me you are . . ." Phylicia stopped talking mid-sentence. "Never mind, you know what? I'm sorry I called you in the first place. Good night." Phoebe heard the phone slam down in her ear.

Three days later, she reluctantly dragged her tattered Louis Vuitton luggage off of a Greyhound bus and hailed a cab. It had taken her that long to sell off several pieces of her furniture and jewelry to buy a bus ticket. She'd hoped to make enough to fly home in style, but the old man at the flea market on the corner refused to even consider the prices she was asking. Taking a loss, she agreed to his extortion and took the money.

After finally climbing out of the backseat, Phoebe paid the cab driver and asked him to leave her luggage on the curb, though he offered to take it inside. She declined because she didn't want to risk him speaking with any of her family and telling them he had picked her up from the bus station. She looked down at her Diesel jeans and her last pair of Jimmy Choo pumps, then slowly walked up the driveway to her former home.

"Mom, who is that lady coming up the driveway?"

Phylicia Morgan motioned for her son to move over as she peered out of the front window and almost fainted. She recognized the woman coming up the driveway immediately. How could she miss the wide, swaying hips and cocoa skin, with her beautiful grey eyes hidden behind Jackie O sunglasses? "It's your Aunt Phoebe. Go open the door and help her with her things, sweetie."

Phylicia could barely believe her sister was really there. After hanging up on her a few nights ago, she'd told her husband Gary that she was sure her sister was not going to come home this time, either. She would be left alone to tend to their mother as always. Her sister was only good for the occasional phone call or Christmas card, and none of them had laid eyes on her in more than twelve years.

Born only three minutes apart, Phylicia and Phoebe were twins. Clinically speaking, they were identical. Their demeanor, attitude, style, and personalities were vastly different. Phoebe had always been the flighty twin, while Phylicia was the stable one. She had made excellent grades in school, and had been on the yearbook staff and student council while Phoebe, barely passing, had been on the drama team.

My sister has always been full of drama, Phylicia thought as she watched Phoebe flounce into the living room, followed closely by her sixteen-year-old son. He had been only four years old when Phoebe left and seemed in awe of his Auntie.

"Phyllie, girl is that you?" Phoebe yelled as soon as she was inside, opening her arms wide. Phylicia stood a few feet away and folded her arms across her breasts. "Hello, Phoebe. How are you?" she said coolly.

Phoebe slowly lowered her arms, keeping the fake smile on her face. "I'm fine; a little jet-lagged. The flight was really bumpy. How is Mother?"

"*Mom* is doing as well as can be expected. I thought you weren't coming. Why are you here?"

Ignoring her question, Phoebe turned her attention to her nephew, who'd been staring wide-eyed at her since the moment he saw her. "Who is this handsome young man?" she asked, practically singing the question.

"Of course you remember Gary Jr., my son." Phylicia looked over at her son. "Say hello to your auntie. Don't be rude Li'l G."

"This big man is Li'l G? Wow, when I left town you were just a baby. Come give me a hug." She opened her arms wide.

Li'l G looked over at his mother for approval before tentatively giving his aunt a hug. He released her, stepped back, and continued to stare.

"Well, what's wrong? Why do you keep gawking at me like that?" she asked.

"You look just like my mom except, well, you're gorgeous."

"What's that supposed to mean?" Phylicia asked.

"Sorry, Mom. I mean she has your face but it's all glamorous with makeup and everything. Not plain like yours. No offense, Mommy. You're beautiful too." He tried to backpedal.

Phylicia knew exactly what her son meant. She and Phoebe may have been identical twins, but Phoebe had always been the glamour girl. Almost from the day they reached puberty she'd begun spending hours practicing her hair and makeup skills. Phoebe could pick up any magazine, newspaper ad, or photo and perfect virtually any hairstyle and makeup trend with little effort. They both were five feet nine inches tall, although Phoebe claimed to be an inch taller. The two of them shared a glowing cocoa-colored skin tone with large, expressive grey eyes. Phylicia's hair was brushed down stiffly and pulled back into a very tight, prim and proper bun, while her sister sported a very long, curly and flowing weave that hung down her back. If they were to stand side by side, Phylicia thought they'd look like the before and after pictures on one of those makeover shows. She would be the before and Phoebe the after. However, as much as she hated to admit it, her son was right. Her sister was gorgeous.

"Why don't you take your aunt's luggage to the guest room?" Phylicia finally managed to mumble to her son.

Li'l G was a lean teen who had been taller than six feet since he was fourteen. He'd inherited his father's thick, black, curly hair along with his lean and muscular build. He proudly flexed, then grabbed the two bags and carried them up the staircase.

As he did, Phylicia watched her sister walk around the living room, seemingly taking it all in. She appeared to be in a trance in the room she'd left so long ago. Slowly, she picked up several pictures on the mantel, staring at each one and then returning it to its place. There was a long pause when she reached a photograph of their father, Pharrell Carson. A tall and muscular unpretentious man, he had loved his daughters dearly. Their mother had divorced him only weeks before their birth, but he'd always been an active part of the girls' lives until his untimely death twelve years before.

Phoebe placed the picture back on the mantel, then dramatically took off her sunglasses and long, flowing faux leopard fur coat, which she laid across the chair before taking a seat. "So, Phylicia, tell me what's going on with Mother?"

Wondering why her sister bothered with a fur coat in early spring, Phylicia stood a few feet away watching her before finally answering. "Before I do that, I'm going to ask you again. Why are you here? Is Christmas early this year?"

"No, it isn't, sister dear, but you said I needed to come, so I came. What's the big deal?"

"I said you needed to come when she had the first heart attack four years ago, and when I gave birth to my daughter ten years ago, and when Aunt Virginia passed away eight years ago, and—"

"Please, Phyllie. Spare me the lecture, okay? You know I have a career. I can't just come home at every turn like you want me to."

"What career? You are not still pretending to be a super-model with those hips, are you?"

"For your information, sister dear, plus-size models are doing wonderful things these days. Haven't you ever heard of Mia Tyler or Toccarra Jones?"

Cringing as she remembered how much she hated to be referred to as "sister dear," Phylicia paused before continuing. "Those are young women. Phoebe, you are thirty-six years old. Way too old to still be a model."

"Whatever. You never had any faith in me or my ability, and I'm not going to sit here and defend myself to you. You called and said Mother was sick and that I needed to come. Now I'm here and you have done nothing but give me the third degree. For the last time, I want to know how Mother is doing."

Phylicia sighed heavily before answering her sister. "Mom's on a respirator. She has been since the heart attack. The doctors are not very optimistic, but she's still alive."

"A respirator? Don't tell me you're keeping her alive artificially. Mother wouldn't want that."

"What do you know about what Mom would want?"

"She's my mother too. I don't want to see her live like some vegetable."

"She's not. The respirator helps her breathe until she can breathe on her own. She is alert and very aware of her surroundings. She was unconscious when she was admitted to the hospital, but not anymore. She's hardly a vegetable."

"Well, in that case I want to go to the hospital and see

her. Let's go right now. I have a doctor friend I can call for
consultation to make sure that she's getting the best care."

"I can't go right now. Besides, she is getting the best
care. She's had the same doctor her whole life."

"Well, maybe that's the problem. What hospital is she
in? If I'd known, I would have had the cab driver take me
directly there."

"She's at Mercy General. I will drive you later, as soon
as Eva gets in from school."

"Mercy General? Why isn't she at Price Memorial? It's
a much better hospital with much better physicians."

"There is nothing wrong with Mercy General."

"There's nothing right with it, either. I don't understand
how you could not even be concerned with the quality of
care she's getting from those people at the Band-Aid Bri-
gade. I'm going to make some calls and see if I can get
her transferred."

"No, you are not. Mom is in no condition to be moved.
Dr. Wallace is taking excellent care of her."

"Dr. Wallace is a thousand years old if he's a day. She
needs someone younger and with a particular degree.
Dr. Wallace is a family doctor. Have you contacted a
heart specialist? She needs a better hospital with more
specialized care."

"Phoebe, I know how to take care of my mother, and I
really resent you coming in here after twelve years questioning and second-guessing my decisions. Just who do
you think you are?" Phylicia had completely lost her cool
and was now screaming at her sister.

Not one to be outmatched, Phoebe stood and screamed
back at her, "This is not about you, Phyllie. I am just as
much her daughter as you are. We came out of the same
womb and I beat you by three minutes. So don't you dare
ask me who I am."

"So what if you are the oldest by three whole minutes?

You've never acted like it. You've never tried to be responsible. I'm the one who has been here while you were off doing God-knows-what with God-knows-who."

"Well, I'm here now!" Phoebe screamed, almost spitting in Phylicia's face.

"Whoa! What is going on in here? Ladies, calm down."

They both turned to look at Gary Sr. as he entered the front door. He was tall, caramel-colored, and sexy in a way that no one would ever guess he was a minister of the gospel. He walked with a swagger and had a smile that could melt hearts and drop panties. Oblivious to his sex appeal, he took his relationship with God very seriously as the pastor of the largest black congregation in their small rural town.

"Phoebe? When did you get into town?" he said with a look of surprise as she turned around.

Phoebe's jaw slowly dropped as she looked at him for the first time in twelve years. Reverend Gary Morgan. The first man she'd ever loved; who was now her sister's husband.

Phoebe's mind raced back so fast she thought she was actually being propelled backwards through time. As she stared at Gary, she remembered the first time she'd laid eyes on him at Brown Bottom High School. She was a pudgy little sophomore and he was a sophisticated senior. Phoebe was trying to get a book to fit inside her overstuffed locker when a group of girls walked by. The leader of the pack, Loretta Martin, hated her because her boyfriend liked Phoebe just a bit too much. Phoebe wasn't interested in the boy at all, but that didn't stop his girlfriend from looking for opportunities to humiliate her.

As the girls walked by, one of them yelled out, "Fat fat the water rat!" and they all broke out in giggles. Phoebe had a lot of confidence in herself, regardless of her size-sixteen jeans, and ignored the remark. She crammed the book inside, then turned around to face the group. "Hello, Rotunda!" Loretta said, using the horrid nickname she'd picked for Phoebe. She encouraged her friends to join in laughing with her.

"Well, if it isn't Low-down Loretta and her band of merry idiots," Phoebe responded.

Without any warning, the group of girls rushed her and quickly had Phoebe pinned against the locker. She struggled to get free but there were six of them against one.

"Talk your mess now!" Loretta yelled.

"Get them off me, so I can kick your butt one-on-one." Phoebe answered.

"Oh, I'm too pretty to fight. We are just gonna mess you up. Gimme the scissors, let's cut some of this nappy hair off and see how she likes that." Loretta motioned to one of her friends.

Phoebe struggled harder, and just when she was about to scream bloody murder, she heard her liberator.

"Loretta, let her go now!" he ordered. All of the girls released Phoebe and backed off. Phoebe turned around and looked into his handsome but angry face. "What do you think you're doing? I'm telling your mom as soon as I get home this afternoon."

"You need to learn to mind your own business, G!" Loretta yelled, rushing down the hall with her friends following closely behind.

"Are you okay?" he asked Phoebe.

All she could do was nod her head. And then as quickly as he had appeared, he was gone.

A few days later she noticed him in the hallway again. He walked by her, barely noticing her staring at him. "Do you know him?" Phoebe asked her friend, Janet.

"That's Gary Morgan. He's on the basketball team with my brother."

"Do you think you could get your brother to introduce me to him?"

"What in the world for? C'mon, Phoebe, I know he helped you, but he's just nice like that. He's a church boy. It didn't mean anything."

"It meant everything to me. After one phone call from him, Loretta's mom grounded her for two weeks, and if she comes near me again, it will be even worse."

"Loretta has always been a bully. So what? Just be grateful she's off your back."

"So, I want to thank him. You know . . . really thank him properly."

"He would not be interested in you. I just told you he's a church boy, and he's a senior."

"So? I go to church." Janet gave her an odd look. "Well, I do. My parents make me. Besides, I've dated older boys before."

"No, you haven't, you li'l liar." Janet nudged her in the arm and giggled.

Phoebe had told everyone in their homeroom class that she'd dated an older boy for three months, but she'd forgotten that her best friend Janet knew that Murry was really her third cousin once removed and they were never dating. She giggled, too, in spite of herself.

"Okay, so you're right. I sleep in church and Murry wasn't really my boyfriend. But I've got to meet this guy. I've just got to."

"Well, not right now. Come on, you're gonna make us late for geometry and then old Mooseface Mrs. Gates will make us do detention."

Phoebe stared in the direction that Gary had gone, then slowly followed her friend to class, dreaming of being wrapped in his arms.

Over the next two weeks, she hung out at the high

school gym, trying to catch him coming out of basketball practice and somehow get an introduction. Daily, he'd come out talking with a group of friends or rush off to his car. He hadn't noticed she was even around. But Phoebe was never one to give up. Her skirts got shorter and her visits to the gym became more frequent. Gary Morgan was the man for her, she'd told herself. She just had to meet him.

She finally got her wish a few weeks later. To her surprise, Phoebe came home from school and found Gary sitting on her living room couch drinking a glass of milk and eating cookies as if he belonged there. She stared at his hair and imagined running her fingers through it, as he looked down at his science book. Suddenly, he noticed her standing there and looked up.

"Wow, you sure changed. What's with the hair and makeup? I thought you were just going upstairs to get some paper," he said, staring at her.

"I was," Phylicia answered as she came down the stairs and brushed past her sister. "This is my twin, Phoebe." She turned to her sister. "Phoebe, this is Gary Morgan."

Gary looked back and forth between the two of them for a moment. Phoebe was dressed in tight bell-bottom jeans, and an even tighter multi-colored sweater. Her hair was cut asymmetrically and teased on top of her head. He tried, but he couldn't count all the colors of eye shadow she had plastered on her eyelids, surrounded by black mascara and long eyelashes that reminded him of spiders. Phylicia, on the other hand, was dressed casually in jeans and a red T-shirt that fit loosely. As usual, her hair was pulled back in a ponytail and she only wore a hint of lip gloss on her lips. "Oh, so this is your sister," he finally said, then turned his attention back to the plate of cookies and then his book.

"You don't remember me?" Phoebe asked Gary.

"Should I?" Gary stared at her again, trying to jog his memory.

"Uhm, Loretta and her gang were bothering me in the hallway at school a couple of months ago and you told her to quit, and then you told her mom."

"Sorry, but that doesn't narrow it down. Loretta is always in some kind of trouble. She lives next door to me and her mom asked me to keep an eye on her. It's gotten to be almost a full-time job. But it's nice to meet you anyway, Phoebe." He munched on his cookie and slid over so that Phylicia could sit down.

Phylicia sat on the couch next to him and picked up her science book, as Phoebe continued to stare at the two of them. "What do you want, girl?" Phylicia finally asked.

"Uhm, where's Mom?" Phoebe asked.

"She's at work. You know that. She's never home before six."

"Well, if Mom's not home what are you doing with a boy in the house? You are gonna get us both in trouble."

"Mom knows he's here. He's helping me with my college prep science class. I want to take the PSAT's this summer. Now go away and leave us alone."

Phoebe took another longing glance at Gary, then headed up the stairs. *Beautiful and smart*, she thought to herself.

Over the next hour, Phoebe managed to come downstairs at least six more times to retrieve items she'd left in the living room and desperately needed. Each time, she tried her best to gain Gary's attention, but he was a dedicated tutor and only had eyes for Phylicia and her books. The last time she waltzed down the stairs after changing into a hot pink tube top and shorts, she was met by her mother at the bottom step. Gary was outside with Phylicia as she walked him to his car.

"Phoebe, what are you doing wearing that outfit? It's only fifty degrees out today. You are gonna catch a cold. Go change. Right now!" her mother yelled as she walked towards the kitchen. Instead of immediately obeying, Phoebe rushed to the front window to watch Gary leave. Her heart crumbled into tiny pieces as she saw him gently peck her sister on the lips before getting into his Mustang 5.0 and drive away.

Phoebe brooded all through dinner trying to figure out what was going on between Gary and Phylicia. Livid that her sister had actually kissed him, she sulked as she washed the evening dishes and put them away. Finally, she decided to confront her sister with what she knew and demand the truth. As she entered their bedroom, Phylicia was standing, staring in the closet. It was her nightly ritual to choose, iron, and lay out her clothes for the next day, while Phoebe usually was late trying to make a last-minute decision each morning. Phoebe waited until Phylicia had chosen a pair of jeans and a blouse and turned around before speaking.

"I saw you today. I'm telling Mom," she blurted out.

"You saw what, Phoebe?" Phylicia asked as she laid her jeans on the nearby ironing board and bent down to plug in the iron.

"I saw you and that boy kissing. You know we are not allowed to date. You said he was here to help with your homework. I'm telling Mom."

Phylicia stared at her sister, then quickly reached behind her and closed their bedroom door. "Please don't tell Mom. She'd never let him come back to study if she knew. Please, Phoebe, don't tell on me," she pleaded.

"Why shouldn't I tell? You'd tell if it was me. Besides,

what else are you two up to?" Phoebe asked, eyeing her sister suspiciously. She'd never seen her excited over any boy, and now she was pleading with her sister to keep a secret.

"We aren't up to anything but kissing. Please don't tell. I'll give you anything you want." Phylicia thought for a moment. "What if I let you keep my Walkman at school all day tomorrow?" she offered.

"You never want me touching your Walkman. What's so special about this boy?"

Phylicia stared dreamily into the air as she began to talk. Phoebe was listening, but she didn't want to hear. Her sister had met Gary months before at a youth meeting at the church when his church's youth group came to visit. Phoebe remembered that meeting. She'd faked a stomach ache in order to get out of it. When Gary met Phylicia, they'd hit it off instantly and became fast friends. They found they had a lot in common, both enjoying the same types of movies, music, and even favorite food: peanut-butter-and-jelly sandwiches with slices of banana. Gary couldn't believe it when Phylicia told him how much she loved them. They talked on the phone and saw each other regularly at the church youth meetings. The twins' sixteenth birthday was a few months away, and that was the time designated by their parents when they each could go on their first official date. Nevertheless, Gary had asked, and Phylicia had officially accepted to be his girlfriend; it had been more than two weeks. He honestly was helping her with her science class, but it was also an excuse to spend time with her.

"Oh, Phoebe, he is wonderful. I've never known a boy as wonderful as him," she gushed. "He's a Christian, he's respectful, and he's so smart. He makes straight As even during basketball season."

Phoebe listened to her sister go on and on about how

wonderful Gary Morgan was, while growing more and more jealous. She wished she had met him first and he'd chosen her. After all, they were twins, she reasoned. If he'd met her first, he would have fallen for her instead of her sister. When she felt she could no longer stomach listening to her sister for another second, Phoebe finally agreed to take the Walkman, a pair of sneakers, and five dollars cash for her silence.

Phylicia invited Gary to the twins' sixteenth birthday party, and while there, he formally asked if he could date Phylicia. Her father was a big fan of Gary and the Brown Bottom basketball team, and her mother admired his academic accomplishments. They both happily agreed. The two of them dated steadily for the next year, falling deeply in love.

As Phoebe's crush and desire for him grew more and more each day, she found herself unable to be happy for her sister. She felt that she was the beautiful one, the sophisticated one. It was she who was in the drama department and had played Dorothy in the high school production of The Wiz. And she was the one who was going to be a famous model, if she could just lose a few pounds. If he'd been given the chance to know her first, Phoebe was sure Gary would have fallen head-over-heels in love with her. How could he resist?

It was that reasoning she used as logic one evening when she found herself alone with Gary at their home. He'd come over looking for Phylicia, who'd come in a few moments earlier in tears, run upstairs to their room, and filled Phoebe in on the night's events.

They'd gone to a party at a friend's house and then back to Gary's dorm room. He was a sophomore at Brown Bottom State College studying psychology. After college, he was planning to enter seminary and become a minister. This particular weekend his roommate was out

of town, and he'd wanted to be alone with his girl. Phylicia cried that the evening had begun innocently enough,
but things quickly got out of hand. Gary wanted to sleep
with her and her Christian beliefs made her say no. She
was upset because she believed that Gary wanted to wait
for marriage as much as she did. When he tried too per-
sistently to convince her to say yes, she'd run from his
dorm room and called a cab to take her home. She was
lying on her bed crying as Phoebe rubbed her back, when
he knocked on the front door. Their mother was not
home and the two girls were alone. Gary pounded
loudly on the door and called out her name. "Phylicia!
Phylicia!"

"Oh, no. Why did he have to follow me? Phoebe, I
can't talk to him right now. Please just go downstairs and
make him go away," she pleaded.

"But, Phyllie, I thought you said you loved him. I
thought you said you wanted to marry him."

"I do love him, and I can't wait to marry him."

"So why won't you sleep with him?"

Phylicia glared at her sister before answering. "I want
to wait until we are married. It's the right thing to do. He
said he wanted to wait too. But he's just like all those
other boys. He doesn't care about me."

"Girl, you've been dating over a year. He's human; he
has needs. C'mon, Phyllie. How could you think that he
doesn't care?"

"I don't know what I believe. I mean, he's going into
the ministry. We are both Christians. How could he ask
me to do something like that?" she said, wiping her tears.

"He's a man, Phyllie. That's what men want to do with
the women they love. It's only natural."

"We are not married and it's wrong. If you stayed
awake at church, you'd know that."

The knocks on the door began to get louder and more urgent. "Phylicia . . . please open the door. Please. I want to apologize," Gary screamed.

"Well, I don't understand why you won't just give him some. That would not be a problem if he was my man. Sometimes you are really too old-fashioned for your own good, Phyllie."

"Call it what you want. I'm just not ready."

"Fine, then you don't have to give him any, but at least go make him stop beating on the door before one of these nosey neighbors calls the police."

"No, I can't. I don't want to even see his face right now. I just need to be alone." she said, grabbing her jacket.

"Where are you going?" Phoebe asked.

"I'm going to sneak out the back and take a walk. Get rid of him for me. Please."

After she watched her sister leave, Phoebe rushed to the bathroom and washed all of the makeup from her face. She quickly brushed down her hair and pulled it into a ponytail. She rushed downstairs and turned off all the lights except for one, dimly lit near the kitchen. Finally, she opened the door to let Gary in.

"Phyllie? Please forgive me, Phylicia. I'm so sorry. Can we talk?"

She didn't answer him. She just reached up and pulled him into a deep kiss, leading him into the house and to the couch. Within minutes they were lying on top of each other and tearing at each other's clothes.

"I thought you weren't ready. I thought you didn't want this," he managed to breathe out between kisses.

Silently she shushed him, by pressing her lips harder to his. Gary gave in to the passion he felt for Phylicia and slowly began to make love to her sister. Their bodies rocked in motion leisurely as he entered her. He expected it to be more difficult, as she was a virgin, but in his lust he didn't care. He entered her completely and they made intense, passionate love. Surprised at her expertise and her passion, Gary quickly lost control. Holding her tightly as they both climaxed, he screamed out her name. "Oh, Phylicia."

"Yes, Gary. That was so wonderful" Phoebe moaned.

As soon as he heard her voice he realized something was wrong. He suddenly stopped, jumped off of her, and reached for the light, flipping it on. "Phoebe? I thought you were Phyllie. Goodness, girl! Are you crazy?" he screamed as he reached for his clothes.

"Wait, Gary, you can't tell me you didn't enjoy that too. Don't leave. I've been dreaming of you since the first time I saw you. Just listen to me."

He ignored her and continued dressing. She tried to touch his arm, and he pushed her away. "You are sick, Phoebe," he finally answered as he reached for the door and rushed out.

Phoebe called him every day for the next several weeks, but he refused to talk to her, or her sister. He'd told Phylicia that after what happened that evening he wasn't sure about their relationship anymore, and he needed some time. Phylicia had cried in her sister's arms not realizing what had happened between the two of them.

Phoebe quickly became exasperated with listening to her sister's cries, and wanted Gary more than ever since making love with him. She dug out the last of her allowance and took a cab to find him at the university. He wasn't in his dorm room, so she wrote a note, folded it, and taped it to his door.

Gary I missed my period. I think I'm pregnant. You have to call me now.

The next morning, he was in their kitchen when Phoebe came downstairs for breakfast. Her mother and father were sitting with him, and as soon as she walked in the room, their eyes turned to her in icy stares. "Phoebe, Gary says that you told him you are pregnant with his child. Is that true?" her father asked.

"I . . . I . . ." Feeling trapped, Phoebe just began to cry. Her mother pulled her into her arms and comforted her.

"Mr. Carson, Mrs. Carson, I'm sorry. I never meant for this to happen. I love Phylicia. I thought she was Phylicia, but I know that still doesn't make it right. I let my lust overcome me and I'm so sorry. That's why I came here today to do what's right. I've told my parents, and I'm gonna drop out of college and get a job to help with the baby, but I can't marry her. Not when I love her sister so much," Gary confessed.

"Gary, I understand." Mr. Carson said. "I married Mrs. Carson because she was pregnant and, as you know, our marriage didn't even last through the pregnancy. We understand, we only expect you to support the baby. Our family does not believe in abortion."

"I understand, and neither do I. I'll support the baby, I promise. I'll do my best to be a good father. I know it's the right thing to do." Gary looked over at Phoebe, still wrapped in her mother's arms. "Does Phylicia know? I mean, I want to be the one to tell her. I should be the one to tell her." He stared at his hands clasped on the table.

"No, she left for school early this morning. If you'll come back this afternoon, you can tell her then," Mrs. Carson stated before turning to her daughter. "Phoebe, you aren't going to school today. I need to take you to Dr. Wallace for a checkup, and then your father and I want to talk to you about, well, about everything."

Two hours later when they returned from the doctor's

office, Phoebe tried to run to her room to escape, but her father was there waiting and her mother explained the truth to him. "Phoebe lied. The test was negative. She is not pregnant. Pharrell, talk to her, because I have tried everything I know to say and I can't make sense out of what she's done."

"Lied? I don't understand." Mr. Carson asked his ex-wife.

"Let her explain it. I have to go call Gary's parents before that boy throws away his future over our daughter's lies," she said as she rushed up the stairs, leaving them alone.

Pharrell looked at his daughter with tears smearing her makeup, and with his eyes, asked the question to which he was sure he knew the answer.

"I love him, Daddy. I can't explain it, but I do," she sobbed.

Now, almost twenty years later, Phoebe stared at Gary Morgan and realized her love had never died. She'd buried it, hoping to suffocate it, but whenever she saw him it would be resuscitated. She'd left town trying to outrun it and be truly happy for her sister. Over the past twelve years she'd believed that she had. She rarely daydreamed about him at all anymore. But standing face to face with him, the door of her heart swung open like the pearly gates and, once again, in he swaggered.

Swallowing hard, she finally managed to speak. "Hello, Gary. I just got in today," she said.

Chapter Two

Slowly and quietly, Phylicia pushed the door to her mother's hospital room. As the door squeaked open, Phylicia heard the raspy sound of the respirator along with the beeps of the various vital signs monitors making a sad symphony throughout the room. Timidly, she walked over to her mother's bed. "Hi, Mommy," she said.

Her mother opened her eyes and smiled at her weakly. "Hi, Phyllie, how are you doing today?" she eeked out in a raspy whisper through the oxygen mask covering her mouth.

"I'm good, Mom. How are you?" Phylicia answered, leaning down in order to hear her weak voice.

"The Lord's not quite ready for me yet, so I'm hanging on. Did you call Phoebe?" she whispered hoarsely.

Phylicia's heart sank. Phoebe was all her mother seemed to care about. She asked for her every day. She didn't seem to care that Phylicia had been there caring for her, praying with her, and loving her alone for twelve years while her sister was traipsing around somewhere pretending to be a model. However, she was relieved that today would be the last day she'd have to hear that question. "Yes, ma'am. She's in the hallway with Li'l G and Eva. I wanted to come in first to make sure you weren't sleeping. I'll go get her now," she said before kissing her mother on the forehead and walking back out to the hallway.

"Can I go in now? Can I see her?" Phoebe asked Phylicia as soon as she stepped through the door.

"Yes, go ahead. She's waiting for you. The kids and I will be in the waiting room down the hall."

Phoebe pushed the door open widely and waltzed dramatically into the room. Immediately, she stopped cold in her tracks wondering who this old woman was lying in the bed in her mother's room. Phoebe stared at the thin, frail person with wispy hair lying in the bed, who resembled her mother, though Phoebe remembered her being plump and busty. This weak and quiet woman could not possibly be the woman whom full of zest and passion she'd admired and feared growing up.

The day she'd left town, Phoebe remembered hugging her mother, then pushing her one or two gray hairs that sat at her temples behind her ear to kiss her cheeks. This woman was completely white-headed. With her caramel-colored skin glowing, she'd waved good-bye as Phoebe took her seat on the crowded Greyhound bus. She didn't look at all like this woman with sickly, yellowish skin barely hanging onto the bones of her face. This person lying here was not the mother she'd left twelve years ago. She stood by the door fighting back tears at the thought of all the years she'd allowed to slip by without seeing her mother.

"Phoebe? Is that you, girl?" Her mother paused and coughed several times. "Come here, baby."

Reluctantly, Phoebe moved closer to the bed and the little old woman who was supposed to be her mother. As she got closer, she stared into her matching grey eyes and the tears began to tumble down her cheeks. "Oh, Momma, I've missed you so much," she blurted out. Ignoring the tubes and wires, she bent down to hug her closely.

Across town in his church office, Reverend Gary Morgan tried desperately to put his mind back on the sermon he was writing and his duties to his congregation. He'd been distracted all afternoon, powerless to escape the fact that seeing his sister-in-law again had shaken him to his core.

Unable to concentrate, he allowed his mind to wander back in time to the day he received the news that Phoebe lied about her pregnancy. Wondering why she'd pulled such an elaborate stunt, he decided it was time he talked to her. He asked her mother to have her meet him at the local park, so as not to run into Phylicia. He was sitting on the bench near a grove of trees when she bounced up to him like Tigger on crack, grinning from ear to ear.

"Hi, Gary, I'm so glad you wanted to see me. Listen Phyllie will be hurt but she'll get over it. You and me, we fit so well together," she said, reaching out to hug him.

Gary swiftly moved out of her reach. "I don't want you, Phoebe. I came to find out what's wrong with you. Why did you do this?"

"I didn't do anything. We did. I felt the same passion you felt. Don't try to stand here and tell me you didn't feel it. You wanted me. I know it. How could you not recognize your own girlfriend?"

"In the dim light, without makeup, and with your hair pulled back, you know you look just like her. You were trying to make me think you were her. I never would have done anything like that with you. Obviously, I love your sister much more than you do."

His words stung, so Phoebe decided to fight back. "I do love my sister, so much so that I'm going to tell her what a rat you are. I'm going to tell her that you slept with me on purpose. I'm going to tell her everything."

"Go ahead and break your sister's heart the same as you did your parents. You should've seen the looks on their faces when I walked in and told them your lie yesterday morning. Go ahead and hurt your whole family if it will make you feel better, but I still don't want you. I never have, and after this, I know I never will."

Phoebe began to cry, and he immediately regretted being so harsh with her. A woman in tears had always been his weakness. Instinctively, he pulled her into his arms. "I'm sorry. What happened between us was wrong, but it wasn't entirely your fault. I never meant to hurt you, but I love Phylicia," he mumbled. He held her for several moments, just listening to the sound of her whimpering, before handing her his handkerchief to dry her tears.

"I won't tell. I promise. I just wanted to be with you so badly. I wanted you so much," she whispered, still holding tightly to him.

"I'm sorry, Phoebe, but it's Phylicia I love."

Gary gently rubbed her back and the smell of her expensive Obsession perfume oil filled his nostrils. The scent reminded him of that night, just a few weeks before when he'd held her even tighter and passionately made love to her. As he relived that moment, he felt an erection stirring in his jeans. Realizing that he needed to end this intimate connection, he reached down and gently lifted her chin for her to look at him. Seizing the moment, Phoebe quickly kissed his lips until she felt him respond. He held the kiss for a few seconds, then abruptly pushed her away and walked as fast as he could out of the park, without looking back.

To this day Gary loved Phylicia with all his heart and soul, but no matter how he tried, he could not get that one night of lovemaking all those years ago with Phoebe out of his mind. When he was with his wife, their lovemaking was gentle and tender. It was endearing, and he fully enjoyed it. But Phoebe had been full of fire and passion and sent sensations through his body he'd never felt before, or since. At first he was angry with her for tricking him into betraying his soon-to-be wife. But eventually he had to admit that just being in her presence made his nature rise. He loved Phylicia, but he couldn't deny lusting for her sister. Realizing how wrong his lust for her was, he spent the next several years finding every way imaginable to simply avoid his sister-in-law altogether. Now she was back in town, and he had to struggle to keep the demons of lust from resurfacing in his life once again. As he sat at his desk, he silently prayed for strength.

Phylicia sat in the hospital waiting room with Eva's head resting in her lap. Li'l G had gone down to the cafeteria for a soda, while Phoebe continued her visit with their mother. As much as she tried, Phylicia could not shake the feeling of apprehension she'd felt the moment her sister arrived. It had intensified during their argument over her mother's care. She was furious that Phoebe would question her after being gone for so long. But the knot she currently felt in her stomach had nothing at all to do with their mother. It began twisting at her guts the moment her husband walked in and looked at her sister. His face was full of surprise, but then it changed. Phylicia didn't know how to describe it, but the look of discomfort that always washed across his face whenever Phoebe was in the room was painfully obvious. She'd almost forgotten it over the twelve years her sister had been gone, but for the first few years of their marriage, it had been a constant barrier between them.

She first noticed it when they became engaged, and Phoebe walked into their engagement party wearing a slinky, silver, beaded gown with a plunging neckline. They'd both been blessed with ample bosoms, but only Phoebe enjoyed showing hers off for company. As Phoebe pranced into the room, all eyes were suddenly on her. Phylicia watched her fiancé's face turn from brown to burgundy in three seconds flat, and then he suddenly left the room. Instead of spending his engagement party by her side as Phylicia thought he should have, Gary spent most of the evening dodging Phoebe.

From that point on, he always continued to find some reason to be excused from the room, or the house, or wherever they were in Phoebe's presence, until the day she left town.

She'd never mentioned it, and neither of them realized she felt that way, but she was certain his constant discomfort and her sister's sudden exit from town meant something. She just wasn't sure what.

When he came crawling back begging her forgiveness and her hand in marriage, she hesitated, momentarily hurt over his insistence that they have sex. He assured her he was in love and willing to wait. She realized that she loved him, and, no matter what, she didn't want to live without him.

Following the engagement party, the doubts began to surface and she wondered if marriage to him was a mistake. She wondered if the apprehension she felt was a sign from God. She prayed and prayed for guidance before she finally decided to go through with the marriage, trying to push that awful feeling from her mind.

But the feeling was back. It had waltzed into her living room wearing a fake fur coat, carrying Louis Vuitton luggage, reeking of cheap perfume; and its name was Phoebe.

Eva sat up as she heard her Auntie entering the waiting room. "How's Grandma?" she asked, rubbing her eyes.

"Oh, she's fine, honey. She is just fine." Phoebe answered.

"What do you mean she's fine, Phoebe? Momma's on a respirator. That's hardly what I'd consider fine."

"Well, she didn't ask you, she asked me."

"Look, I really don't want to argue with you yet again." Phylicia stood up from her chair and grabbed her purse. "Eva, come on honey; let's go see your grandma." She walked swiftly, then stopped near the door. "Phoebe, when Li'l G gets back would you send him in the room, please?" Phylicia asked, then walked out of the waiting room.

Phoebe watched her stalk away down the hall, then took a seat. Almost as soon as she did, she felt her stomach rumbling and realized she had not eaten in more than twenty-four hours. She hadn't had any money to buy food on the trip there, and she was too proud to tell Phylicia that she was hungry when she'd arrived. Instead, they'd rushed over to the hospital and decided to eat dinner later. As she sat wondering if her stomach would quiet down until they returned to the house for dinner, Phoebe heard whistling, and realized her savior was on the way up the hall. Her nephew sauntered in and grinned at her before taking a sip of soda.

"Li'l G, where did you get that soda?" she asked.

"There's a cafeteria in the basement. If you'd like, I could go get you one."

"Would you, sweetie? Bring me a bag of chips, too.

Just to pass the time until your mom and sister come out." Phoebe began dramatically searching through her knock-off Coach bag for change.

"If you don't have any money, I'll buy it for you," Li'l G offered.

"Well, of course I have money. I just don't think I have any change. I don't want to put you to any trouble, but if you could get it for me, I'd appreciate it."

"It's no trouble at all. I don't mind. I'll be right back," he said, and grinned at her again.

Phoebe could not get over how much he looked like his father when they'd first met. And he'd certainly inherited his father's killer smile. She had to remind herself he was her nephew. "Thanks, sweetie, Auntie would appreciate that," she replied.

The moment he returned, she ripped open the bag and ravenously dug in. She'd stuffed several chips in her mouth and was crunching loudly before she realized he was watching her strangely. Wiping crumbs from her face, she looked over at him.

"Aunt Phoebe, you sure are hungry. Do you want me to get you anything else?"

"No, sweetie. I just skipped breakfast 'cause I had an early flight. That's all. This will hold me until dinner. Now you go on in and visit with your grandma."

Li'l G gave her another strange look, then did as she asked.

She was just finishing up the potato chips and gulping down the soda when she heard her phone ringing inside her purse. She checked the caller ID and then looked down the hall to make sure her family was not coming before she flipped it open. "Hello?" she whispered.

"Phoebe? Where are you, girl? I came home and the apartment was cleaned out. What's going on?" Phoebe stared at the phone, willing herself to speak, but the words would not come. "Phoebe? Do you hear me? What's going on?"

"Uhm, I'm down south. My momma's sick. I had to come see her. The furniture was all I had to sell for a bus ticket," she finally blurted out.

"Yo' momma? You told me yo' momma was dead. What are you up to, Phoebe? How you gonna sell the furniture right out from under me?"

"It's mine. I own every piece of it. I had every right to sell it."

"And what am I supposed to do until you get back? You expect me to sleep on the doggone floor?"

"Sleep wherever you've been sleeping the past two weeks. It certainly hasn't been in our bed."

"Phoebe, look, I had some things going on. You know I always come back. What in the world has gotten into you?"

Phoebe heard footsteps in the hallway and panicked. "I gotta go. I'll call you tomorrow." She hung up the phone and quickly threw it back inside her purse. She looked up as an elderly white man walked in and took a seat a few feet away from her. Phoebe silently breathed a sigh of relief. She sat in scared silence, hoping her phone would not ring again, until finally she heard Phylicia and the children talking as they came down the hallway.

"Aunt Phoebe, we're ready to go," Li'l G said.

The four of them left the hospital and rode home. As soon as they entered the house, the children went upstairs to their rooms. Phoebe was about to follow them to the guest bedroom when her sister stopped her. "Phoebe, could you sit down with me for a minute? We need to talk."

Phoebe sat down on the chair across from her sister on the couch. As she sat, she remembered she'd always loved this chair. It had huge overstuffed pillows and wide arms. It had been her favorite to sink down into when they were growing up. Sinking into this chair made her finally feel that that she was home. She felt so comfortable in it; she decided to extend the olive branch. "Phyllie, I'm sorry. I know I came in here like Cleopatra floating down the Nile and began barking orders and demands. I was just worried about Momma. I hope that I didn't offend you. She was in good spirits and I know that you've taken good care of her."

Phylicia was surprised and taken aback. "Well, thank you for saying that," she muttered with a shocked look on her face.

"You don't need to thank me. I know I've been gone a long time. It's not that I haven't wanted to come back; it just never seemed like the right time. But now that I'm here, I'm sorry that I put it off for so long. Your children are beautiful, and you have taken good care of Momma as well as the house. I love the new bedrooms and sun porch you added."

"Thank you. A lot of it was Momma's idea. She wanted us to live here with her rather than buy our own home. It made sense while Gary was building his ministry. His first appointment was a small country church that couldn't afford a parsonage. We've enjoyed living here. It's a good school district and the kids have made good friends. Of course, now with Gary pastoring Freedom Inspiration, we could probably afford to buy two or three houses, but we love it here and Momma loves having us around."

Phoebe felt a slight twinge of envy at the reference to their financial success. She knew Phylicia had never worked because of their mother's health and her various duties as first lady. Their mother always bragged about Phylicia leading a ladies' group meeting, hosting a ladies' luncheon, collecting clothes for the church clothing drive, or feeding homeless people in the soup kitchen. Phoebe was jealous that Gary had done so well, although she'd always believed he would. Trying hard to hide her feelings, she smiled at her sister. "Well, I'm glad that you're happy here. But I'm a bit tired. I want to lie down until dinner. I'm going to head up to that gorgeous guest room you added."

"Wait, Phoebe, that's what I wanted to talk with you about; the guest room."

"What about it? You don't have to change the sheets or anything. I'll just lie down on the comforter and you can change them later."

"No, that's not it. I don't want you to stay in the guest room. I . . . I want you to go to a hotel."

"Did you say a hotel? What are you talking about?" Phoebe asked with a surprised look on her face.

"I just think it would be better for everyone if you stayed at a hotel while you're in town. There's a new Marriott out by the interstate. It has lovely rooms and it's not too far from the hospital. I think you would be much more comfortable there."

"Phylicia, I just apologized for our fight and now you ask me to go to a hotel? I can't believe you."

"It's not about our fight. The last time you lived here it was just you, me, and Mom. But I'm married now, and I have two children. There are four of us here."

"And you've added three extra bedrooms and two extra bathrooms to what was here before. I don't understand. There's plenty of room. Who do you think you are asking me to leave my own mother's house?"

"Phoebe, this is my home."

"No, it's Mom's home and I have as much right to be here as you do. Just because you've been here all this time and think you have squatter's rights or something doesn't mean you can just put me out." Phoebe stopped speaking as she heard the front door open and Gary walked in. She took one look at him and realized why her sister did not want her staying in her home. She knew he'd asked her to do this. She almost agreed with her that it was a bad idea for her to stay, but she had no money and no place else to go.

"Another argument and so soon?" he said.

"Gary, please let me handle my sister, okay?" Phylicia answered.

He raised his hands in front of himself as if to surrender. "I'm sorry. I'll go check on the kids. Call me when dinner's ready."

They stood in silence until both were sure he was all the way upstairs. While they waited, Phoebe searched her brain for something to say that would convince Phylicia to let her stay. Before she could, her sister spoke up. "Phoebe, listen, I just think this would be better for all concerned."

"Well, I don't have enough cash on me to rent a hotel room, and surely you know they won't accept an out-of-town check. I'll have to at least stay the night then go to an ATM tomorrow morning. I've taken out my limit for today in order to buy the plane ticket."

"I've already reserved you a room, and charged it to Gary's and my credit card. You can stay there as long as you like and pay us back later."

"You've already reserved it? Well, why didn't you say something sooner? What was the point of having me put my things in the guest room if you were just going to throw me out?"

"I'm not throwing you out. I was thinking while you were in with Mom, and it just makes more sense for you to stay at a hotel. I called and made the reservations and I'll drive you over after dinner."

"No. Don't bother. I don't want any dinner. I'll just call

myself a cab. That's if I can still use the phone in my mother's home."

Phylicia sighed loudly. "Why do you always have to be so dramatic? Of course you can use the phone, but you don't have to leave now. "

"I think I should," Phoebe said, moving toward the phone.

Exasperated, Phylicia stood up and walked to the base of the steps. "Li'l G? Li'l G, would you come here, please?" she called up the steps.

Her son came bounding down the stairs chewing on an apple. "Yeah, Mom?"

"Your Aunt Phoebe is going to be staying at a hotel. Would you get her things and drive her over to the Marriott on Clover Street? You can take my car."

"Do you want me to go right now? I thought we were gonna have dinner soon," he asked.

Phylicia reached into her jeans pocket, pulling out a fifty dollar bill. She handed it to Li'l G. "Why don't you stop and get you both something on the way," she said, then walked into the kitchen, leaving them alone.

Chapter Three

"You are a very good driver for a teenager," Phoebe said, admiring her nephew.

"Thanks. I got my driver's license a few months ago, but Dad's been letting me drive since I was tall enough to see over the steering wheel."

"That must have been fun. Your grandparents were really strict. Your mom and I didn't learn to drive until we were almost eighteen. Well, your mom learned a little earlier because she had your father to teach her. I learned later on that same year."

"Can I ask you something, Auntie Phoebe?"

"Sure, honey, anything."

"Why don't you and my mom get along?"

"Of course we get along, honey. Things are just a little tense right now with your grandma being sick and all. Sometimes we don't agree, but we get along just fine. Why would you think we don't?"

"I mean, she's never sent family to a hotel before. Even when our cousin Yolanda came from Texas that she hadn't seen since she was four, she put her and her husband in the family room. Then spread her kids out with me and Eva. And that time that Daddy's Uncle Cleophus was here for the church conference, that's when she suggested to Grandma to have the guest room built with a private bathroom for family."

"Honey, I can't explain all that."

"C'mon, Auntie Phoebe, I'm sixteen years old. I'm a man. You can tell me the truth."

Phoebe chuckled to herself at his self proclamation of manhood. "I realize that you are mature and a very intelligent young man. But honestly, your mother and I get along fine."

"Then how come you never come to visit?"

"You sure do ask a lot of questions, don't you?" Phoebe laughed, trying to lighten the mood. "Hey, do you like pizza? Let's stop for pizza for dinner."

"No, I don't eat pizza. I'm allergic to tomato sauce. You'd know that if you'd ever been to visit."

"Li'l G, it's not that simple. I have a busy career, and when I had the time to visit, sometimes it wasn't the best time for your family and the years just got away from me, that's all. Please try to understand that."

"Mom says you left to be a model, but I've never seen you in an ad or a commercial or anything."

"I don't do that type of modeling. I'm a private model."

"What does private model mean? Are you a . . . a porn star or something?"

"Of course I'm not! What in the world do you know about porn stars, young man?" Phoebe asked, suddenly shocked by his words.

"Nothing, really, it's just some of the guys at school pass around pictures and stuff and it's usually marked private. I'm sorry. I didn't mean to insult you. What exactly is a private model?"

It was a fancy way Phoebe had found for saying that she had a portfolio full of expensive pictures but had never been hired. She'd pounded the pavement relentlessly and been swindled out of almost all of her father's insurance money when she first moved away, until finally giving up on that dream. At the present time, she wasn't modeling anything but the latest in waitress uniforms.

"Uh . . . I do fashion shows for department stores and boutiques. That's why my schedule is so busy. The shows are usually booked around holidays when everyone else is home with their families." Phoebe liked the sound of her latest lie, and decided to remember it for later use during her visit. "So when I do have free time, it's spent resting and getting prepared for the next show. I have dozens of clients, but if I want to keep working, I have to be dependable."

"So how were you able to get away this time?"

Li'l G was beginning to annoy her. He was so much like his father in that he needed a logical explanation for every movement a person made. Gary never could just let things go.

"Well, I told my agent that my mother was sick and I needed to be here. Your grandmother is seriously ill, Li'l G. I wanted to make sure I got a chance to talk to her, well, you know, just in case she doesn't make it. I don't mean to scare you, but your grandmother is knocking at death's door." She finished with her added flair of drama.

"It doesn't scare me. I'm not afraid of death. Daddy explained to us and everyone in the church that death is a gateway to heaven. I'll miss Grandma when she goes, but I know she'll be rejoicing."

Phoebe was beginning to understand that Li'l G was wise beyond his years. "Well, that's good. And if it makes you feel better, let me just say that I regret not coming home sooner. I've missed my family."

"Even my dad?"

Phoebe's heart jumped into her throat, almost choking her. She began to cough uncontrollably. Li'l G reached into the car console and handed her a bottle of water. She drank it slowly, trying to regain her composure.

"Are you okay?" he asked with a worried look on his face.

She nodded her head but did not speak. She was afraid to, so she kept drinking the water until she saw the hotel lights up ahead. When Li'l G pulled the car into the circular driveway, she finally spoke again. "Your mother has me all checked in. You can just pop the trunk and the attendant will get my luggage," she said, trying to rush out of the car.

Li'l G got out of the car with her, unlocked the trunk, then handed the bellhop the two suitcases. "What about dinner? Aren't you hungry?" he asked.

"Well, I suppose I could call room service or something."

Li'l G reached into his pocket and retrieved the fifty dollars his mother had given him. He added another twenty dollars of his own money and handed it to his aunt. "Here you go. I overheard you telling Mom you hadn't been to the ATM. Order yourself a large pizza," he said with a wink and a smile.

Phoebe turned her back and walked into the hotel, following the bellhop with her luggage and desperately trying to hide the tears that were falling down her face.

When Li'l G returned home, he parked the car in the garage and entered the house through the kitchen. He was busy fixing himself a plate of cold chicken from dinner when he heard his parents' voices floating down the stairs.

He took his plate upstairs and closed his bedroom door, drowning out the noise with his television as he turned on the music channel.

"Phylicia, what has gotten into you? How could you send your own sister to a hotel? What will the parishioners think knowing that we have this large home and the first lady doesn't want her own sister to stay here?"

"I don't care what they think and neither should you. It's just better that she not stay here."

"Better for who? I don't understand. You are just going to have to run out to that hotel every day to pick her up and go to the hospital. It's a waste of time and money. Thank goodness she can afford it."

"We're paying for it," Phylicia mumbled.

"What did you say?"

"I charged the room to our credit card."

"You did what? Why would you do something like that? This makes even less sense now. You mean to tell me after all the money we've spent remodeling this house you are spending more putting your sister up in a hotel for God knows how long? What kind of sense does that make?"

"Gary, lower your voice. The children will hear you."

"Don't talk to me about my voice. You've been yelling at your sister all day and now you're worried about what the children will hear? Explain to me why you did this. Why couldn't she just stay here?"

"When did you become a fan of my sister? In all the years we've been married, you've never had more than ten nice words to say about her or to her for that matter. Whenever she's around, you are not. I didn't want to go through that again."

"What are you talking about? I don't have a problem with your sister. She's the one who hasn't been around for all these years. What does this have to do with me?"

"Don't play games with me, Gary. Since we first got

engaged there has been tension between you and my sister. She'd walk flirtatiously into a room and you'd walk out. When she calls, you hand me the phone without even so much as a hello to her. I didn't imagine it all those years ago and I didn't imagine it this afternoon. You spoke two words to her, then suddenly had to rush back to the church on some emergency. I don't know what it is between you two that you can't be in the same room, but I know I cannot deal with it. Not right now, not with Mom so sick. So I asked her to leave so that you didn't have to."

Gary was stunned. He'd spent all afternoon at the church praying for a way to deal with his feelings for Phoebe without making his wife uncomfortable. He loved his family. He knew there was no chance of an indiscretion happening, but he prayed for the strength to deal with the tension. He finally found comfort in scripture by reading Luke 14:27.

> *Peace I leave with you, my peace I give unto you: not as the world giveth, give I unto you. Let not your heart be troubled, neither let it be afraid.*

Gary read the scripture over several times and prayed. When he'd finally come home, he'd felt he was prepared to deal with Phoebe without losing his cool. He'd found his peace; now he had to help his wife find it also. "Honey, I'm sorry. I never meant to make you feel this way. I just never really got to know your sister, that's all. So I was hoping with this visit, with her in the house, maybe all of that would change."

"So are you saying you want me to ask her back? How am I supposed to do that?"

"No, you don't have to do that. I'm sorry I just didn't understand. Let her remain at the hotel and we'll have her over for dinner or something. I promise I'll make a better effort to stay around and get to know her," he said, pulling Phylicia into his arms. "We'll do whatever makes you comfortable, sweetie. That's all that matters." As he held her, Gary began to pray silently that Phyllie could find the peace of mind and strength he'd found.

Phoebe walked around her hotel room from corner to corner, touching things. She ran her fingers across the rich mahogany of the desk, then let them linger on the luxurious seat of the chair. Next she walked over to the bathroom and sunk her face deep into one of the plush white towels before staring wide-eyed at the Jacuzzi jets in the bathtub.

Phoebe walked back into her room and plunged head first into the queen-sized bed as if it were a pile of leaves gathered in the fall of the year, then rolled around in the soft comforter. When she was done, she ran a hot bath. While waiting for the tub to fill with water and strawberry-scented bubbles, she peeled off her clothes and tied her weave up on top of her head. She covered it with the complimentary shower cap before turning on the Jacuzzi jets and sinking down into the steaming water. It soothed her aching muscles and massaged every pore of her body. Phoebe lay there, deeply inhaling the sweet strawberry aroma, unable to remember when she'd felt so serene.

She'd been soaking almost an hour when there was a knock at her door. Momentarily, she wondered who it could be, before remembering that on the way up she'd asked room service to bring her dinner. She stepped out of the tub, wrapped herself in a lavish hotel bathrobe, then answered the door. The waiter brought the tray in and set it on a round table near the window. He carefully arranged everything neatly on the table, then stepped closer to the door, where he stopped and waited patiently for his tip. Reaching into the deepest bowels of her purse, Phoebe finally found fifty-four cents to give him. He looked disappointed, then left.

She felt bad. Being a waitress, she always liked to tip well, but the seventy dollars she'd received from her nephew along with five dollars left after the cab ride to her mother's house was all the cash she had, and she wasn't going to give him that. When he was gone she lifted the silver cover from her plate and dug into her dinner. She'd ordered steak well-done, with a baked potato, mixed vegetables, and a large slice of cheesecake. *Forget the diet,* she'd thought when she ordered; however, she did request a diet soda to go along with the meal. She decided while soaking in the tub that as long as her sister and brother-in-law were footing the bill, she was going to enjoy herself. It had been years since she'd been able to enjoy the finer things in life and Phoebe had severely missed them. Staying at a hotel was turning out to be even better than she could have imagined.

Phylicia awoke early the next morning and snuck out of bed before her husband had awakened. She was still tired, as she'd had a fitful night's sleep, but was anxious to get to the hospital to visit her mother. After waking both kids and getting them off to school, she returned upstairs to shower and get dressed.

She walked out of the bathroom a few moments later wrapped in a thick purple towel and saw her husband sitting on the edge of the bed. Phylicia thought he'd left for work already, and wondered why he was sitting there staring into his hands. "Gary, what are you still doing here?" she asked.

"We need to talk, Phyllie. There's something I need to tell you."

"Can it wait? I'm on my way to visit Mom at the hospital," she said, opening her dresser drawer and pulling out a matching bra and panty set. She kept her back to her husband as she put them on and let her towel drop.

"No, it can't. I'll talk while you dress."

"Fine, but make it quick. I'm almost done." She walked to the closet and pulled out a pair of grey slacks and a pink blouse.

"I just wanted to say, about your sister, you were right. I have been avoiding her and I honestly can't say why. I've never liked her and just thought avoiding her was best."

"I know that, Gary. What I don't know is why you never liked her. I mean, Phoebe is a spoiled little brat, and she can be flighty and selfish, but she's my sister and I still love her. I don't understand why you can't too."

"I don't know, Phyllie. Here I am pastor of a congregation of more than six hundred members and I can't even get along with my sister-in-law. I realized there was no excuse for it. That's what I wanted to tell you. I apologize. There's no reason why I should not be able to get along with your sister. You have my word that while she's here visiting I will do my best. Phoebe and I will become the best of friends. I promise."

Phylicia stopped buttoning her blouse and stared at her husband. "You don't have to go that far. My sister and I have our issues, too. But your tension with her only adds to that."

"You're right, and with Mom in the hospital, who needs that? I'll follow your lead as far as your sister is concerned and no more disappearing acts. I give you my word, honey."

Phylicia slipped into her shoes, grabbed her purse, and kissed her husband on the lips. "Thank you, sweetie, I'll call Phoebe from the car and see if she wants to go with me to the hospital. Will you be by later?"

"I have a marriage counseling session with Shanice and Jeremy. This was the only day they both could take off work. They are so young to be considering marriage, but since they're expecting their second child, both their parents and I agree it's best that we give them a good foundation and proceed with the wedding. When I'm done, I'll be over."

"They aren't much younger than you and I were when we got married, but I see your point. I guess I'll need to call Shanice's mother when I get in this afternoon." She kissed her husband once more, then rushed down the stairs and out the door. Feeling contented at last, the butterflies that had taken up residence in her stomach seemed to float away. She felt she could finally put all those ill feelings about the two of them behind her.

As soon as she pulled into traffic, she pressed her On-Star to contact the hotel and Phoebe's room. A very sleepy Phoebe answered the phone on the fifth ring. "Hello."

"I'm on my way to visit Mom. Do you want me to pick you up?"

"What time is it?"

"Almost nine. Are you still in bed?"

"Yes. I mean it's not like I had to go to work this morning." Phoebe stretched and yawned loudly into the phone receiver.

"So I guess that means you're not going with me. I'm not surprised at all."

"I didn't say that. I'm getting up now. Come on up to the room when you get here. I'll leave the door unlocked; it's room four thirty-seven," she said, and hung up.

Phoebe really didn't want to get up and go, but she couldn't stand the tone in her sister's voice. She was the oldest, but Phylicia always had a way of talking down to her that made her feel like a little kid. Reluctantly, she crawled out of bed and popped open her suitcase. She dug around in it, tossing items until she found the perfect outfit: Tommy Hilfiger hip-huggers and a red, low-cut peasant blouse. She dug around some more until she found a red thong and push-up bra to match, then rushed to the bathroom, leaving everything scattered all over the bed. She was dressed and just beginning to apply her mascara when she heard Phylicia enter the room. "I'll be out in a minute," she yelled.

"You know, you really need to clean up this mess before we go," Phoebe heard through the door.

Annoyed, she chose not to answer. *If Phyllie wants the room clean, she could clean it herself the way she did when we were kids. She probably is doing that right now and if I stay in here long enough, the room will be spotless,* she thought as she picked up her eyeliner.

She'd successfully lined one eye and was just beginning on the other when Phylicia burst into the bathroom, causing her to draw a black line all the way down her cheek. "Girl! What in the world are you doing in here? Look what you made me do. I told you I'd be out in a minute."

"Where did you get this?" Phylicia demanded.

"Get what?" Phoebe was busy trying to wipe the black line from her cheek and it was smudging. Out of the corner of her eye, she caught a glimpse of her sister in the mirror holding up a white handkerchief, waving it as if she were surrendering in battle. She froze momentarily, then quickly made up a lie. "That old handkerchief? I don't know. I've had it forever."

"I made this handkerchief," Phylicia said, her voice trembling.

"Well, then I probably got it from you. What's the big deal?"

Phoebe tried to go back to her makeup, hoping her sister would leave, but she knew it was no use. She heard

Phylicia speaking very low, her voice trembling and breaking between words as she tried to choke back tears.

"I made this for Gary. It took me three weeks to get the embroidery right for his initials. GDM is not as easy to sew as it looks. I had to take the stitches out and redo them several times, and even had to get help from Momma. When I finally got it right, I gave it to him for his high school graduation. He told me he loved it. He used to carry it with him all the time because he said it made him feel as if he were carrying me with him. Every day for over a year he carried it in his pocket, then one day it was gone. He told me he'd lost it. He couldn't remember where or when and he didn't want to talk about it." Phylicia took a deep breath. "Tell me the truth. Where did you get this?"

"Phyllie, I told you I don't remember. He probably lost it at the house and I picked it up. Why are you freaking out over a simple handkerchief?"

"It's not just a simple handkerchief. It's the handkerchief I spent weeks making for my husband. It's the gift I gave him that he told me he treasured as much as he treasured me and our relationship. Now stop lying and stop playing games with me! Where did you get this?" she shrieked.

"Phyllie, you are getting hysterical. Look, if it means that much to you and it's going to make you this upset, you can have it. Tell Gary you found it."

"Oh, I'm gonna tell him I found it all right. Then he or you or somebody is going to tell me the truth."

"What truth? What are you talking about?" Phoebe asked, feigning innocence.

"I could feel it. Phoebe, we are twins. Do you think I haven't felt the tension between you two all these years? Do you think I don't see the look in both your eyes when you are in the same room?"

"Phyllie, you really need to calm down. You know, now that I think about it, Gary did give it to me. Remember that time I didn't get the spot in the fashion show? He came by the house looking for you. Uh . . . I was crying and he gave it to me. I just forgot to give it back, and after all these years I forgot where I got it. So see, there's nothing to be upset about."

"Then why did he lie and say he lost it?"

"He probably forgot just like I did. C'mon, give me a few minutes to repair my makeup and we can go see Mom. I promise I'll be right out." Phoebe smiled weakly at her sister as she watched her back out and slowly close the bathroom door. She quickly wiped the black mark from her cheek and reapplied her foundation, then her eyeliner. She decided that under the circumstances, she wouldn't go through the ritual of adding any eye shadow. She pulled the wrap off of her weave and fluffed it out, then walked out of the bathroom to her room.

The door was standing open and Phylicia was gone.

Chapter Four

Phylicia parked her car in the church parking lot and sat quietly for several minutes, hoping to calm her nerves. She deeply regretted compulsively cleaning her sister's hotel room. As she had begun to repack the things scattered on Phoebe's bed, she couldn't believe she'd found her husband's handkerchief in her sister's suitcase nestled in amongst her panties and bras. The most intimate thing she'd ever given him was touching her sister's most intimate apparel. The symbolism of the situation sickened her. She'd almost forgotten about the handkerchief over the years and had even made him a new one, but now she realized what a fool she had been. Obviously he'd given it to her sister and they'd kept it a secret from her for almost twenty years. What she didn't understand was why. Slowly opening her car door, she got out and walked around the side of the church to the office, intent on finding out what else the two of them had kept from her.

Mrs. Farmer, her husband's elderly secretary, greeted her warmly as she entered.

"Good morning, Sister Phylicia. How are you doing?" she said with a boisterous smile.

"I'm just fine. How are you?" she answered unenthusi- astically.

"Oh, I can't hardly complain, child. How's your momma doing?"

"She's as well as can be expected under the circum- stances."

"I understand. We all have been praying for her. I was just telling my sister last night that it's rare for a person to get over two heart attacks, but if anybody can, it's your momma. She's a strong woman."

"Yes, ma'am, she is. We certainly appreciate your prayers. Is my husband alone in his office? I really need to speak with him."

"You just missed him. He said he was going over to the hospital to visit your mother. I believe he thought you were there."

"What about the counseling session with Shanice and Jeremy?"

"Those two children called at the last minute and can- celled on him. It's the third time they have cancelled this week. I just don't know about young folk these days. They have no respect for appointments and certainly not their elders. But if you hurry, I'm sure you can catch up to him. He hasn't been gone more than ten minutes."

"Thank you, Mrs. Farmer. I'll do that," she said, rush- ing out the door.

Phylicia had been so upset when she drove up, she hadn't even noticed that her husband's Acura Legend was not parked in its reserved space. Sitting inside her car, she debated with herself whether to follow him to the hospital, or wait there until he got back. Deciding there was no way she'd confront him in front of her mother, and needing time to calm down and think, she started the engine to go back home. Just as she did her cell phone rang.

"Hello," she said into the receiver.

"Phyllie, why did you leave me? I thought we settled this handkerchief business. Come back. I want to go visit Mother," Phoebe said.

"We didn't settle anything, and I'm not coming back."

"What has gotten into you? I can't believe you are this upset over a handkerchief."

"Good-bye, Phoebe," Phylicia said, then hung up the phone.

As she pulled into her driveway several minutes later, Phylicia noticed an old, beat-up Cadillac parked out front with a suspicious looking man sitting inside. Wondering what he was doing there, she closed and locked the garage door before getting out and entering the house. By the time she walked into the kitchen, the man was ringing her front doorbell.

He was dressed roughly in a dirty football jersey and blue jeans, and looked as if he had not shaven for several days. His small afro was uncombed with tiny specs in it; Phylicia could not tell if they were grey hairs or lint. He stood about six feet tall and was the color of burnt toast. Phylicia memorized all of these details while peering at him through the peephole. She'd been taught by her husband to be observant just in case, because the police would want to know all of that.

She backed up a few feet from the front door and yelled out, "Who is it?"

"Phoebe, is that you? Open the door."

"Phoebe's not here right now. Can I give her a message?"

"Okay, so you wanna act funny? I saw you drive up in

that fancy car. Open the blame door. I'm not playing with you. I'll kick it in." The man slammed his hand against the door. "Open up, Phoebe!"

Phylicia grabbed her cordless telephone from the table by the door and quickly dialed 911. "Phoebe is not here! You'd better leave; I have the police on the line," she yelled.

"Police?" The man violently kicked the door. "You better not call the freakin' police. I drove all night long just to get down here and you are acting like a lunatic." He kicked the door again. "Open up, I said!"

Phylicia ran upstairs and locked herself inside her bedroom as the police dispatcher advised her. She also advised her to stay on the line until an officer arrived, as the man continued kicking the door and screaming, "Phoebe, quit acting crazy and open this door! Phoebe!"

"I'm alone and I'm scared. Please can you call my husband?" Phylicia asked the dispatcher.

"What's the number, ma'am? We'll get him on the line. Just stay in your room until the officers arrive."

Phylicia gave the dispatcher her husband's cell phone number, as she heard her front door lock breaking and the door crashing in. "He's inside! Oh, God, he's in the house," she screamed into the phone.

"The officer is just a few blocks down the street. I'm gonna stay right here with you on the line. Just try to stay calm and as quiet as you can."

"Okay, I will," she whispered.

"Tell me what's going on now, ma'am. Is he still downstairs?" the dispatcher asked.

"Yes. I can hear him screaming my sister's name and walking through the house. Oh no, he sounds like he's coming up the stairs. I've got to hide somewhere else. I've got to run," she whimpered.

"The officers are onsite. Stay where you are, ma'am. Stay where you are."

Phylicia heard a struggle on the stairs and voices, and then she heard a gunshot. She screamed into the phone, dropped it, and ran into her walk-in closet, locking the door behind her. Huddled in a corner, she laid her head on her knees, crying and praying for the next half-hour until she heard her husband's voice.

"Phylicia, where are you?" Gary called out.

"I'm in here," she yelled as she got up and rushed to open the door.

"Oh, thank God you are all right." Gary breathed a deep sigh of relief and pulled her into his arms, holding her tightly.

Relieved, Phylicia collapsed against him, consumed by tears of fear and relief. When she was finally calm, Gary led her downstairs to speak with the officers. As they walked, she saw splatters of blood against the wall, the carpet on the stairs, and the railing.

"My wife was hiding in the closet. She's okay. She's shaken up but she's all right," he told the officer as he led Phylicia to the couch.

"What happened? The blood, I heard a gunshot," she said.

"The suspect was just starting up the stairs when we arrived and realized he was armed. He resisted arrest and wounded my partner in the leg before we were able to subdue and arrest him."

"I just can't believe a stranger would break into our home like that in broad daylight. The world has gone crazy," Gary said.

"This is gonna sound weird, sir, but he claims he's not a stranger," the officer replied, then turned to Phylicia. "Mrs. Morgan, he says that he knows you."

"No, no he doesn't. He thinks he does, but I'm not her."

"I don't understand, ma'am."

"My sister; he was looking for my sister, Phoebe. He thought I was her. We're twins. I don't know who he is but he must know her. He kept calling me by her name."

"Phoebe Cox? Is that your sister?"

"Yes, but her name is Phoebe Carson."

"Ma'am, the suspect, Maurice Cox Jr., says he's her husband."

Both Gary and Phylicia looked at the officer in stunned silence. They were both dumbfounded to think Phoebe was married to this man who had just broken into their home.

"Did you say her husband? How is that possible? My sister has never told us she was married," Phylicia said.

"Where is your sister now?" The officer asked.

"She's staying at the Marriott out by the highway in room four thirty-seven. Are you sure he said 'husband'?"

"Yes, ma'am. He claims she left town a few days ago after selling all of their furniture. He called and she told him she was visiting her sick mother. He went through her address book and followed her here. That's why he kicked your door in. He was angry with his wife."

"Oh, my goodness, I can't believe any of this," Phylicia said.

"Ma'am, I have to ask: since this is your brother-in-law, do you want to press charges for breaking and entering? We will still detain him for resisting arrest and assaulting an officer, but the other charges are up to you."

"Yes, of course we want to press charges," Gary answered. "This maniac broke into my home and scared my wife almost to death. My children will be home this afternoon and there's blood all over the place. Why wouldn't we want to press charges?"

"Gary, wait. If he's Phoebe's husband, maybe we shouldn't."

"What are you saying, Phyllie?"

"I mean, it's not like he's going to go free. I just don't want to make it worse for him. If he'd just told me who he was, maybe none of this would have happened. Or better yet, if my sister weren't such a liar, we . . ." Phylicia's voice trailed off as she suddenly remembered the handkerchief.

"We what, Phyllie? Your sister has been gone for years and we don't know this man. Are you sure you want to just let him get away with what he did?"

"I don't know, Gary. Do we have to decide right now?" she asked the officer.

"No, ma'am, you don't. As stated, he won't be going anywhere for a while. You can let us know in a few days. I'll go over to the hotel to speak with your sister and let her know where her husband is," the officer said.

"Phylicia, maybe you should go back upstairs and rest awhile. I want to get a bucket and some bleach and try to get these walls and carpet cleaned before Eva and Li'l G get home."

"Reverend Morgan, if you could hold off on that for a while, our forensics officers will need to take a few photographs before you clean up," the officer said.

"Wait, for how long? I don't want my children to see this."

"Actually, I think it would be best if you and Mrs. Morgan came with me to the hotel and checked in. We won't be clearing the crime scene today. I'm sorry, sir, but it's part of the investigation."

"We can't go to a hotel. What about the kids? What about our things? How can you ask us to leave our home?" Phylicia wailed.

"Phyllie, calm down, sweetie." Gary turned to the officer. "Why do we need to leave our home? Isn't there someway you can avoid that?"

"An officer has been wounded, that makes this much more than a simple breaking and entering case. I'm sorry for the inconvenience, Reverend, but it's necessary."

"Okay, I'll pack us a quick bag." Gary answered.

"Reverend, we really need you to leave now. If you remain in the house it could possibly disturb some evidence," the officer said.

Gary sighed, then looked over at his wife, who was still visibly shaken. "I guess we'll have to purchase some items for the night." He turned to his wife. "C'mon, Phyllie, let's get out of here and let the officers do their job."

"Thank you for understanding, Reverend Morgan." The officer ushered them out.

Chapter Five

Pacing back and forth in her hotel room like a caged tiger, Phoebe was sure she'd soon run a groove in the carpet. She wondered what was going on with Gary and Phylicia; surely they had talked by now. Had he confessed everything, or did he even remember the handkerchief? *Of course he remembers. How could I have so carelessly left my suitcase open when I knew Phylicia was on her way over?* Phoebe knew exactly how much it meant to both Gary and Phylicia.

A few days after he had left her in the park, Gary had called and asked for his handkerchief. He'd told her it was a very special gift from her sister and she'd been asking what happened to it. Phylicia had also mentioned to her that it was missing and Gary acted oddly whenever she asked about it. There was no doubt how valuable of a keepsake it was.

Desperately wanting to see him again, Phoebe asked him to meet her at their home when she knew everyone would be gone. It was Wednesday night, and her mother and Phylicia never missed Bible Study; they had long stopped bugging her to go. Her mind was still reeling from the kiss she and Gary had shared and she felt if she got him alone, it wouldn't take long for her to seduce him again. After that he'd be so in love with her he'd forget all about her sister.

She lit scented candles all over the family living room, dimmed the lights, and dressed in a tight black sweater dress that showed all of her curves.

When she heard the doorbell, she struck a sexy pose on the couch before seductively saying, "Come in."

"Dang, baby, is all this for me?"

Surprised, she looked up not at Gary, but at his best friend and roommate, Tino. He was tall and lean and almost as sexy as Gary, but he wasn't who she was expecting. He told her Gary sent him to collect the handkerchief, but she refused to give it to him. It still smelled of Gary's cologne, and if she couldn't have Gary then she'd at least have it.

For years she'd carried it with her no matter where she was. It had become almost like a security blanket for her, much more than a good luck charm. It represented Gary, what they shared, and she could never let go of it. Even now she felt lost without it, and wished she'd never allowed her sister to find and leave with it.

Reaching for the phone, she decided to give Phylicia another call, hoping her sister had calmed down. She'd just dialed the number when she heard a knock at her door. She placed the phone back in the cradle and called out, "Who is it?"

"It's the police, Mrs. Cox. We need to speak with you about your husband."

Phoebe rushed to the door and flung it open. "Maurice? What's going on? Is he okay?" Stunned, she noticed Phylicia and Gary standing behind the officer.

"He's fine, ma'am. He's at the county lockup. He shot a police officer and has a court appearance in the morning for a bond hearing for breaking into your sister's home."

"Broke in? I don't understand. What is he doing here?"

"We were hoping you could tell us that. He claims he was looking for you, and according to your sister, he mistook her for you and broke into the house. Why would he do that, Mrs. Cox?"

Phoebe's husband, Maurice, had been hot-tempered and violent since the day she met him while waiting tables at Denny's almost five years earlier. It was what had drawn her to him. A customer became rude and grabbed her arm. Without a word, Maurice yanked the guy off of his feet and punched him in his face, causing him to tumble to the floor like a deflated balloon. She'd never been so impressed with a man and his strength in her whole life. But it wasn't long after their wedding six months later before his strength no longer impressed. It petrified her.

"I . . . I don't really know. I suppose he followed me." She looked over the officer's shoulder. "Phyllie, Gary, I'm sorry. I'm really sorry," she whined.

"Well, I guess that's not your fault, Mrs. Cox. We just needed to confirm his story. However, he shot an officer so he's in a good deal of trouble." The officer reached into his pocket and pulled out a card with his name and title printed on the front. He turned it over and scribbled on it before handing it to Phoebe.

"Ma'am, this is the name of the judge he'll go before tomorrow. Be there at nine AM if you wanna post bail, but I have to warn you, it could be high. He's charged with resisting arrest and aggravated assault of a police officer. You may want to bring a bail bondsman with you."

"No, I won't be posting bail for him. But thank you, Officer. Thank you for coming by," Phoebe said and smiled weakly.

"Reverend, Mrs. Morgan, you should be free to return home in the morning, and we'll have an officer clean up the spatters of blood for you. We apologize for the inconvenience," he said before walking back down the hallway.

Phoebe saw the looks of rage in her sister's and brother-in-law's faces and wanted to rush after the officer for protection. Instead, she backed into the room and waited for the main event to begin.

"You're married and you never told us? Phoebe, this is ridiculous even for you," Phylicia said. Her voice was low and strained as she tried to contain her anger.

"Phyllie, just listen . . ." Phoebe began.

"Where did you meet such a thug? He practically tore our door off the hinges trying to get to you. What kind of crazy person are you involved with?"

"I don't know why he—"

"Why do you always do this? I called you because Mom is sick, and instead of coming to help, you cause chaos." Quickly losing her cool, Phylicia began screaming at her sister. "I have to wonder why you even bothered to waltz your thickly made-up, overdressed, loud-mouthed, weave-wearing self into town!"

"I haven't done anything. I came to visit my mother. You called me and told me to come and you've done nothing but make me miserable since I got here, with your condescending voice and your constant bossiness. So I'm married. I don't have to tell you my every move." Phoebe turned her back and walked behind the bed. Phylicia followed closely behind her.

"No, you certainly don't, but your lunatic husband didn't

have to tear the door off our home either. He scared me nearly to death. Thank God the police got there in time."

"I'm not responsible for that. You shouldn't have walked out on me in the first place. If you'd just listened to me, we'd be visiting mother right now. You are the one who ran out of here like a crazy person. No matter what happens, you always find a way to twist it into being my fault. How can you blame me for what he did?"

"I blame you because you are dishonest, Phoebe. If you'd told us you had a husband this whole incident never would have happened. Or better yet, if you had not run out on him after selling your furniture. What's that all about?"

"Just leave me alone, Phyllie. I did what I had to in order to see Momma." Phoebe pointed her finger at Phylicia's nose. "Don't you dare stand there and judge me with your five-bedroom home, your wallet full of credit cards, your Donna Karan outfit, and your six figure-earning husband. Don't you dare!"

"This isn't about money. If you needed money to come home, all you had to do was say so. Instead, you've been lying about having some great modeling career for all these years."

"I do have a career! My money is just tied up right now. In . . . It's in investments. So I didn't have much cash on hand. The furniture I sold was old anyway."

Phylicia threw her hands in the air in exasperation. "When are you gonna stop living in a fantasy world? I swear you'd think we were still nine years old the way you act sometimes."

A bellhop peeped into the door and interrupted their screaming match. "Ladies, I'm sorry to bother you, but some patrons on this floor have complained about the noise," she said.

"I'm sorry. We're sorry," Gary apologized. He reached into his pocket and handed the bellhop a five dollar bill. "It won't happen again. My wife and I are going to our room. C'mon, Phylicia, let's just go."

"You go to the room. I'm going down to the lobby to get a cab to the hospital. Phoebe and her antics have delayed me long enough," Phylicia snapped.

"What do you mean my antics? You are the one who came here raving like a mad woman!" Phoebe shot back.

"Ladies, please. I think you've both said enough. Phylicia, let's just go to the room," Gary interrupted.

"No, I'm going to the hospital." Without waiting for a response from her husband, Phylicia stormed down the hallway toward the elevator, leaving Gary and Phoebe alone.

"You two have a room here?" Phoebe asked as soon as her sister was gone.

"Yes, your husband decided to repaint our walls with a police officer's blood so we have to spend the night here," he said, turning to walk away.

"Gary, wait. Can we talk before you go?" she asked tentatively.

"Talk about what?" Gary snapped before he remembered his promise to Phylicia to be nice to her sister. He sighed. "What is it, Phoebe?"

"She knows about the handkerchief. She found it in my suitcase."

"What handkerchief? What are you talking about?"

"Your handkerchief; the one you gave me that day in the park. That day we kissed. Don't you remember?"

Gary remembered all too well and was becoming uncomfortable alone in the room with Phoebe. "You still have it? Why in the world have you held on to it?" he asked, astounded that she'd kept his handkerchief for more than a decade.

"That's not important. Listen, she was pretty upset, and I told her that you gave it to me when I didn't get into a fashion show. Just repeat that and we'll be fine."

"We? Since when is there a 'we,' Phoebe. I told Phylicia I lost it, and as far as I'm concerned, it's still lost. I have to go."

"Wait! Phyllie was furious with me. Could you at least back me up and smooth things over?"

"Smooth what over? I honestly had completely forgotten about that handkerchief, but the fact that you kept it certainly does not look good to my wife. Your husband just broke into our house and shot a cop. So now our home is a crime scene and we can't go back until tomorrow. Even you have to admit you've brought quite a bit of drama with you on this trip. I don't think there's anything I can do to fix it."

"I'm sorry, Gary. I just wanted to see my momma. It's been twelve years."

"That was your choice, Phoebe. No one ran you out of town or made you stay away."

"No, but . . ."

"Look, I really have to go." Gary reached inside his jacket pocket. "Here, take my card just in case you need someone to talk to."

"Gary, you mean I can call you and . . ." she asked, suddenly perking up and taking it from his outstretched hand.

"No. That would not be a good idea, but my associate pastor's number is on there. She is a wonderful counselor and great with people. Call her and she'll be glad to talk with you. Good-bye, Phoebe."

Phoebe watched him walk down the hallway before closing the door to her room. Then she ripped the card into tiny little pieces before throwing herself on the bed and bursting into tears.

* * *

When she arrived at the hospital, Phylicia went to the ladies' room to freshen her lipstick and put drops of Visine in her eyes before going in to see her mother. She'd been praying and crying the entire way over in the cab. Crying because she was hurt and confused when she'd found the handkerchief. She wondered if she'd made a big deal over nothing. She was also crying because she was so thankful her sister's husband had not hurt her. Phylicia had never experienced such fear in her life, and even though it was over, her heart still seemed to be beating at an irregular pace.

As she rode, she'd wiped her tears, stared out the window, and prayed. She prayed a prayer of thanksgiving, then she prayed for strength and clear thinking. She heard God speaking with her and dealing with her but she didn't want to listen, so she began crying again until the cab finally stopped in front of the hospital.

She blinked several times to make sure the redness was gone from her eyes, then, taking a deep breath and putting all of that behind her, Phylicia put on her best fake smile and walked into her mother's room. "Hi, Mom," she said as cheerfully as she could.

"Phyllie, I've been waiting for you girls all morning. Where's Phoebe?" her mother asked.

"She didn't come with me, Mom. It's just you and me today."

"Why didn't she come? Has she left town already?"

"No, Mom. She's still in town. Uhm . . . She's at the hotel."

"What is she doing at a hotel? Why isn't she staying at the house with you, Gary, and the kids?" her mother asked, then began coughing heavily.

Phylicia quickly poured her mother a cup of water

then removed her oxygen mask to help her swallow it. "Mom, please calm down. Gary and I paid for her to get a room there. We thought she'd be more comfortable."

"I need to speak with both of you girls. I want you to go get Phoebe and bring her back here. Go now."

"But, Mom, I just got here. I'll bring Phoebe by to see you tomorrow, okay?"

"Phylicia, it's time for me to go home. The Lord is calling me. Please go get your sister. I need to talk to both of you girls. Tomorrow will be too late."

Phylicia felt tears stinging her face. "Don't talk like that. You are going to be just fine. You are going to get stronger. Soon you'll be home and cooking fried chicken with molasses breading and laughing with me and the kids."

"Baby, I'm sorry, but it's my time. I've accepted it and you've got to accept it too. This old body is tired and weak. I'm ready to go, baby. But first I need to talk to my girls. Go get Phoebe, please?" her mother pleaded.

Phylicia wiped away a tear. "Okay, Mommy, I'll call her; but only so you'll stop talking like this. I'll tell her to take a cab here. That will be quicker. I'll be right back."

Phylicia walked out of the room and made a beeline to the nurses' station. "Can I see my mother's doctor, please?" she asked.

"Dr. Wallace is out of town. Dr Chang is taking his calls for today," the nurse replied.

"Well, then I need to see him. I need to see whoever is in charge of her care."

"Dr. Chang is on rounds at the moment. Can I help you, Mrs. Morgan?"

"My mother is talking about dying. I need to know her condition. Has it changed, and if it did, who told her? Who told her she's going to die? I need some answers and I need them now!" Phylicia didn't realize she was crying, screaming, and banging on the nurses station desk.

"Mrs. Morgan, your mother suffered a massive heart attack. Dr. Wallace advised you that it was very serious. That has not changed. We are making her as comfortable as possible, but until she gets stronger, that's all we can do."

"What about the surgery? Wasn't a specialist supposed to check her out for surgery?"

"I'm sorry, but she is too weak for open-heart surgery. At this point, her age combined with the damage done by the previous heart attack makes it too risky."

Phylicia tried to respond, but her words were lost in the tears that were now choking her. She walked away from the nurse's station and found the nearest chair. As she sat weeping, she noticed someone handing her a small Styrofoam cup. She looked up as the nurse smiled at her. "Here, Mrs. Morgan, take a few sips of water."

Silently she drank, wondering if she was only refilling her tear ducts for another round. "Can I get you anything else or call somebody for you?" the nurse asked.

"Please call my sister. Her name is Phoebe Carson Cox and she's at the Marriott on Clover Street. Just tell her to get here as soon as she can."

Gary stared at his watch as he stood in the check out line at Wal-mart. It was almost two o'clock, and if he didn't hurry, he would not get to the elementary school before Eva was dismissed from class. The last thing he wanted was for her to take the school bus home into pandemonium.

While there, he'd picked up jeans and T-shirts for the kids, extra toothbrushes, pajamas, socks, and underwear. Then sweat suits and personal items for himself and

Phylicia. He'd also stopped in the food aisle and grabbed some microwave popcorn, soda, cookies, and chips, then visited the DVD section for a few movies. It was only one night, but he felt if he made it fun, the kids would accept the transition better.

He still had not figured out what he was going to tell them, but he wanted to get to them first. Annoyed, he checked his watch again as the line inched up. No matter what time of day, Wal-Mart was always overcrowded and the elderly cashiers moved extremely slowly.

Relieved when it was finally his turn, Gary quickly paid for everything with his credit card, signed the receipt, and rushed to his car with the bags. He pulled up to Brown Bottom Elementary just as Eva was heading for her bus. He honked the car horn to get her attention, then waved.

"Hey, it's your dad," her friend Jayla said as they both turned.

"He must have come to give me a ride home. I wonder why."

"Eva, I thought we were gonna ride the bus together."

"Don't worry. I'll ask my Dad if you can ride home with us. C'mon," she said as they both walked toward the car.

"Hi, girls." Both girls waved at Gary. "Eva, sweetheart, wanna ride home?"

"Reverend Morgan, can I get a ride home too?" Jayla grinned and the sun bounced off of her braces.

"I'm sorry, Jayla, but we aren't going straight home tonight. I promise you can go with us next time," he said as he leaned over and opened the door for Eva.

Jayla looked at Eva sadly, and silently pleaded with her eyes. "Can't we drop her off on the way, Dad? It's not that far," Eva asked.

Trying to keep his cool and not worry his daughter,

Gary sighed. "I really hate to say no, pumpkin, but we've got to pick up Li'l G at the high school, then meet your mother." He looked over at Jayla. "I'm sorry, Jayla, really I am."

He watched as the two girls whispered and huddled for a few moments, then Eva finally got into the car. She watched out the back window as Jayla slowly walked toward the bus and got on alone. Then she turned around in her seat. "What are all those bags in the back seat?" she asked.

"I did some shopping today."

"You never go shopping. That's Mommy's job. Where is Mommy?"

"At the hospital with your grandmother, and I've been shopping plenty of times."

"Oh, so that's what's going on. Mom's busy, so you have to do women's work." She giggled.

"Yeah, that's exactly it." Gary shook his head at his daughter's joke.

A few moments later they pulled in front of Brown Bottom High School where Li'l G was a sophomore. He came bounding down the school steps and noticed them immediately. He rushed over to the car and snatched open the front passenger side door. "Get in the back, runt," he ordered his little sister.

"Dad!" she whined.

"Go ahead, Eva. Get in the back. I need to talk to you both. No arguing today."

Eva grudgingly obeyed and crawled over the seat. Li'l G settled into the front seat just as his Dad pulled out of the school driveway into the street. "What's going on, Dad? It's all over school that there were police cars and an ambulance at our house this morning. Jamal said they were still there at lunchtime and it's closed off with yellow tape," Li'l G blurted out.

"Did you say police cars and an ambulance? Is Mommy okay?" Eva screamed.

"Somebody was gunned down in a hail of gunfire is what I heard."

"Where's Mommy?" Eva asked frantically.

"Stop it, Li'l G. You're scaring your sister. There was no hail of gunfire," Gary said.

"So what happened? Is Mom all right?" Li'l G asked.

"Yes, your mother is fine. She's at the hospital visiting your grandmother. Listen; there was an altercation at the house today between your . . . uhm. Well, a man tried to break in, and he shot a police officer in the leg. There was no hail of gunfire, but the police have our house closed off for the rest of the day. We'll be staying at a hotel tonight."

"That's crazy. This is Brown Bottom, Louisiana. Since when do people break in during the middle of the day? Where were you and Mom?" Li'l G asked.

"Your mother was home, but she hid in the bedroom closet. The police called me and I came home. It's all over now."

"Did the cops catch him? What did he look like? Was he one of those crackheads from downtown? How he'd get all the way out to our house? What kind of gun did he have?" Li'l G asked all in one breathe.

"I wanna stay at the hotel forever. I don't wanna go home," Eva said as tears streamed down her face.

"Li'l G, stop with all the questions. Look what you're doing to your sister." Gary looked at his daughter in the rearview mirror and tried to make eye contact. "Honey, there's nothing to be afraid of. It's all over now. Don't cry, pumpkin."

"But what if he comes back? What if he tries to get in again?" Eva sniffed and wiped her nose on her sleeve.

"Sweetie, that won't happen. He has been arrested and

is in jail. He can't hurt us. I promise you. Listen, tonight we are gonna relax at the hotel. I got us a big suite that has a TV with a DVD player. I bought that new movie you wanted, and some popcorn, and we will order room service and it will be just like going on a mini-vacation. Then tomorrow we'll go back home. There's nothing to be afraid of, sweetie."

Eva wiped her face and nose with the back of her hands and seemed to calm down a bit. Gary breathed a sigh of relief.

"Yo, Dad, can I use your cell? I wanna call Jamal and tell him what happened. He's gonna freak when he hears this," Li'l G said, grabbing the phone that was resting in its holster on the dashboard.

"No! Call him later. I just got your sister calmed down. Put my phone back."

"Hey, did you know you have seven missed calls? Your ringer is turned off."

Gary had completely forgotten that he'd turned it off right after leaving the hotel. He'd left word with his secretary that he would not be back for the rest of the day and wasn't in the mood to speak with any of his parishioners. He'd already gotten one call from nosey Mrs. Edwards who lived down the block and she had spent more than fifteen minutes berating him on the seriousness of police officers visiting the pastor's home. When she'd finally stopped to take a breath, he'd politely explained to her that his family experienced a break-in. He'd immediately regretted it as he spent another fifteen minutes listening to her cry, rant, and scream about the evils of the world. When she'd finally hung up, he'd called his secretary and shut off his phone.

"Will you check the log and see if any of them are important? If not, I'll call them back later."

Li'l G looked through the phone log. Then he checked

the back seat and noticed his little sister staring out the window, lost in her own world, before he leaned over and whispered, "They're all from Mom's phone except one. I don't recognize that number."

"Call her back then give me the phone. We're only a few blocks from the hospital. I pray nothing is wrong."

Li'l G pressed "send" then waited. "She's not answering. Do you want me to try the other number? It might be the hospital." Li'l G dialed the phone, then handed it to his father as soon as he heard a nurse pick up.

"This is Reverend Gary Morgan. I believe someone at this number called me."

"Uhm, yes we did, Reverend Morgan. Your mother-in-law has taken a turn for the worse. Your wife and her sister are with her now. She asked me to call. You need to get here as soon as possible."

"Tell my wife I'll be right there." Gary answered.

Phylicia held her mother's hand and rubbed it gently. On the opposite side of the bed her sister sat mirroring her image and actions. Tears streamed down both of their faces, Phoebe's looking like an abstract painting as her makeup ran.

When she'd received the phone call from the nurse, she'd tried to reach Gary in their hotel room to give her a ride, but he was already gone from the hotel. Instead, she asked the concierge to get her one of the hotel cars, and was pleased to learn the short trip to the hospital was only an eleven dollar flat fee. She'd arrived to find Phylicia sitting in the hallway in a puddle of tears. Gently, she touched her shoulder, and for the first time in more than twelve years, her sister reached out and hugged her tightly, then began sobbing in her arms.

"Phyllie, what's going on? Is Mom okay?" Phoebe asked her.

"She said it's time for her to go home. She said the Lord is calling her. Phoebe, she's dying. Momma is really dying." Phylicia clung to her sister.

"It's okay, Phyllie. She's not gone yet."

Phylicia sniffed loudly. "I don't know why I'm acting this way. I've known since she first had the heart attack that it could be fatal, but I guess I just didn't want to believe it."

"I didn't either. I've wasted so many years away from her."

"She said she needs to talk to us both before . . . before she's gone." Phylicia sniffed and wiped her nose on the tissue the nurse had given her, which was now ragged. "That's why I had the nurse call you."

"I have some fresh tissues in my purse. Let's get your face cleaned up and we'll go in to see her, okay?"

As they stood quietly at her bedside, their mother weakly told them what she needed to say. "Phoebe, it's time to tell your sister the truth. I can't go home peacefully unless she knows."

"Don't try to talk, Mom. We're both here. That's all that matters, okay?" Phoebe answered.

"No. I need you to tell her. It's been too many years of secrets and lies. Please just tell your sister the truth."

"Mom, I'm confused. I don't know what you mean." Phoebe said amidst tears.

"Pharrah, tell her about Pharrah," she whispered, as Phoebe's eyes grew wide as saucers. She rubbed her mother's hand and kissed her forehead. "Don't worry about that right now, Mommy," she said.

"What is she talking about, Phoebe?" Phylicia asked, confused.

Phoebe's eyes darted back and forth from her mother to her sister, then she finally shrugged her shoulders. "I don't know," she answered

"Phoebe, promise me you'll tell her. Promise me," her mother whispered.

Phoebe looked over at her sister, then back at her mother. She leaned down and kissed her mother again. "I promise, Mom. Whatever you want, I promise." She looked at her sister, and then turned back to her mother. "Just don't try to talk too much right now, okay?"

Their mother nodded, then slowly turned her face towards Phylicia. "Phyllie, I want you to be strong. I hate to leave my girls, but I know it's time. You two have to hold on to each other, and hold on to God. That's the only way you'll make it. You have to stop fighting with each other and learn to lean on one another."

"Yes, Momma," Phylicia said as the tears dropped off her face.

They both watched in pained silence as their mother's eyes slowly closed, and her breathing became heavy and labored as it slowed down.

They stood there quietly, unsure of how much time passed until the door flew open and Gary and the kids rushed in. "How is she?" Gary asked breathlessly.

Phylicia went to her husband and he enveloped her into his arms. "It won't be long now. She's dying," she whimpered. As she watched her mother struggling to breathe with the help of the respirator, Phylicia whispered to her husband, "Maybe the kids shouldn't be in here. I'm not sure they should see her like this."

"They should be here. They need a chance to say . . . to say good-bye." He turned to his children. "Li'l G . . . Eva . . . go talk to your grandma," he instructed.

The kids moved to each side of their grandmother's bed and took their mother and aunt's places as they both stepped back. Phylicia watched them sobbing uncontrollably as they each whispered in her ear and gently kissed her. Her eyes opened momentarily and she smiled weakly at both of them. She mouthed the words, "I love you," before closing her eyes again.

Eva joined her parents and buried her face into her father's side, soaking it with her tears. Gary held them both tightly. Seeing her standing all alone, Li'l G offered his broad shoulder to Phoebe, and she gladly took it.

The entire family stood weeping as Gary prayed for her peaceful transition, and Gertrude Evangeline Carson crossed over and went home.

Chapter Six

The next morning, Phylicia awoke suddenly, wondering where she was. She frantically looked around the strange room before remembering they'd spent the night in a hotel. After leaving the hospital, contacting the mortuary, family, and friends, it had been well past midnight when they'd finally gone to bed. Phylicia lay awake in the dark until almost daybreak before finally drifting off. As her husband lay still, sleeping, she checked the bedside clock and realized that she'd only been asleep for two hours. Exhaustion had overtaken her and she was drained physically and mentally, but she knew that sleep would not come. Slowly, she peeled back the covers and climbed out of bed.

"Where are you going, sweetie?"

"I'm sorry, I didn't mean to wake you. I'm gonna take a shower. We should get packed and back to the house. Mr. Watkins will be by with the extra chairs and the wreath for the door at nine-thirty. I'm sure we have tons of messages from family and friends. Will you go wake the kids and order them some breakfast from room service? I'll be out and dressed in a minute."

Gary tried to stop her and say something, but he knew his wife. Keeping herself busy and moving was the way she dealt with grief. He'd watched her operate on autopilot like a robot twelve years earlier when her father passed, but he'd hoped with her mother she'd show more emotion. After the initial tears, Phylicia shut down her heart and put her mind and body into full gear. Gary knelt beside the bed and prayed. He knew they'd both need God in order to get through the next few days.

Still dressed in the clothes from the day before, lying on top of the covers, makeup smeared across her face, Phoebe stared at the ceiling. She'd dozed on and off all night, but never really slept. She was no longer crying, but it was only because she'd run out of tears. For twelve years she'd told herself that her mother would always be there and she could always go home. That was no longer true. She felt lost and alone. Her thoughts briefly wandered to Maurice, until she remembered he was in jail.

In her mind, she rewound the last few moments of her mother's life and the words she'd spoken. *Tell her about Pharrah* echoed over and over. Suddenly, Phoebe sat upright in the bed and reached for her purse. Anxiously, she searched for her cell phone, dumping her purse contents all over the bed. When she finally found it, she realized she'd forgotten to charge it the night before and the battery was dead. She was rustling through the items lying on the bed searching for her calling card when the phone on the hotel nightstand rang. She let it ring four times before she finally decided to pick it up. "Hello."

"Phoebe, it's me. We're ordering breakfast. Can we get something for you?"

"Thank you, Gary, but I'm not really hungry."

"You have to eat; you need to keep up your strength. How about a fruit salad? You can join us in our suite for breakfast, then we're all going back to the house."

"Well . . . I'm not sure."

"Listen, I haven't mentioned this to Phyllie, but I will as soon as she gets out of the shower. I want you to come back to the house with us and stay in the guest room." There was a long pause as he waited for her to answer. "Phoebe, are you there? Did you hear me?"

"Yes, I'm sorry. I was just a bit surprised. Are you sure you shouldn't discuss this with Phyllie first? She asked me to leave."

"I know all about that, but it was before Mom passed. The family needs to be together now all in the same house. After breakfast I want you to come home with us. I know that's what your mother would've wanted."

"All right, I'm getting dressed. Go ahead and order me the fruit salad and some pancakes, too," she said, grinning from ear to ear as she hung up. She still felt grief for her mother, but having Gary personally invite her back into the house sent joyous chills up and down Phoebe's spine. Gleefully, she hopped off the bed and began getting ready.

"So when were you planning to tell me about all this?"

Gary turned around; Phylicia was out of the shower. "As soon as you got out of the bathroom; I think it's for the best," he answered.

Ignoring him, Phylicia grabbed the Wal-Mart bag her husband had brought and dug inside for her clothes. "What is this? You of all people should know I don't wear synthetic underwear. I need a cotton panel, Gary," she screamed.

"I'm sorry. I was in a hurry and—"

"And what is this, a bulky sweat suit? It's spring. I'm going to burn up in this thing."

"It was on sale. Clearance, I guess," he said weakly.

"The temperature is going to be well above seventy today, Gary. Were you even thinking? Honestly, how much thought does it take to get cotton underwear and spring clothing? What did you get for the kids? I'm gonna have to get dressed and go check it out. No! Forget it. I'll just put this on and go shopping myself for them."

Gary sat quietly on the bed as his wife ranted. He realized her anger was not about the clothes or directed at him, so he silently allowed her to vent.

Completely dressed, she went to the mirror. She stood there, aggressively brushing her hair. "We wouldn't even be here if it weren't for Phoebe. Why did I even bother calling her? She's been nothing but trouble since the moment she strutted through the door!" Suddenly, she turned to face Gary. "Why in the world did you invite her back to the house? Why?" she screamed.

Standing slowly, Gary walked over to the mirror and wrapped his arms around his wife. "She's your sister, Phyllie. She's all you've got now," he whispered.

"No. I still have you and the kids," she said, clinging tightly to him.

"I promised you before; if this is about me, she can stay at the house. I will not leave your side for a moment."

"She's hiding things, Gary. Her husband, and before you came in, Mom urged her to tell me the truth about something. She promised she would, and then she stopped talking. Mom's dying wish was for us to get closer, but I don't know how. I don't know if I can even trust my sister."

"Does all of that matter right now? The next few days are going to be difficult for all of us. Let's just call a truce between you and your sister, at least until after the funeral, okay?"

Phylicia looked up at her husband with a tear-stained face, and slowly nodded her head.

"I'm gonna order the food and get showered. The kids are up and getting dressed." Gary reached for his pants that were lying across the chair and dug into the pocket. He retrieved his handkerchief, slowly wiped her tears, and handed it to her, then went to the phone.

As he dialed and spoke with room service, Phylicia stared at it in her palm. It was the one she'd made for him when he "lost" the first one. She held it to her chest as she heard the Spirit speaking to her. It was all connected somehow. The handkerchief, the secret, and her sister's exit from town were all intricate pieces of a clandestine puzzle. As soon as she laid her beloved mother to rest, she was determined to get answers from them both.

Maurice Cox sat in the courtroom silently staring at the judge who was about to pronounce his bail. While there, he'd sat through the bond hearings of a drunk driver, a trespasser, and two hookers. It was all pretty boring and he struggled to stay awake. He perked up when he realized the judge was finally speaking to him. "Mr. Cox, do you have anything to say before I set bail?"

"Uhm, it was an accident. Things just got out of control, Your Honor, sir."

"According to the report, you broke into a home and shot an officer. How was that an accident?"

"That woman in the house was my wife. It's her momma's house. I was trying to get in to uhm, to help her. I heard her screaming and I thought something was wrong."

"Why did you shoot the officer?"

"I didn't mean to shoot him. I had my gun drawn, because like I said; I thought my wife was in danger. I'd do anything to protect her. It went off by accident when the officer grabbed me on the steps. I swear I would never shoot no cop."

The elderly Asian judge shuffled through his papers, then turned to the arresting officer. "Was the gun drawn when you approached the suspect?" he asked.

"I can't be sure, Your Honor. My partner went up first. There was a struggle on the stairs and I heard a shot, then I noticed he was wounded. It all just happened really fast."

"Like I said, Your Honor, it was an accident. I didn't shoot that cop on purpose," Maurice said interrupting.

"You've had your chance to speak, Mr. Cox," the judge answered before turning back to the officer. "I don't see any breaking and entering charges here. All I have are the resisting arrest and assault charges. Where is the paperwork for the other charges?"

"The owners of the home, Reverend and Mrs. Morgan, are reluctant to press charges since he is family. They may change their minds later but right now—"

The judge held up his hand to shush the officer. "I don't need to hear anymore. There are no charges here." He turned to Maurice. "I don't know if what you are saying is true; that will come out in court. However, under the circumstances, I will set bail at five thousand dollars on the resisting arrest charge, and five thousand dollars on the assault charge." He banged his gavel and signaled the bailiff to bring him the next case.

Maurice grinned as the detention guard led him back to his cell. He knew he'd only need a thousand dollars to get out, and he knew just who he'd call to get it. As soon as the cuffs were off, he rushed to the pay phone in the inmates' area and dialed the number. It rang several times, then he waited for the operator to introduce him. He heard her hesitate, before she finally agreed to accept the charges.

"What in the world are you doing in jail in Louisiana?"

"Hello, to you too, babygirl."

Pharrah cringed, as she hated when he called her that. "What do you want?" she asked.

"I need your help. Can you get me out of here?"

"You still haven't told me why you are in there."

"It's a long story. Just help me get out and I'll explain it all. My bail is only a grand. I know you've got that."

"Where in the world would I get a thousand dollars? I'm a student."

"Don't play with me. I know your mom sends money to you at that fancy college, and I know you've got a job, too. Just help me out this time. I promise it will be the last."

"That's what you said last time, Maurice, and the time before that. Besides, why didn't you just call Mom and ask her?"

"Uhm . . . well . . . okay, I didn't want to tell you all this, but you forced me to. Your mom is acting crazy. She's in some hick town down here pretending to be some rich bougie woman. She wouldn't even talk to me when I went by there. She had me arrested. Can you believe that?"

Pharrah could not only believe it, she was relieved her mother had finally had the courage to do it. Maurice had been a thorn in both their sides since the day her mother married him, when Pharrah was just fourteen years old. She'd never seen him strike her mother, but she knew that he did. There were only so many lies she could make up to hide the bruises, the cuts, and the burns. For whatever reason though, Maurice had never laid a hand on her, and she was grateful when she'd been able to leave just a few years later for college. She was currently a junior at Southern University and enjoying her time away from him, although she missed her mother.

"What town? Where are you?" she asked.

"Brown Button or something like that."

"Do you mean Brown Bottom? What's Mom doing there?"

"Yeah, that's it. Your mother is lying as usual. She said her momma's sick, but you know as well as I do that her momma been dead. She sold all our furniture and just took off. Then when I get down here she's riding around in this new car and pretending to not even know who I am. Your momma's gone crazy, I tell ya. I think she got another man or something. C'mon, babygirl, help me out of here so I can find out what's really going on."

"Grandma's sick? Oh my God. She has to be really sick for Mom to go back to Brown Bottom."

"What are you mumbling about, girl? There was nobody at that house but your momma. She was driving a Navigator and looking all plain Jane."

"You went to Grandma's house? Maurice, tell me everything you know."

"I don't know nuttin' 'bout no grandma."

"You went to the house, you must know something."

"I don't know nuttin'; but I need a grand to get out. Help me and I'll tell you anything you wanna know."

"I gotta go," Pharrah said, then hung up the phone. She immediately dialed her mother's cell phone and heard it click over to voicemail. She was just about to leave a message when she realized that if her mother had not told her she was going there, she would not return her call. Instead, she hung up and called her best friend.

"Hey, Kelli, you feel like skipping class today and going on a road trip?" Pharrah asked.

"Well, right now I'm on my way to physics, but after that you know I'm always down. Where we headed?"

"Brown Bottom, Louisiana."

"That's at least three hours from here and way back up in the sticks. Who do you know that lives way out there?"

"My grandmother . . . and I think my father."

Chapter Seven

Phylicia felt as if she were in a dream as she watched the procession of family, friends, and church members file into her house with their hugs and well wishes. Each of them had a warm, funny, or endearing story to tell about her mother, and she smiled politely at each one. The living room, family room, dining room, kitchen, and even the garage were packed full of funeral home chairs and guests. She didn't want to appear rude, but she'd insisted that no one other than immediate family be allowed upstairs. She'd wanted to be able to retreat to the calmness of her bedroom if the throng of people got to be too much for her. So far, that had only been a wish, as she had not a moment to sneak away. Her refrigerator, dining room table, kitchen table, and kitchen counters were stuffed way beyond the legal capacity with chicken, hams, pies, vegetables, casseroles, breads, desserts, and drinks. She'd sent Li'l G to the corner store for paper plates, cups, and ice. Gary and the children were trying to feed as many people as they could in order to lighten the load.

Phoebe sat in her favorite chair in the living room, vividly entertaining her cousins with stories of life in New York and working as a model. Phylicia knew they were mostly lies, but, for once, she was grateful that her sister was garnering lots of attention. Having her there meant there were less people she had to mingle with and talk to. Phylicia greatly appreciated the condolences, but she wasn't in a particularly chatty mood. Noticing that Gary finally had an orderly food line, she caught his attention and mouthed words to him. He immediately joined her by the stairs.

"Are you okay, honey? Can I get you something to eat?" he asked as he wrapped his arm around her waist.

"No, I'm fine. I just need to go upstairs for a few minutes. I feel like being alone."

"Do you want me to come with you?"

"How can I be alone if you come with me?" she laughed. "I just didn't want you to worry. I need to go through Mom's things and pick out a dress to take to the mortuary. Then I need to find the insurance policies, write the obituary and program for the service, and—"

"Stop it right there. All of that can wait until later. You need to lie down. C'mon, I'll take you upstairs, then I'll come back to our guests."

Gary refused to leave their bedroom until Phylicia was lying down. He covered her with the quilt from the foot of the bed and gently kissed her forehead. "Just get some rest, honey. I can handle things downstairs, then later I'll come up and help you with everything else."

She nodded her head and waited until she heard him descending the stairs before she threw back the quilt and got up. She went over to her closet and walked the full length of it to the back corner. She knelt down and retrieved the tin box her mother had given her a few months before. It contained all of the family's important papers, including birth, death, and marriage certificates, insurance policies, letters and old report cards of her's and Phoebe's. Sitting on the floor, she crossed her legs and fumbled with the lock until it finally opened. She took a long, deep breath, then began to thumb through it. Within a few moments, she found the four life insurance policies her mother had told her were there. She opened each one and read the amounts and beneficiaries. The first had her name and was for $20,000. Her mother had advised her it was to cover funeral expenses, and the remainder was to be donated to the church. She laid it aside for the mortuary. The next two were for $150,000 each and also listed Phylicia as the beneficiary. Phylicia knew her mother bought these two policies for Eva and Li'l G. She'd told Phylicia to use it for their college educations. "Thank you, Mommy," she whispered into the solitude of the closet.

Finally, she picked up the last one, read it, and then stared at it in total shock. She turned it over and checked the dates. Her mother had paid it religiously and the premiums were up to date. Unable to believe her eyes, she read it aloud, hoping it would sound different than it looked. "$150,000 dollars, beneficiary Phoebe Carson Cox."

"I knew you wouldn't listen. What are you doing in here?"

Phylicia looked up as her husband walked in. "I'm sorry, I just couldn't rest. I needed to pull out these insurance policies. You've got to see what I found." She handed the policy to her husband.

"So, your mother left Phoebe some money. It's not a big deal. It's not like we need it, and from the things we've learned since she got back, maybe your sister does."

"She's been gone twelve years, Gary. All Mom has gotten from her in all that time have been some rinky-dink Christmas cards and the obligatory Mother's Day call.

I've been here caring for her, cooking and cleaning for her, nursing her when she was sick, and even wiping her behind when she couldn't do it for herself. How could she slap me in the face like that and leave all this money to Phoebe? How could she?"

"Phyllie, you are getting upset over nothing. We don't need any money. My salary at the church is almost double the amount of that policy. What are you so concerned about?"

"It has nothing to do with the money. It's the principle of the whole thing. Phoebe has done nothing for Mom and I've done everything. It's not fair, Gary. It's just not fair. Daddy left us equal amounts. He didn't play favorites at all. He had policies for both of us with the exact same amounts on them!"

Gary stared at his visibly upset wife, then noticed the other policies lying on the floor. "What are those? Maybe one is yours," he offered meekly.

"Those are for the children and the funeral. There's nothing here for me. Nothing! After everything I've done for and been to her, how could she do this to me? How could she love Phoebe more than me?"

Gary sat down on the floor beside his wife and wrapped his arms around her. "Don't doubt for one second that your mother loved you. You and she were like best friends. She depended on you and she loved you for being here for her all these years. Do you really believe her love is measured by the amount of money she left you?"

"I don't know what to believe anymore. This is just so shocking. I never expected Mom to leave me any money. She'd told me she wanted to take care of her grandchildren, her funeral, and nothing more. But she lied, Gary. She wanted to take care of Phoebe, too."

"What about the house? Maybe she left the money to Phoebe because we have the house."

"The deed is in both mine and Phoebe's name. The house belonged to Daddy. He just let Mom keep it after the divorce, since he'd had it built for her and us girls. You and I don't even own this house, and Mom left Phoebe all this money. It just doesn't make sense."

"Listen, honey, I know your mom, and I know she had a good reason. Like I said before, Phoebe probably needs the money. We both know she's no model like she claims. We also know she had to sell her furniture just to get here. Not to mention that low-life she married. You and I are well taken care of financially. God has and will continue to provide. Don't let this make you doubt your Mom or your relationship. She loved you very dearly. If I don't know anything else, I know that."

"Do you think Mom was in touch with Phoebe, I mean more than she told us about? This policy lists her married name, and we didn't even know she was married. Obviously Mom did."

"I don't know, maybe. What difference does it make? Look, do you want me to call Phoebe up here? You can give her this and she can tell you just how much your mom knew."

"She won't tell me anything. I wasn't going to bring this up again, but I have to. Last night when Phoebe and I were alone with Mom, she asked her to tell me the truth about Pharrah. Mom begged her to tell me the truth. Phoebe played dumb, but I know she knew what Mom meant. I could see it in her face."

"Who's Pharrah?"

"You remember my little cousin. Mom used to have her baby picture on her dresser."

"Wasn't she your Aunt Philomena's daughter?"

"Yeah, she should be in college now. She'd be around that age anyway. I'm not sure what happened to her after her mother died."

"Well, why don't you call her, tell her about your mom. Maybe she'll want to come and we can get some answers."

"I wouldn't know how to reach her."

"Maybe you can look through Mom's things for a number later. But for now, let's get out of here. The children are probably going crazy trying to fend off all those people downstairs."

Phylicia gathered up all the insurance policies and followed her husband out of the closet. As they neared the bedroom door, she suddenly stopped. "Wait! Let's not tell Phoebe about the policy yet. Not with all these people here. I'll talk to her about everything later. I couldn't stand the embarrassment of all these people knowing Mom left her something and me nothing."

"Phyllie, I think you're overreacting, but I do agree that family business should be discussed with family."

Phylicia placed the policies inside her dresser drawer, then followed Gary downstairs just as the front doorbell rang. She walked past it, motioning for him to answer. He pulled the door open and looked into the face of a young woman he did not recognize. Her cocoa-colored facial features seemed familiar, and he instinctively knew by her grey eyes that she must be a relative of the Carson family. "Hello, may I help you?" he asked.

"Is this the residence of Gertrude Carson?"

"Yes it is, well, it was."

"Was?"

"I'm sorry. Mrs. Carson passed last evening. Are you family?"

Pharrah did not answer. She slumped into Gary's arms as she fainted.

Phoebe stood in the garage pretending to be engrossed in her latest tale of glamour and glitz as a model. She'd seen the commotion in the living room and immediately darted through the kitchen, out the back door, and into the garage, trying to think. She couldn't believe that Pharrah had just fainted at her sister's front door and that at any moment she would wake up and start talking.

"Auntie Phoebe, my mom wants you in the living room."

She heard Li'l G talking, but pretended not to. She continued flailing her arms dramatically as she told a much-worn, fabricated tale of a fashion show she had done for Versace. Her cousin, Ophelia, looked back and forth between her and Li'l G before interrupting her. "Phoebe, he said Phyllie wants you. You can finish telling me this story later."

"No, I'm almost to the end." She finally looked in her nephew's direction. "Li'l G, tell your mom I'll be in there in a few minutes." Phoebe continued her story as her cousin stared wide-eyed, obviously impressed, until Li'l G returned. He stood in the doorway watching her for several moments before he finally spoke.

"Aunt Phoebe, she says it's important and could you come now, please?"

Reluctantly, Phoebe stopped her story and followed him into the living room. She stood back, unsure of what to say. She watched her daughter, Pharrah, sipping a cup of water as Mrs. Farmer fanned her with a paper fan with Martin Luther King Jr.'s picture on it.

"Phoebe, look who's here," Phylicia said as she noticed her. Phoebe didn't answer. She only stared with a bewildered look on her face. "You probably don't recognize her. This is our cousin, Pharrah, Aunt Philomena's daughter."

Phoebe swallowed hard before extending her hand. "Hello, cousin Pharrah. How are you?"

Pharrah stared at her mother, realizing that her visit did not mean things had changed. On the drive up, she'd told Kelli the whole story of her birth, her paternity, and the secrets. She'd hoped since her mother had returned to Brown Bottom that finally she had stopped all the lies and come clean. Obviously, she had not.

"Hello, it's nice to see you," she finally said.

"Pharrah fainted at the doorway. She didn't know Mom was sick and was surprised to get here and find out she'd died. Apparently she and Mom have kept in close contact over the years." Phylicia spoke slowly, watching her sister's face for reactions.

"It is rather shocking, isn't it? I guess I would have fainted too," Phoebe said weakly.

"Mom mentioned you last night, Pharrah, right, Phoebe?" Phylicia said, then looked back and forth between the two of them.

"She did? What did she say?" Pharrah asked.

"It was just ramblings. We aren't really sure what she meant. Who is this other young lady with you?" Phoebe said, quickly changing the subject and pointing to the red-haired, fair-skinned young woman sitting next to Pharrah.

"This is my roommate, Kelli Liddle. We attend Southern University in Baton Rouge together."

"It's amazing that you decided to make a surprise visit at this time, isn't it, Phoebe? I mean it's almost like she knew something was wrong. What brought you here, Pharrah?" Phylicia asked.

Realizing her roommate was a lousy liar and backed into a corner, Kelli decided to bail her out. "She's with me, really. I met a guy on the Internet who asked me to come down for the weekend. Pharrah just thought she'd drop by and say hello to her, uhm, aunt while we were here. We had no idea what was going on."

"Uhm, she's right, we really didn't. But I'd like to attend the funeral, if it's okay with you guys," Pharrah said, staring at her mother.

"Well, of course it's okay. Where are you staying?" Phylicia answered.

"Uhm, do you know of a cheap motel nearby? We don't have much cash on us," Kelli answered for the both of them.

"Why can't they stay here, Mom?" Li'l G said, suddenly speaking up. He and his father had been standing by watching the exchange. He realized Pharrah was his cousin, but he was impressed and had developed a mini-crush on Kelli in the few moments she'd been in their home.

"Li'l G, I'm not sure we have room with your Aunt Phoebe in the guest room," Phylicia answered.

"What about Grandma's room?" Li'l G suggested.

Phylicia looked at him, surprised. She had not even opened the door to her mother's bedroom since returning to their home. It hit her once again that her mother was not coming back. "Uhm . . . I need to . . . we haven't cleaned . . . I uhm . . ." she stammered.

"Hey, I've got a better idea. If you girls don't mind, the couch in the family room opens up to a comfortable queen-sized bed. You're welcome to use it until after the funeral. After all, you are family," Gary said.

Pharrah suddenly noticed the handsome man who'd answered the door and caught her when she fainted. Unbeknownst to her, he'd carried her to the couch and summoned Phylicia. When she awoke, she thought she was looking at her mother momentarily, then realized it must be her mother's twin. She had not yet been introduced to him, but she was sure he must be Gary Morgan; the man she'd been told was her natural father. She smiled broadly at him. "That would be great. We'd love to stay here."

* * *

Late that night, when she felt everyone in the house was fast asleep, Phoebe crept out of bed and tipped downstairs to the family room. The door was ajar, so she slowly pushed it open to see if Pharrah and Kelli were awake. She was surprised to see Pharrah sitting up in bed staring at the doorway, as if she were waiting for her. "I knew you'd be down here. Mom, you've got a lot of explaining to do."

"Me? No, let's start with you, young lady. What in the world are you doing here? Don't give me that Internet story again, because I'm not buying it."

Kelli turned over and looked at them both. "Do you want me to leave while you two talk?"

"Yes," Phoebe said immediately.

"No. I've told her everything, Mom. I'm not good at keeping secrets."

"What secrets?"

"The ones you've been keeping from me my whole life. I thought that since you were here maybe Grandma had convinced you to come clean."

"I came here because she was sick, but I never expected you to show up. How did you find me?"

"You two need to talk," Kelli said as she rolled out of the sofa bed. "I'm going to the kitchen for a slice of cake and to leave you alone."

As soon as she was gone, Phoebe sat down on the bed next to Pharrah. "Okay, spill it. What do you mean you know everything?"

"Maurice called me to bail him out of jail and told me you were here. I decided it was time I met my family."

"Great, first Maurice follows me, then he sends you here."

"He didn't send me. I've known about Grandma for a while. It all started when I applied for college and sent away to the Florida state capital for a copy of my birth certificate."

"You already have a birth certificate. I got it for you when you applied for your driver's license."

"That one only lists your name, my date of birth, and my name. I needed an actual hospital copy for the admissions office at college."

Phoebe stared at her with her mouth gaping open. "You've seen your hospital birth certificate?"

"Yes, and it doesn't list my father as the dead man you've always told me he was."

Phoebe swallowed hard before speaking again. "How did you find out about your grandmother?"

"After I was away at school, I decided to do some research. I wanted to know why my father's name was different than what you told me, so I put his name into Google and did a search. That's when I found my father's Web site for the church. I wasn't sure if it was the same person since you'd told me you grew up in Georgia somewhere, not Louisiana. It wasn't easy working with the stories you'd told. I did another search and came up with this address and phone number; when I called, Grandma answered." Pharrah paused momentarily and looked over at her mother who was staring at her with a combined look of confusion, amazement, and fear.

She sighed loudly, then continued. "Grandma told me that Reverend Gary Morgan was indeed my father. When I asked who she was, she told me that she was your mother. Of course, she was shocked to hear that you'd told me she was dead. Then I asked her if I could leave a message. I told her I wanted to meet my father. That's when she explained that he was your twin sister's husband. At least part of what you'd told me was true, in that you were sent to Florida to stay with Mom Philomena. She kept me and raised me as her own, and when she died, you brought me to New York to live with you. Grandma didn't know what had happened to me after Mom Philomena died. She had no idea I was with you."

Phoebe willed herself to speak, but the words wouldn't come. Instead, she just stared at Pharrah with her mouth open. She closed it again when she realized she could not form words.

"I've kept in contact with Grandma the entire time I've been in college. We talked at least once a week, sometimes more. She was planning to come visit me soon. Neither of us could understand why you tried to keep me from her. We knew you had to keep the secret from my dad, but she knew everything. You could have at least let her be a part of my life, Mom. I can't believe she's dead and I never got to meet her." Pharrah brushed away a tear, as her mother finally managed to form a sentence.

"I didn't know what else to do. When Philomena died suddenly, there was nowhere else for you to go. Child Protective Services put you in foster care. But then Daddy died just a few weeks later and he left me enough money to move away. I wanted you to be with me. I love you!"

"I love you too, and I'm glad that you came and got me. Otherwise, I would never have known you either. What I don't understand is why didn't you just tell Grandma that? Why have you been lying to me since the day you picked me up from Florida?"

"Pharrah, listen, you should not have just shown up. Why didn't you call me when Maurice called you? How do you just jump in the car and show up on someone's door step?"

"I'm glad I did. At least I'll get to pay my last respects to my grandmother."

"Can't you see what a huge can of worms you've opened by showing up here out of nowhere, introducing yourself to people who barely even knew you existed?"

"They think I'm their cousin and even though I don't like it, I don't plan to tell them any differently."

"Do I have your word on that?"

"I promise you, Mom. I'm just glad I got a chance to meet him and know him, even if he doesn't realize who I am." Pharrah grinned.

"Who are you talking about?"

"I can't believe I stood face to face today with my own father, Reverend Gary Morgan. I've been dreaming of this day for a long time," she said, beaming.

Phoebe stared at her for several moments before answering. "It's been a long, exhausting day, Pharrah. I'm going to bed." She leaned in and kissed her daughter on the cheek, left the family room, and tiptoed back up the stairs without noticing Li'l G lurking in the shadows.

In their bedroom, Phylicia and Gary lay awake in the darkness talking about the day's events. "There's something going on, Gary. I can feel it. Did you see the look on Phoebe's face when she saw Pharrah?"

"She looked surprised. Is that what you mean?"

"No, it was much more than surprise on my sister's face. She was like a deer caught in headlights."

"You are overreacting again, Phyllie. We were all surprised to see your cousin, especially with her fainting like that."

"What about what Mom said about her telling me the truth about Pharrah? Then Pharrah suddenly turns up on our doorstep. That's no coincidence."

Gary rolled over in the darkness and pulled Phylicia closer to him. He snuggled against her neck. "Honey, whatever it is, she'll be here until after the funeral on Monday.

That gives you plenty of time to talk with her and find out."

"I tried to talk with her all evening. Every time I went near the girl, Phoebe would rush her into another room or steer the conversation into a different direction. Those two are hiding something."

"Well, your son is certainly smitten with her roommate. Did you notice how he followed her around like a lost puppy?" Gary said with a laugh.

"Yes, I noticed. He will have lots of crushes, and the girl is way too old for him."

"I know, but I think this is his first real crush on an older woman. Did you hear him tell Kelli to call him Gary Jr. instead of Li'l G? Our son is becoming a man."

"Eva's been awfully quiet all day. Do you think she's okay? She was very close to Mom, but she's hardly said a word since we left the hospital last night."

"Yeah, I noticed that too. You want me to go and check on her; make sure she's sleeping okay?"

"Would you mind?"

"No, I'll be right back."

Gary got out of bed and put on his robe. Li'l G was standing outside his room as Gary entered the hallway. When he noticed his father, Li'l G quickly tried to wipe away the tears that were streaming down his face.

"Are you okay, son?" Gary asked.

"I hate you!" he hissed before rushing into his room and slamming the door.

Kelli had just returned to the family room and was crawling into bed next to Pharrah when they both heard a door slam. A few moments later they heard a blood-curdling scream come from upstairs.

"What do you think is going on up there? Should we go check?" Kelli asked. Pharrah was not listening, as she'd already left the room and was headed to the base of the stairs with Kelli close on her heels. As they reached the top, she saw Phylicia in the hallway, and Phoebe's door was opened as she peered out.

"Is everything okay? We heard a door slam and a scream," Pharrah inquired.

"Yes, it's fine. Eva had a nightmare. Gary's with her now. All of you can go back to bed."

"Are you sure? Do you want me to get her something from the kitchen? Maybe she'd like a glass of warm milk," Pharrah offered.

"Thank you, but she's a daddy's girl. She has everything she needs right now. Good night," Phylicia said, then went inside Eva's room, closing the door behind her.

Pharrah and Kelli returned downstairs and climbed back into bed. As she reached for the light, Kelli noticed that Pharrah was crying. "What's wrong?"

"She said that Eva's a daddy's girl. She has a nightmare and he's right there to make everything all better. I can't believe how much my mother cheated me out of by lying to me all these years."

"Don't you have a step-father? Isn't your mom married?"

"I have a step-jerk named Maurice. I've never had a father."

"You have one now. He's right upstairs. All you have to do is go up and talk to him."

"I promised my mom I wouldn't say anything."

"You did what? On the way here that's all you talked about: finally meeting your grandmother and your father. Your grandmother's dead, but your dad is here. That's one promise you need to break, girl."

"I can't. My Aunt Phylicia doesn't know about me. It would break her heart. Anyway, he's a minister of a huge congregation. How will it look if it got out he's got a grown daughter with his wife's sister?"

"Look, your aunt and the church busybodies will get over it. Besides, you said he doesn't know either. It's not like he abandoned you. That's gotta count for something."

"Maybe you are right, but I just want to enjoy being in his home and getting to know him. If I told him, I might not get that chance. It's better this way. Turn off the light. Let's get some sleep."

Chapter Eight

Gary awakened early the next morning and tiptoed out of bed while Phylicia was in the shower. He was anxious to speak with Li'l G about his words the previous evening. He was just about to follow him into his room to find out what was wrong when Eva screamed out. She'd had a horrible dream filled with dragons breathing fire, and Gary and Phylicia had spent over an hour in her room getting her calmed down and back to sleep. He'd wanted to go in and speak with Li'l G, but his light was off. He decided it was best to wait until morning.

After he tied the sash on his robe, he tapped on Li'l G's door. When there was no answer, he pushed it open and walked in. He was surprised to find Li'l G's bed empty and completely made. Gary backed out of the room and closed the door. He started downstairs, then remembered he had a house full of guests and decided to get dressed.

"You're up early," Phylicia said as he entered the bedroom. She was completely dressed and standing at the dresser, pulling her hair back into a ponytail.

"I need to talk to Li'l G. I went to his room but he's already up and downstairs. He even made his bed."

"Our son made his bed? He really is smitten. He's probably downstairs making goo-goo eyes at Kelli."

"I'm gonna take a quick shower and hurry and get down there."

"Is something wrong?"

"No, well maybe, honestly I don't know." He sighed.

"You're not making sense. Why do you need to speak with Li'l G so urgently?"

Gary hesitated before answering as Phylicia turned from the mirror and looked at him. "Last night, when I was on my way to Eva's room, I saw Li'l G in the hallway. He was crying, so I asked him if he was okay. He just stared at me, then I think he said, 'I hate you.' Then he went into his room and slammed the door."

"He hates you? You must have heard him wrong. He probably thought he was in trouble for being up so late."

"Well, I was going to ask him, then Eva screamed and it got so late. I think I need to speak with him this morning. 'Hate' is not a word we use in this house, no matter if he is angry or upset."

"Go ahead and take your shower, you can speak with him later. I'm going down to start breakfast. Then I have to pick out a dress to take to the mortuary for Mom. Our appointment is at eleven."

"Why don't you ask Phoebe to do that while you fix breakfast? You really don't have to do everything yourself."

"No, I want to do it. I'll see you downstairs in a little while." Phylicia gave her husband a quick peck on the lips then left their bedroom.

When she got downstairs, Kelli, Pharrah, and Li'l G were sitting on the living room couch looking guilty. "Good morning," she said.

"Good morning, Phylicia," both of the girls said, while Li'l G just stared at her.

"Li'l G, your father wants to speak with you. He's taking a shower, but he'll be down soon. What would you all like for breakfast?" she said as she walked toward the kitchen.

"Whatever you cook is fine," Kelli answered.

"I agree," Pharrah chimed in.

Phylicia turned around to ask Li'l G what he'd like, when she realized he had gotten up and was headed upstairs. "Li'l G? Do you want eggs or anything?"

"I'm going to talk to Dad," he said without turning around.

When Gary stepped out of the bathroom with a fluffy towel wrapped around his waist, he was surprised to find Li'l G sitting on the bed waiting for him. "I was going to come down and get you as soon as I got dressed," he said, walking to the closet to retrieve his clothes.

"I couldn't wait. I had to know and I had to know now."

"Know what?" Gary yelled from inside the closet.

"Are you Pharrah's father?"

Gary pulled on his underwear and trousers before stepping out of the closet and staring strangely at his son. "Am I what?"

"Are you Pharrah's father? Tell me the truth."

"Of course I'm not! Where would you get a crazy idea like that?" Gary walked across the bedroom as he pushed his arms into the sleeve of his shirt and began buttoning it up the front.

"I got it from Pharrah herself. I heard her and Aunt Phoebe talking. I heard her tell her she knew that you were really her father. She said Grandma told her. That's why she came here. She wanted to meet Grandma and her real father."

Gary sat down on the bed next to his son as he continued dressing. He pulled on a pair of clean, black socks and reached for his loafers. "Are you sure you heard her correctly? Why would she tell Phoebe I'm her father?"

"Aunt Phoebe is her mother. She's been living with her these past twelve years in New York until she went away to college. Aunt Phoebe is her mother and you are her father. I heard her say it, Dad."

Gary suddenly stopped dressing as his mind went back to that fateful night with Phoebe on the couch downstairs. Pharrah was certainly the right age, and he had to admit the family resemblance to Phoebe was uncanny. He'd been told Phoebe had lied and was never pregnant. *How could she have had a daughter, our daughter?* he wondered.

"Li'l G, you must be mistaken. I've known your aunt and your mother for more than twenty years. I'd know if she had a daughter."

"I asked Pharrah myself just a few minutes ago."

"What did she say?"

"She didn't say anything, but I could read it all over her face. Then Mom came down, so I came up here to ask you. You promised me a long time ago that you'd never lie to me, Dad. Is she your daughter?"

"Li'l G, I swear to you, I barely knew Pharrah existed until yesterday. I don't know what this is all about. I have to talk to your aunt Phoebe."

"So are you saying it's true?"

"No, I didn't say that."

"Are you saying it's possible? Did you have an affair with Aunt Phoebe?"

"Li'l G, I told you, I don't know what's going on. I need to find some things out."

Li'l G stood up and began screaming at his father. "How could you? How could you do that to Mom?"

"Calm down and lower your voice."

"You told me Mom was your first love and your only girlfriend. All those man-to-man talks about purity and saving yourself for the woman who's gonna be your wife. How could you look me in my face and say those things after what you'd done with Aunt Phoebe? She's Mom's sister. I never thought you'd be such a hypocrite."

Gary stood and put his hand on his son's shoulder. "Li'l G, sit down and listen to me. You want the truth, I'm going to tell you the truth. But you have to promise this will stay between you and me until I have a chance to talk to Phoebe. Do I have your word, son, man to man?"

Li'l G moved away from his father, but sat down on the bed as he asked. He folded his arms across his chest. "What's the truth?"

Gary took a deep breath, then for the first time in more than twenty years, he spoke about the night with Phoebe on her parents' couch. As he spoke, he silently prayed his son was mature enough to comprehend. When he was finally finished, he searched his face for understanding, and waited for him to speak.

"So you thought she was Mom? She tricked you?"

"Yes, not that it makes having sex with her right. But I would never cheat on your mother. I swear to you, son, I intended to do the right thing by Phoebe, but your grandmother called and told me she wasn't pregnant. She told me it was all a lie."

"What about Pharrah?"

"I don't know. She's the right age, and Phoebe did move away shortly after Philomena died. I need to talk to Phoebe or Pharrah or both. But until I do, you cannot breathe a word of this to your mother."

"Don't you think she has a right to know if you have another child?"

"Of course she does. It can't be true, but if it is, I will tell your mother everything. Your grandmother just died, your mother is grieving. We can't dump this on her now."

"I understand, Dad. Uhm . . . I'm sorry for what I said last night. I could never hate you. I was just confused and—"

"You don't have to explain. I'm not a perfect man, G. I've made some mistakes, and that night with your aunt was one of them. God forgives us for our mistakes, but we have to forgive ourselves and we have to make them right. Do you understand?"

"Yeah, I get it." Gary pulled his son into a tight bear hug just as their bedroom door opened.

"That's what I love to see: the men in my life hugging." They both turned to Phylicia and smiled. "Breakfast is ready. Everyone else is downstairs. I hope you're hungry because I made pancakes, sausage, and eggs."

"That sounds great, Mom," Li'l G said as he bounded out of the room. Phylicia waited until he was gone, then turned to Gary.

"Is everything okay with you two? Did you find out what he was upset about?"

"Yes, I did. We talked and everything's fine."

"Oh good, c'mon, let's eat." As they walked hand in hand down the hallway to the stairs, Gary silently prayed for forgiveness. He had never lied to his wife before.

Later that morning, Phylicia stood at the door to her mother's bedroom for five full minutes before she finally found the courage to turn the knob and enter. It was the first time she'd been in the room since her mother had been taken away by ambulance following her heart attack. As she stood in the middle of the room, she could still hear the sirens and the voices as the paramedics frantically tried to keep her mother alive. She'd stood by the doorway clinging tightly to Gary, while Mrs. Farmer kept the children upstairs and away from the commotion. Phylicia could still vividly see the stretcher being rolled out of the door with her mother's listless body lying on it.

"Phyllie, are you okay?"

She turned around and suddenly realized her sister had followed her into the room. "Not really," she whispered.

Instinctively, Phoebe walked over and held her sister. It was only the second hug they'd shared in many years, and they each held tightly, afraid to let go as the tears flowed freely from their eyes. Finally, after several moments, they broke free and smiled at each other.

"I've missed my big sister," Phylicia said as she wiped her wet face.

"I'm only three minutes older than you." They both laughed heartily. "So, what are you doing in here anyway?"

"I need to pick out a dress for Mom, for the funeral, and some jewelry."

Phoebe walked over to the closet. "Mom was the sharpest dresser in the family. This closet is full of nice things." She flipped through the dresses, then looked up on the shelf. "Is that Mom's collection of church hats?"

"Yes. She wore one every Sunday. It's a shame she can't wear one for the funeral. Those hats were a signature touch to each outfit. You know Mom always had to have the dress, the shoes, the hat, the gloves, and the matching purse, or she felt half naked. Do you remember that dance when she let you borrow an outfit and told you, 'If you want to look sophisticated you have to wear one glove and carry the other?'"

"Yes, I remember. Mom was my first fashion stylist. You didn't go anywhere with her unless you were pressed, pleated, and shined." Phoebe laughed as she continued searching through the closet. "What do you plan to do with all of this stuff? I mean after the funeral?"

"I don't know." Phylicia shrugged. "Maybe donate it to charity or something. I haven't thought that far ahead. It's taken everything I have just to come in here and look at her things."

"Would you mind if I took one outfit and a hat? I don't wanna wear it; I just want something that was hers, you know? I need a memento of some sort."

"Take anything you want."

"Hey, do you remember this?" Phoebe said as she pulled a dress from the closet and began twirling around, holding it up to herself.

Phylicia took one look at her and burst out laughing. "I can't believe Mom saved that thing."

"Mom was a pack rat. She saved everything. I wonder if the wig is here, too," Phoebe said, reaching to the back of the closet. "I found it!" She pulled out the tattered grey wig and put it on top of her weave. She held the dress up and began speaking in a high, squeaky voice. "Children, I told y'all. Sanny Claus won't wake up. No presents for you this year," she said, imitating her mother's voice to a T. The long, red dress with puffy lace at the bottom and wig was the costume their mother had made and worn in the Christmas play at church when the girls were twelve years old. She'd played Mrs. Claus to a sleeping Santa.

"You sound just like her." Phylicia laughed then suddenly became serious. "I'm gonna miss hearing her voice in this house. Her laughter could light up a room. Do you remember how she used to sing in the kitchen when she was cooking?"

"No, she didn't sing. She moaned, remember?"

" 'Cause when you moan, the devil don't know what you're talking about," they both said in unison, then doubled over laughing again.

"There are a lot of great memories of Mom in this house. Her spirit is in every room," Phylicia said.

"You have a lot more than me. I can't believe I've stayed gone for twelve years. I've missed out on so much. I'm sorry, Phyllie. I should have been here."

"Why'd you stay gone so long?"

"That's not important. Just know that I'm sorry. I'm sorry for a lot of things," Phoebe said quietly, then went back to browsing through the closet. "How about this?" she said after finally choosing an outfit.

It was a powder blue suit with blue pearls on the lapels and cuffs. Phylicia had given it to their mother on her last birthday and she'd only worn it once.

"Yes, that's perfect. I'll get the matching gloves from her dresser. I guess there's no need to take the hat and shoes to the mortician," Phylicia answered.

"I think I'd like to have them if you don't mind. That way I'm not breaking up a set."

"Good idea." Phylicia handed her the shoe and hat boxes that were marked with their contents.

"Always organized; now that's one trait of Momma's that you got, but it completely skipped over me," Phoebe commented.

"Yeah, you were always a slob."

"Hey, why should I clean up when I knew you'd come along and do it for me? That was the great part about having a neat freak for a twin. My room was always clean and I never had to clean it."

"Remember the time I was away for the summer at band camp? I came back after three weeks and thought you were trying to grow a garden in our bedroom it was so filthy."

"It wasn't that bad. Was it?" The two of them looked at each other, nodded, then burst out laughing again.

Phoebe and Phylicia sat in their mother's room reminiscing and laughing for almost an hour until Gary finally interrupted them. "Hey, we have twenty minutes to get to the mortuary for our appointment. What's going on in here? You two sound like you're at a comedy show."

"My sister and I have twelve years to catch up on. We were getting a head start," Phylicia said as she put her arm around Phoebe on the bed. "I forgot Mom had all these old photo albums down here. Look, here's me when I was four in my pink Easter dress." She pointed at the picture.

"That's not you, that's me," Phoebe corrected.

"It can't be you. There's no weave or makeup." They both laughed loudly again.

"I'm sure it's me. I bet I can even remember my speech." Phoebe stood up and cleared her throat before she began reciting:

When they asked me to act like an angel, and welcome you
    today,
my sister said it wouldn't work. Wasn't that an odd thing
    to say?
But I won't pay any attention; I'll just hurry on to say:
we're very glad to have you here, and Happy Easter Day.

Phoebe curtsied as Gary and Phylicia laughed heartily at her.

Gary hated to interrupt them. He couldn't remember

the last time the two of them had been laughing and getting along so well. It had to have been years, even before he and Phylicia married. He smiled happy to see them finally putting the past behind them and moving on together. It made him feel very contented with himself and his family.

"It's great to see you two getting along so well, but we've got to get out of here," Gary stated. "C'mon, we'll take my car. Li'l G will be staying here with Pharrah and Kelli in case any more visitors drop by. I gave Eva permission to go to Jayla's for a while since it's Saturday. I hope that's okay, honey?"

"Yes, that's fine. You are right, we need someone here. I'm sure the throng of visitors has not stopped. We chose this dress. Would you mind putting it in the car? I'm going upstairs to change shoes and then I'll be ready." She turned to her sister. "Phoebe, do you need to freshen up?"

"No. I'm gonna put these photo albums back. I'll meet you guys at the car," Phoebe replied.

As soon as Phylicia was out of the room, Gary closed the door and turned to his sister-in-law. "We need to talk, Phoebe."

"What about? If it's the handkerchief business, let's forget it. Phyllie seems to have done that already."

"No, it's not about the handkerchief, well, not exactly. Uhm, I don't know how to put this, so I'm going to come out with it. Is Pharrah your daughter? Is she our daughter?"

Phoebe stared at him without answering for several seconds. "Who told you that?" she finally said.

"Not that it matters, but Li'l G overheard your conversation last night. Is what he heard true?"

"Pharrah is my daughter, yes, but I really don't think this is the time or place to get into all of this, Gary."

"It all makes sense now. I understand why you kept my handkerchief and why you left town for so long. But why didn't you just tell me you were pregnant with my child?"

"Are you saying you want to be a father to Pharrah? Have you forgotten about Phylicia? My sister and your wife."

"I never wanted to hurt Phyllie, you know that. And I think it's best if we don't tell her anything about this, at least until after the funeral. I just couldn't wait to get some answers. I love Li'l G and Eva. I don't understand why you didn't give me a chance to love our child, too."

Our child. Those two little words sounded like an angel's symphony to Phoebe's ears. Even after twenty years, being around Gary made her feel like a teenager again. As she looked at him, she became the girl he left in the park all over again. She still wanted him more than anything else in the world.

"Phoebe? Is it true? Am I her father?" Gary asked, interrupting her thoughts.

Phoebe smiled her sexiest smile, then nodded her head.

Chapter Nine

On the afternoon of their mother's funeral, the sun shone brightly into the windows of the long, black limousine as they rode to the services. The sisters had only one fight while making the funeral arrangements. Phylicia wanted an early morning funeral in order to get it over and done; while Phoebe, who was never a morning person, preferred to have a late-afternoon funeral. Because of their newfound friendship, they easily reached a compromise, and laid their mother to rest at one that afternoon.

Gertrude Evangeline Carson attended Freedom Inspiration since the day her son-in-law took over as head pastor, but the girls knew her final wish was to be taken back to her home church, St. James Christian Fellowship. The immediate family, along with two hundred and fifty of her closest relatives and friends, had crowded inside the tiny wooden structure like matchsticks. It was early spring, but the combination of the bright sun and the collection of people made the temperature inside the small building rise. The single air conditioning unit they had installed a year earlier was pumping beyond capacity. Throughout the service, paper fans wagged as everyone tried to find some relief. They were all grateful when it was finally over and they were sitting comfortably inside the coolness of the limos, traveling up the winding dirt road back to the house.

No one spoke as they all stared out of the windows, each feeling their own grief and anticipating the days ahead without the family matriarch.

Gary had spoken with Phoebe again the previous evening, and told her that after the funeral he was going to tell Phylicia about Pharrah. He wanted to be the one to break the news to her. As much as he knew it would hurt her, he was looking forward to having his daughter be a part of his life. It had taken all the strength he had over the weekend not to run to her, and hold her in his arms, and tell her that he knew he was her father and he was glad. But he realized it was too soon. Instead, he'd found every possible moment he could to talk with her to begin building a relationship.

Pharrah welcomed the conversations and the attention. Gary beamed with pride when she told him she was a pre-med student and planned to be a pediatrician. She'd told him she received straight As and was on the dean's list. He knew she'd inherited both his and her mother's height as she stood almost six feet. During a pickup game of basketball late Sunday afternoon, the two of them came within a few points of beating Li'l G and Kelli. She was good, really good. Almost as good as he'd been in college. They didn't speak the words, but somehow he felt the connection and the bond growing. Phylicia liked her also, and he felt the relationship they'd built over the past few days would help soften the blow of finding out she was his daughter. He held tightly to Phylicia's hand as they rode, praying for God to give him the right words to say to her.

Directly behind them in the limousine, Phoebe's head swirled with fantasies of her and Pharrah's life with Gary. She completely blocked out the marriage and family he already had, in favor of the new one she was creating in her mind. There was no reason for her to return to New York City, she reasoned, since Maurice was still in jail and Pharrah was at Southern University. She would move back to Brown Bottom so that when summer break began, Pharrah could stay with her. She was sure Gary would come by several times a week to see them. She almost hated that Pharrah was too old for her to file for child support payments, but she knew Gary was a reasonable and generous man. He would have no problem with supporting them until she got on her feet. Phoebe even imagined the used car she would have Pharrah ask him to buy for them. It was a dark blue, 1998 Honda she had seen with a "For Sale" sign on it at a neighbor's house, that was right next to a duplex with a "For Rent" sign. She was planning to live right down the street from Phylicia. She knew Gary would want them close. It had taken almost twenty years, but she felt she was finally going to have the life and family she'd always imagined, with Gary by her side.

Phylicia held tightly to Gary's hand, desperately trying not to cry. She had broken down several times at the funeral and had finally regained her composure near the end of the service. She watched her husband in the pulpit brush his eyes with his handkerchief only once. Eva and Li'l G had spent the entire funeral with wet faces, and she wanted to be strong for them. As the limousine pulled away from the cemetery, she suddenly realized she was

leaving her mother behind and a huge knot began twisting in her stomach. She glanced back at Phoebe who had
a goofy grin plastered across her face as if she were daydreaming about cotton candy and ice cream. She wished
she could be as strong as Phoebe, who'd only broken
down once during the services. Maybe it was because she'd
been gone so long and would be leaving in a few days.

Maybe Phoebe would not feel the loss as much as they
did, Phylicia reasoned. She was glad that her sister had
come home in time to say good-bye, and realized she
was ashamed of how she'd overreacted to the handkerchief and the insurance policy she'd found. It was still
tucked inside her dresser drawer, but she had decided
that before dinner she would present the ones for the
children as well as Phoebe's to each of them. Spending
time with her sister and laughing with her again had
erased the spirit of jealousy she'd felt. She felt sad at the
loss of her mother, but, for the first time in years, Phylicia
felt content with her relationship with her sister.

Chapter Ten

"We've got to leave tomorrow. I can't miss my econ class on Wednesday," Kelli said as they changed out of the clothes Phylicia had loaned them for the funeral.

"I know. I wish we could stay longer, but you're right. Finals are in a few weeks. We'd better leave early tomorrow morning."

"Are you still planning to keep that promise you made to your mother?"

"Yes, I have to. But you know, I've noticed something. It's as if he knows. He's been wonderful to me these past few days. That's the way I've always imagined a father would be."

"Yeah, he's a great guy. I noticed you two seemed to bond. Maybe Li'l G told him."

"Maybe, but I don't care. I'm just glad that I came and was able to spend so much time with him. Speaking of Li'l G, what's up with you two? He's been on you like white on rice, girl."

"He's sixteen, there's nothing up. He's a sweet kid, but that's where it ends."

"That's not how it seems to me. I mean, you've spent a lot of time with him this weekend. Are you sure there are no sparks?" Pharrah teased.

"Not even a flicker. I could never be interested in someone so young, you know that. I've been trying to run interference for you so that you could have time with your dad. I am not at all interested in Li'l G. Trust."

"Well, my little brother is definitely a cutie. He's gonna be a heartbreaker one day."

The girls stopped talking as they heard a knock at the door of the family room. "Come in," Pharrah yelled as she pulled her T-shirt over her head and straightened the hem. "Cousin Phoebe, what is it?"

Phoebe stepped into the room and closed the door tightly behind her. "You won't have to call me that much longer," she said, grinning from ear to ear.

"I know. We're heading back to school in the morning."

"No. You can't. I mean, when are you coming back?" Phoebe asked frantically.

"What do you mean we can't? What's going on?" Pharrah raised an eyebrow as she waited for an answer.

Phoebe looked back and forth before leaning in and whispering to them both. "I've spoken with Gary. He knows about you and he's happy about it. He plans to tell Phylicia soon. We just wanted to give her time to get through the funeral."

Pharrah's eyes lit up like Times Square on New Year's Eve. "He knows? Are you sure about this?"

"Yes, I talked to him myself."

"He's not mad about all the lies, and the secrets?"

"No. Honey, you will find that Gary is a kind, reasonable man. He was very understanding of everything. He wants us to be a part of his life."

"What do you mean us?" Pharrah gave her mother a suspicious look.

"I'm going to move back here to Brown Bottom. That way, when you take summer vacation in a few weeks, you can stay with me and we'll be close to Gary. What do you think?"

"What about Maurice? He's going to be out of that jail soon."

"I called the courthouse before we left for the funeral. Unless he can make bail, which I doubt, Maurice will not be getting out for a long time. I'm having him served with divorce papers."

"You are really planning to divorce Maurice? I don't believe it!"

"I know you never liked him, and since you've been out of the house, things have not been good with us." A look of complete sadness suddenly washed over Phoebe's face. "I don't think I ever loved him. I married him for all the wrong reasons. I thought he would take care of us. It was a mistake," she said quietly.

Pharrah reached over and pulled her mother into a hug. "It's okay. I understand why you did it, Mom."

They broke apart quickly when they heard another knock at the door. "We sure are popular today," Kelli said as she walked over and opened it up.

"Oh, Phoebe, I didn't know you were down here." Phylicia said. "That's good; I can tell you all at once. I'm really sick of donated chicken and ham, so if nobody minds, I was going to cook us all something for dinner tonight. My jambalaya is legendary."

"That sounds delicious, Cousin Phylicia," Pharrah answered.

"Are you gonna make Mom's hot water cornbread to go with it?" Phoebe asked.

"You know it, girl. I'm gonna hook up a salad and probably some honey-lemon tea, too."

"We are in for a treat tonight, ladies. Can I help you do anything, Phyllie?" Phoebe asked.

"My sister wants to help in the kitchen? Will this weekend of miracles never cease?"

"Very funny, Phyllie, but I can cook. Can't I, Pharrah?" she said without thinking, then suddenly wished she could pull the words back inside her mouth.

"Uhm, how would I know, Cousin Phoebe? Unless you mean that ham sandwich you made me yesterday," Pharrah answered nervously.

"No, that's not what she means. How would she know, Phoebe?" Phylicia folded her arms across her chest and stared at her sister.

"She wouldn't. It was a slip of the tongue. That's all." Phoebe tried her best to sound convincing, but it wasn't working.

Phylicia walked into the family room and took a seat on the sofa. "Come here and sit with me, Phoebe," she said, patting the cushion.

Phoebe looked at Pharrah and Kelli, then at her sister. Finally, she walked over and sat with her. "It was a slip of the tongue, Phyllie. Don't make a big deal out of it."

"Stop it. Stop it right now. This has gone far enough. I know that you knew this girl before she came here. There is a connection between you two. Mom mentioned her on her deathbed for a reason and you promised her you'd tell me the truth about Pharrah. Now is the perfect time. Tell me the truth, Phoebe."

Phoebe took a long, deep breath, then looked at Pharrah and Kelli, then Phylicia. She took another deep breath before speaking. "Okay. You are gonna find out eventually anyway. Do you remember that summer you got engaged and I spent it in Florida with Aunt Philomena?"

Phylicia nodded her head. "Yes, you left right after school let out. Mom said I couldn't go because I was going to band camp and I was busy planning my wedding."

"Well, that wasn't the only reason they didn't want you to go. The thing is, Mom and Dad sent me down there, because . . . because I was pregnant and they didn't want anyone to know."

"What? You were pregnant?"

"Yes, I was, and while I was there, I had a daughter. Pharrah is my daughter."

"You had a baby? This beautiful girl is your baby?" Phylicia said as her eyes welled up with tears.

"Yes. The plan was for me to stay there until the baby was born, then put her up for adoption. But as you know, Aunt Philomena never had any children of her own, so she asked if she could adopt her. She reasoned that by doing that I'd always know where she was and that she was taken care of."

"Aunt Philomena has been dead for years. Where's she been? Who's she been with?"

"She's been with me. After Aunt Philomena died she was put in foster care. I couldn't stand the thought of not knowing where my child was. So I went down to Florida and got her, then we moved to New York City. She lived with me until she left for college two years ago."

"Wow, I can hardly believe this. Pharrah, come here." Phylicia stood up and wrapped her arms around her. "I can't believe I have a niece," she said, then hugged her tightly again. "Phoebe, you didn't have to keep this from me. We're family. This is wonderful news."

Pharrah hugged her aunt back while staring over her shoulder at her mother, wondering how long Phylicia's joy was going to last once she found out who her father was.

"Now this makes sense," Phylicia said, reaching into her pocket. "Mom must have bought this for you, Pharrah." Phylicia handed her the insurance policy.

"This can't be mine. It has Mom's name on it," Pharrah said, staring at it.

"I know, but your grandmother left one for each of my children, so I'm sure this one was intended for you. It's to help with your college education. Your grandmother always said she wanted to help her grandchildren."

Pharrah stared wide-eyed at all the zeroes on the policy. "The last time we talked, I told her I had taken a part-time job to help with expenses. She told me not to worry; it would all be taken care of. I can't believe she did this for me."

"Your grandmother was just that type of person, Pharrah." Phylicia said.

"I'm sorry I never got a chance to meet her face to face. We talked often, but I never imagined she'd do this," Pharrah said quietly.

"I'm sure she loved you very much," Phylicia said.

"Thank you, Phylicia," Pharrah answered.

"No, that's Aunt Phylicia to you now," she said smiling. "I can't believe how wonderful these past few days have turned out to be. I didn't know what I was going to do if I lost Mom, but God has given me back my sister, and a beautiful niece. This dinner is going to be a family celebration. What's your favorite kind of cake, Pharrah? I owe you nineteen years' worth of birthdays."

"Uhm, German chocolate," she answered absentmindedly, still staring at the insurance policy.

"That's Gary's favorite too. I have a great recipe for it." She hugged her niece once more, then her sister. "I'm going to start dinner. Let's wait and announce this to everyone after we eat when I bring out the cake. I'll put candles on it, too, just like it's your birthday party."

"Phyllie, wait. Maybe we shouldn't do this," Phoebe began.

"Are you kidding me? This is going to be great!" Phylicia said, before rushing excitedly out of the room.

"A dinner celebration? I hate to be the bearer of bad news, but the grits are about to hit the fan," Kelli said.

Pharrah chewed her dinner very slowly as the family sat around the large dining room table. She hoped if she could prolong dinner, then maybe she could put off her aunt's announcement. She couldn't believe her mother had not tried to stop Phylicia and tell her the whole truth, but she'd reasoned it wasn't her place. Gary should be the one to tell her the rest. Several times, she noticed Phylicia had grinned and winked at her, full of excitement. Inside she felt conflicted between finally having the father she'd always dreamed of, and breaking the heart of a woman she'd come to care about. She almost wished she'd stayed on campus and not ventured out this weekend. She felt as if she were the engine of a speeding train that was rushing along peacefully, but unbeknownst to the passengers, it was about to hit a serious curve, sending it careening off-track.

Before dinner, Pharrah had wanted to talk to Gary, and let him in on what Phylicia was planning, but he'd spent the remainder of the afternoon at the church. As pastor of a large congregation, he couldn't afford to take whole days off, even if it was to bury his mother-in-law. Mrs. Farmer had called to tell him that several parishioners were sick, one was in the hospital, and another had a child in jail. All were in desperate need of his guidance and prayers. He'd rushed out, promising to return in time for dinner.

When he did, everyone was already gathered in the dining room and it was too late.

"I smell chocolate cake," he said, sniffing the air. "That's my favorite. What's the occasion, Phyllie? I didn't think you'd be up to cooking tonight."

"I didn't think so either, but I've gotten some great news and we are celebrating. Everyone sit down, and I'll tell you all about it later."

Later was coming closer and closer and Pharrah took slow, tiny bites trying to postpone the inevitable. She noticed her mother had eaten quickly and cleaned her entire plate. Phoebe was hyped and ready for the show to begin. The moment Phylicia excused herself from the table and returned to the kitchen, Pharrah glanced over at Kelli, her eyes pleading for help. Kelli shrugged her shoulders and they waited.

Everyone's eyes followed Phylicia as she dramatically entered the dining room, carrying the cake with candles glowing on top. She circled the table before finally stopping and placing it in front of Pharrah. "Happy Birthday for the last nineteen years," she said, then leaned down and kissed her on her cheek.

"What's this all about?" Gary asked as Pharrah stared wild-eyed at the cake and candles.

"My sister shared a secret with me this afternoon and I thought it would be appropriate to share it with everyone over dinner. I just found out that Pharrah is Phoebe's daughter. Aunt Philomena adopted her as a baby, but she's with Phoebe now. It's her first day as an official member of this family, so I wanted to celebrate. Happy Birthday, Pharrah! Don't just sit there, go ahead and blow out your candles."

Everyone stared at Phylicia beaming, until Pharrah finally bent over and blew. The candles seemed to flicker and finally go out in slow motion. Everyone just stared until Gary finally spoke. "Li'l G, take your sister upstairs. I need to speak with your mother."

"I want a piece of cake," Eva whined.

"I'll cut us all a piece in the kitchen, then take it up with us," Kelli said suddenly, grabbing the cake from in front of Pharrah and motioning to Li'l G to follow her.

"C'mon, runt, I'll get you some milk," Li'l G said as he grabbed Eva's hand, and the three of them left the dining room.

"Gary, why did you send the kids out? I thought we'd share this as a family. I mean, Eva's a little young, but Li'l G understands about a woman having a baby without a husband."

"Phyllie, come sit down next to me. There's something else you should know," Gary said gently.

"What's going on?" she said, finally dropping the smile that had been plastered on her face. Confused, she walked over and sat in the chair beside her husband.

Gary reached out and held Phylicia's hands in his, as Pharrah and Phoebe looked on in anticipation. He chose his words carefully and spoke slowly. "Pharrah is not just Phoebe's daughter. There's a reason she's had to keep her a secret from everyone for so long. It's the reason your parents sent her away." He paused for several moments then finally whispered, "Pharrah is my daughter too. I'm her father."

"What did you just say?" Phylicia snatched her hands away from Gary, and looked back and forth at the three of them.

"Phyllie, listen. I didn't know until this weekend. Your parents and Phoebe kept this secret from me as well as you. Please, just let me explain."

Phylicia pushed her chair back from the table and stood up slowly. "You slept with my sister?"

"Phyllie, just let me explain."

"Answer me!" she screamed. "Did you sleep with my sister?"

Gary slowly nodded his head. "But it wasn't like you think, Phyllie."

Phylicia didn't wait for him to finish. She ran from the dining room and rushed up the stairs.

Chapter Eleven

Gary reached behind his back and slowly rubbed the sore spot right above his hips at the base of his spine. It had been more than a week since Phylicia had thrown him out of their home, and his back ached from sleeping on his office couch. After running upstairs, she'd locked herself inside their bedroom, and when she finally came out, she was carrying his suitcases. She promptly walked down the stairs, opened the front door, and tossed them out on the lawn where one burst open, scattering his clothes before she returned upstairs. He tried to stop her, and plead with her to listen, but her anger allowed her to move with the swiftness of an Olympic sprinter.

He was outside gathering his things and placing them in his car with Pharrah, Kelli, and Phoebe's help, when they heard something rumbling down the staircase. They rushed inside and saw Phylicia pitching the rest of Phoebe's tattered Louis Vuitton luggage down the staircase.

"Phyllie, please just listen to me!" Gary pleaded.

"Get out! Get out and take your whore and her bastard child with you. Get out now!" she screamed before rushing back to the bedroom and slamming the door.

He'd finally stopped calling the house after the third day that Phylicia would not speak to him. He didn't know how to get through to her, to make her listen and understand, but he knew that he had to. Somehow he had to find a way to put his marriage back together. He looked up at Mrs. Farmer as she entered his office, carrying a steaming cup of coffee that she placed on his desk in front of him. He smiled and thanked her.

"Reverend, maybe I'm just an old busybody, but I have to say something."

"What do you mean, Mrs. Farmer?" He blew his coffee then took a sip.

"I know you've been living in this church office. I'm no fool. You look tired and haggard. Your clothes are wrinkled and unprofessional. Your hair needs a good combing and you've had a five o'clock shadow for three days. I don't mean to pry, but why aren't you going home at night?"

Gary looked up at Mrs. Farmer, wondering if he could confide in her. She'd been a close friend of his family since he was a child. As an only child, he'd spent countless afternoons playing basketball in her backyard, as her sons were among his closest friends. Since he'd lost his own mother only a few weeks after Li'l G was born, she'd been the surrogate. Mrs. Farmer stepped in to take care of him, Phylicia, and the children whenever he needed it. Realizing she would understand, he asked her to close his office door, then offered her a seat.

When he was done explaining, she slowly shook her head. "Phoebe has been fast and hot in the pants as long as I can remember. I'm not surprised that she'd trick you like that. Have you explained all of that to Phylicia?"

"I've tried, but she won't talk to me. I call and she hangs up on me. I went by the house and she let me see the children, but she locks herself in her bedroom and won't come out. I don't know what else to do."

"Where are Phoebe and this girl staying?"

"Pharrah is back at college. She's a junior; pre-med," he said, unexpectedly glowing with pride. "I put Phoebe up in a hotel after Phyllie threw her out. I felt it was the least I could do."

"No, the least you could have done was let her fend for herself. But I understand you wanted to do the right thing."

"Yes, ma'am, I just never expected Phyllie to get so upset. I knew she'd be hurt and feel betrayed, but if she would just talk to me I could explain it all."

"Give her some time. She's had a rough few weeks with losing her momma and then finding out about this. It has to be difficult for her to take it all in."

"I supposed you're right. I'm planning to take Li'l G and Eva out to dinner and a movie this weekend. Maybe she'll talk to me then."

"I hope so, Reverend. In the meantime, you've got to get yourself together before folks begin to talk. Was that hotel you put Phoebe in all out of rooms or something?"

"No, ma'am. I just couldn't stand the thought of checking into a hotel. It makes us seem as if we're separated or something, and we definitely are not. I thought it would only be a day or so."

"Well, you can't continue to stay here. If one of the parishioners sees you like this they'll have the rumor mill talking about your divorce in just a few hours. I have a room; it's yours if you want it."

"Mrs. Farmer, I couldn't put you out like that."

"You wouldn't be putting me out. I'd love the company. It gets kind of lonely now that Luke has passed. I'd be glad to have you, Reverend."

"Are you sure? I don't want to be a burden on anybody, but it does seem as if Phyllie is going to need some time to deal with all this."

"You are not a burden at all. You need to get yourself together so you can work things out with Phylicia. Now, I won't take no for an answer."

"All right, I guess I could stay a few days. Thank you."

Phylicia piled the last box of shoes into the hallway. She'd decided that today was the day she was going to clean out her mother's room. She really had no plans for the room, but keeping busy helped her block the images that were dancing in her head. Several members of the ladies society of the church had called for her advice and assistance on church projects, but she'd made up excuses. She preferred to stay inside her home and busy herself with chores. Whenever she allowed herself to be idle, her mind would conjure up images of her sister and her husband in bed together, their bodies writhing in pleasure. Whenever they were done, she'd see them relaxing and laughing at her. She couldn't believe what a complete fool she'd been. It had never dawned on her to ask who Pharrah's father was. Kicking herself over and over, she hated that she'd welcomed her so happily without once questioning why Phoebe had hidden her.

As she cleaned the room, the past twenty years slowly came into focus. The spring she and Gary became engaged she'd noticed that her sister was putting on weight. Her face looked puffy and her nose began to spread closer to her ears. Phylicia thought it was because she was eating so much; now she realized she had to have been pregnant with Pharrah. As soon as school was out, she was on a bus bound for Florida for the summer, while Phylicia stayed home planning her wedding. Phoebe returned home the night of Phylicia and Gary's engagement party, and that night her husband began the first of years' worth of disappearing acts. He and Phoebe would share awkward glances, then he'd rush out of the room.

Her mind fast-forwarded eight years, and she remembered the phone call her father had received telling him that his sister, Philomena, had died from complications of diabetes. She'd wondered why Phoebe was so anxious to join her father on the trip down for the funeral, as they barely knew their aunt. But she assumed they'd grown closer during the summer she spent there. It was less than a month later that their father's truck skidded off a dirt road during a heavy rainstorm and flipped several times, killing him instantly. Within a week, Phoebe had taken her share of the insurance money and left town. For twelve years she'd asked herself over and over why her sister could not return even for a short visit. Now it was all so clear.

Phylicia looked around her mother's room and the tears flowed freely. She had boxes stacked in the hallway filled with all of her mother's belongings from her closet, dresser, and underneath her bed. She heard the front doorbell, and she took one last glance around the room before closing the door. She rushed to answer the bell as she'd called the local Salvation Army to come by for the boxes. Reaching for the knob, she turned it, then swung open the door, surprised to see Mrs. Farmer standing on the other side.

"Hello, Sister Morgan. Can I talk with you a few moments?"

She hesitated momentarily before inviting her in. "Have a seat. Can I get you something to eat or drink?"

"No, I'm fine. But you . . . you look worse than the reverend." Mrs. Farmer shook her head.

"What are you talking about?"

"Your eyes are bloodshot, your clothes are unkempt. I can tell you've been cleaning, but this isn't like you, Phylicia. Reverend Gary told me everything and I'm here to talk some sense into you, girl."

"Mrs. Farmer, I'm sure Gary told you his version of the truth. I've listened to his lies for twenty years. I don't care to hear anymore."

"Reverend Gary doesn't have a lying bone in his body and you know it. Don't you at least want to know what happened?"

"I know all I need to know. He slept with my sister and they have a child together. It's difficult enough without having to endure the sordid details."

"Did you know that your sister tricked him?"

"I know my sister has been lying to all of us for years. That doesn't excuse him."

"No, I mean did you know that when he slept with your sister he thought she was you? He never would have done it otherwise."

"How could he think she was me?"

"Phylicia, you are twins. Except for the flair, the hair, and the gobs of makeup, the two of you are identical twins. No one but your parents could tell you apart when you were little. Over the years you've both changed quite a bit and each taken on your own style, but back then it was difficult to tell one from the other. Your sister got him alone, in the dark, without makeup, her hair pulled back, and made him believe she was you."

"How could he not know it wasn't me, Mrs. Farmer? Shouldn't my own husband know me and my body?"

"You were not his wife then, and from what I under-

stand, the two of you had never been intimate. It's not totally his fault, Phylicia. He was wrong, but I know he's
sorry. Maybe it's not my business, but you need to forgive your husband."

Phylicia suddenly began to cry, and laid her head on
Mrs. Farmer's shoulder. "I can't. It just hurts so much.
Every time I think of the two of them together, the pain
just shoots through my body. I've never been with anyone but my husband, and I believed he'd never been
with anyone but me."

"I know you've been hurt, honey, but you gotta forgive
him. He made a mistake, but he didn't do it for lack of
loving you. You have to go to him and fix this, Phylicia."

"I don't even know where he is." She sniffed.

"I do. He's at my house. I invited him to stay and he's
been there for a few days. I've cooked dinner and left
him a note to go ahead and put it on the table. He is expecting me. Now won't it be a wonderful surprise if you
show up instead?"

"I'm not sure about that. I don't know if I'm ready for
him to come home. He has another child. This changes
everything. Our marriage will never be the same after this."

"I understand that, honey. Just go talk to him. Try to
resolve some things. He can stay with me for as long as
you need time, but at least make an effort to start repair-
ing things."

"I guess you are right. We do at least need to talk. Will
you stay here with the kids until I get back?" Phylicia
said as she wiped her face with her hands.

"Of course."

"How long are you going to mope around this room?"
Kelli asked as she walked in and noticed Pharrah lying
across her bed staring at the ceiling.

"I'm not moping. I'm thinking."

"About what?"

"I never meant for things to happen like this. My dad is staying at his secretary's house and it's all my fault. We should have kept it a secret. "

"It's not your fault. He and his wife have some things to work out. Besides, did you just hear yourself? You said 'my dad.' Doesn't it feel good to know you have a dad?"

"Yes, it does. He's been just wonderful through all of this. He's called every day to check on me, and reassure me that things are going to work out. He's invited me to stay with him after finals are over next week. Li'l G even called and said that even though his mom is upset, he and Eva are happy to have me as their big sister."

"Then why all the moping . . . I mean, thinking?"

"I just keep wondering why my mom did what she did. I mean, she says that she loved him, but he was her sister's boyfriend. It was probably nothing more than puppy love. It hurts knowing I was the product of a scheme to break up the two of them. A scheme that took twenty years, but apparently worked."

"Speaking of your mother, is she still at the hotel?"

"Yes, basking in the luxury of it all. She has no remorse. I don't understand her at all. Her sister is heartbroken, and all she can talk about is how delicious room service is."

"Yeah, she does seem a bit self-centered," Kelli said, just as their phone began loudly ringing on the wall. "I got it." Kelli walked across the room, picking up on the third ring. "Pharrah, it's your dad," she said grinning from ear to ear.

"Hey, honey, how are classes?" Gary said as soon as Pharrah had picked up.

"They're great! I have one paper to turn in, then all I'll have left is finals. How are you and . . . well, everything?"

"Everything is getting better. Phylicia and I finally talked last evening. She's not ready for me to come home, but we're working on it."

Pharrah breathed a long, slow sigh of relief. "I'm sure it will happen soon."

"I'm sure of it too. I just wanted to check in with you and make sure you were okay. That's a father's job, you know."

Pharrah grinned as she talked with Gary for the next half hour about school, basketball, and her plans for the summer. By the time the conversation ended, they'd planned a trip to Six Flags for him and the kids, and hopefully Phylicia if things were better by then. The last thing she asked was if it was okay to call him "Dad." He happily agreed. She hung up the phone and excitedly filled Kelli in on the details.

Phylicia left and returned to the hotel lobby three times before finally taking the elevator upstairs to Phoebe's room. She wasn't sure about coming over, but she knew that before she could forgive Gary and move on with her marriage, she had to confront her sister. Her brain told her to do it to confirm Gary's story, but her heart insisted she do it to understand her sister's motives. She knocked, then waited patiently until she finally heard the doorknob click, and the door opened. Phoebe stood staring at her with her hands folded across her chest.

"What do you want, Phyllie? You threw me out of the house again; what more is there?"

"We need to talk. Can I come in?"

Slowly, Phoebe stepped aside and allowed her to enter the room. "Phylicia, let me say I'm sorry. Mom and Dad made me keep this secret for so long. I wanted to tell you in the beginning. It was them and Gary who thought it would hurt you too much."

"I don't care why you didn't tell me, Phoebe. What I want to know is why you did it in the first place. Why would you seduce my boyfriend?"

"Seduce? Is that what he told you?" Phoebe didn't know why, but she wasn't prepared to take the blame all alone for her night with Gary.

"That wasn't the word he used exactly."

"Well, what word did he use?"

"Tricked. He says you tricked him. You pretended to be me in order to get him to sleep with you. Is that true?"

Phoebe looked into her sister's eyes and decided to add her usual bit of drama and flair to the details of that night. "That's not how I remember it. Okay, he said that he thought I was you, but honestly, Phyllie, I didn't buy it. Gary wanted me for a long time. I mean, back then you were walking around like a nun or something. The man had needs and I fulfilled them. So if he wants to hold on to that tired old line, let him. It doesn't matter to me anymore."

"How could you do that to me, Phoebe? You knew how much I loved him. I was saving myself for marriage, marriage to him."

"And so you got to be a virgin on your wedding night, Phyllie. Good for you. You were always the good twin, couldn't let a little thing like sex throw you off course."

Phylicia suddenly became angry at her sister's words. "And you were always the bad seed. You never cared about anyone or anything but yourself. Nothing was off-limits if you wanted it. Not even Gary. You are the most self-centered, egotistical, pompous witch I've ever known in my life!"

"Is that what you came here for, to scream and call me names? Well, you can save it. Do you know who's paying for this hotel, Phyllie? Your husband is . . . or should I say my baby daddy." Phoebe smirked at her sister.

Phylicia's hand left her side before she realized it, and was on its way to violently slap her sister's face. She suddenly stopped it in mid-air only a few inches from Phoebe's jaw. Slowly, she lowered it, as the look of fear in her sister's eyes changed to smug satisfaction when she realized she wasn't going to hit her. Phylicia stood staring at her for several moments, trembling as she tried to regain control. Finally, she spoke. "Honestly, Phoebe, I came here to talk to my sister, but now I realize that I don't have one. I never did." Quietly, she turned and left the room.

Chapter Twelve

Eva put the last book on her shelf, then climbed down from the stool she had used to reach it. She smoothed out the covers on her bed, and straightened the pillows and stuffed animals. Prior to that, she'd picked up all of her toys from the floor, dusted all of her shelves, and neatly organized her clothes in her closet. Finally finished, she stood and smiled triumphantly at the work she'd done. The only thing left to do was vacuum the rug, and she realized she'd need Li'l G's help to get the machine up the stairs. She walked across the hallway and knocked on his door.

He opened it a crack and peeped out at her. "What you want, runt?"

"Can you bring the vacuum upstairs for me?"

"What for?" he asked, eyeing her suspiciously.

"What do you think? I wanna vacuum my room. Will you bring it up for me?"

"No. Mom will vacuum your room on Saturday like she always does," he said, then started to close the door.

Eva pushed her small foot in and stopped it.

"I can't wait until then. I have to do it now."

Li'l G had been watching music videos in his room and was annoyed by his sister's interruption, but suddenly he noticed the urgency in her face and eyes. "What's going on with you? You never clean your room," he said, finally opening the door all the way.

"I just want my room cleaned. What's so wrong with that?"

"You're up to something, runt. Tell me what it is and I'll get it for you."

"Forget it. I'll get it myself," she said, then turned and walked down the stairs.

Li'l G shrugged, then closed his door. He was just settling down on his bed when he remembered the look in his sister's eyes and decided that he needed to investigate further. As he approached the top of the stairs, he saw Eva struggling to get the vacuum cleaner onto the first step. She panted and heaved, but the heavy machine would not budge. He walked down to her. "Give it to me." He leisurely picked it up and carried it up. He stopped with it in front of her room and leaned on the handle.

"Thanks. I can take it from here," she said as she caught up with him. Eva reached for the vacuum, but he blocked her by stepping in front of it.

"Not until you tell me what's going on." He pushed open her bedroom door and pulled the cleaner inside. "Whoa! You've been a busy beaver. This room hasn't been this clean since you moved in."

"So what? Can you just leave me alone now? I have to finish before she gets here."

"Before who gets here? Pharrah? Why are you cleaning up for her? She's staying in the guest room."

During dinner the previous Wednesday, their father had told them that Pharrah would be spending the summer with them. After Phylicia had finally allowed him to move back into the house, he was anxious for them to grow and bond together as a family. With Phylicia's blessing, he'd asked Pharrah to spend her entire summer vacation with them. Li'l G was disappointed that Kelli would not be joining her, but otherwise the whole visit meant very little to him. The initial excitement of having an older sister had quickly worn off, and was no big deal as far as he was concerned.

"It's not for her. I just want my room cleaned before she gets here. Now give me the vacuum," she said, trying to pry it from his hands.

They stood in the doorway struggling back and forth while she yelled, "Gimme!" and he responded, "No!" over and over.

Hearing the commotion, Phylicia rushed into the room. "What is going on in here? Stop it, both of you!"

"I just wanted to vacuum my room and he won't let me," Eva whined.

"She's up to something, Ma. She never cleans her room. I just wanted to find out what."

"Li'l G, go to your room. I want to talk to your sister for a minute."

"Now you're gonna get it, runt." Li'l G smirked as he walked back across the hall to his room.

Phylicia tried to choose her words carefully. She was glad that Eva was cleaning her room, but like Li'l G, she realized it was certainly out of the ordinary and it most definitely meant that something was going on. "Eva, honey, I was going to vacuum your room tomorrow. You don't have to do it. I'll just put this away," she said, cautiously reaching for the vacuum.

"No, Mommy. I have to do it. I have to do it." Eva had a look of panic in her eyes that troubled her mother.

"Why do you have to do it? What's going on?"

Exasperated, Eva sat down on her bed and began

bawling. She was speaking, but Phylicia could barely understand the words through her sobs and tears. As she watched her she thought she heard the words "other daughter" and "love her more." She sighed as she went over and pulled her into her arms. "Eva, honey, are you upset about Pharrah coming to spend the summer with us?"

"No. I like Pharrah. I'm just scared."

"Scared of what?"

"That Daddy will love her more than me. She's going to be a doctor, and she makes straight As. I can't even keep my room clean. He's so proud of his 'new baby girl.' I'm not gonna be his pumpkin anymore," she said as she buried her wet face in her mother's side.

Phylicia sighed. This was one of her fears when she'd first learned of Pharrah's paternity. She couldn't get past how it would affect her own children and their relationship with their father. She struggled for the right words of comfort. "Eva, your daddy is very proud of you, and he loves you very much. Pharrah is not going to replace you; she's just going to be an addition to the family."

"That's right, honey. You are the only pumpkin in my life." They both looked up and saw Gary standing in the doorway. He'd been watching and listening. He held his arms open to Eva. "Come here."

"Daddy, I love you!" she said as he closed his arms around her.

"I love you too, pumpkin. Don't you ever worry about that. I have enough love for you, your mom, Li'l G, and Pharrah. There's plenty to go around." He looked at Phylicia and gave her a reassuring smile and a wink. "Listen, Eva, why don't you ride with me to the airport to pick up Pharrah? We can stop at Wendy's and get Frosties first, just you and me. How's that sound?"

"Let me get my shoes on," she squealed as she ran to her closet.

Phoebe rolled over in bed and leisurely picked up the phone. She'd spent the morning watching game shows and was now engrossed in her afternoon nap. She answered it while yawning loudly. "Hello."

"Hey, babycakes."

Phoebe bolted upright in bed at the sound of his voice. "Maurice?"

"Yeah, baby, it's me. Aren't you glad to hear from your husband?"

"When did you get out? How did you get out?" she stammered.

"No thanks to you. I called in some favors and managed to make bail. I go to trial in a few months, but until then I'm free as a bird."

"Uhm . . . Didn't you get the papers?"

"Yeah I got them, and I threw them away. You are not serious about divorcing me, are you? Look, girl, we belong together. I can't leave town until after I go to court, so I figured we'd chill out here in the boondocks until then, just you and me? Whaddaya say?"

Phoebe didn't answer him immediately. She was distracted by a knock at her door. Reluctantly, she got up to answer it after asking Maurice to hold the line. She opened the door to the hotel concierge. "Can I help you?" she asked politely.

"Mrs. Cox, we received a phone call from your sister, Mrs. Morgan. She will no longer be covering the cost of your stay here. I need to get another credit card number for your expenses."

"There must be some mistake. Reverend Morgan assured me that he would cover my stay here."

"Yes, ma'am, originally he gave us his credit card number to charge everything to, but as of today that is no longer the case. If you are going to continue staying here, we need another card."

Phoebe stood at the door of the hotel room, fuming. She could not believe that Gary and Phylicia were putting her out with nowhere else to go. "Can I get back to you a little later?" she asked, trying to stall for time.

"Yes, ma'am. Your room is paid up through tonight, and checkout time is eleven tomorrow morning."

Phoebe closed the door slowly and leaned against it to think. She had no money, no credit cards, and nowhere to go. Frantically, she searched the room for something she could take to the pawnshop before remembering that she'd left Maurice on hold. She rushed to the phone and picked it up.

"Maurice, where are you staying?"

"It's not as fancy as your place, but I got me an extended-stay motel room. Why?"

Phoebe swallowed hard before answering him, trying desperately to get the words to come out. "Do you have room for me?" she finally choked out.

"Sure, babycakes. Take a cab over, and I'll pay him when you get here. Get a pen and paper to write down the address."

"Wait a minute. Where are you getting money from?"

"I told you before; I got contacts all over the country. I'm taking care of business. Look, I overheard your little conversation and I know you don't have no place to go. Since you let me sit in that jail all these weeks, I should just let you sleep on the sidewalk, but I'm an old softie. Call a cab. I'll be waiting for you."

"Uhm, I can stay here one more night. Give me the address and I'll be over tomorrow."

Reluctantly, Phoebe wrote down the address of the

motel where Maurice was staying. She'd been away from Brown Bottom for many years, but she knew that the address was in the seediest part of town. She'd believed she could stay at the hotel for as long as she wanted after learning that Pharrah was spending the summer with Gary and Phylicia. She'd hoped her sister's forgiveness extended to her, but apparently it did not. Immediately after hanging up with Maurice, she angrily dialed Phylicia's number. She answered on the third ring.

"First you throw me out of the house, now this!" Phoebe yelled as soon as she'd said hello.

"Phoebe, I take it you've spoken with the concierge?"

"Yes, I have, and he says I have to be out by tomorrow morning. Where do you expect me to go?"

"Go home, Phoebe. You haven't lived here in years. What are you hanging around for?"

"Pharrah will be here in a few hours. I want to be close to my daughter."

"Well, then you need to find a place to stay, because Gary and I are through paying the bill. Honestly, Phoebe, you've racked up room service nightly, emptied out the minibar, and used laundry service. What were you trying to do, bankrupt us?"

"Don't lecture me, Phyllie. You threw me out of the house and Gary told me I could have whatever I wanted. So I got it. I thought he was being generous, but now I see you two wanna play hardball."

"What are you rambling about now, Phoebe? It's not up to us to support you."

"Maybe not, but I'm tired of you calling all the shots."

"What's that supposed to mean?"

"It means that I know the deed to that house has my name on it, and I want my share. You had no right to throw me out."

"I told you before; this is my home, Phoebe."

"No, it's our house. I want you to sell it and give me what's coming to me." Without waiting for an answer, Phoebe slammed down the phone.

"Who was that on the phone? My goodness, you're shaking," Gary said as he walked down the stairs with Eva close on his heels.

"No one. I mean, it's not important. You two better get going. You know how difficult it is to get into the airport these days."

"Eva, wait for me in the car. I'll be right out." Gary waited until his daughter was safely outside before continuing. "What's going on?" he asked.

"That was Phoebe on the phone. The concierge just told her she has to move out of the hotel. She is so spiteful, Gary. She wants me to sell the house and give her half. This is all so ridiculous."

"She actually said that?"

"Yes, she did. She's upset that we cut off the hotel stay, and she wants to stay in Brown Bottom to be near Pharrah."

"We've looked at other houses before, Phyllie. Maybe it's time to sell this house and move to our own place."

"No. This is our own place. Besides, I have so many memories of Mom right here. I don't want to live anywhere else."

"Then we'll buy her out of the house. We have enough money. You know your sister; she'll blow it all by the end of summer anyway."

Phylicia took a moment to think about what her husband was saying. They had more than enough in savings to give Phoebe what she was asking. Maybe it was worth it to just get her off their backs. "All right, I'll contact an attorney tomorrow to draw up the paperwork."

Gary smiled, then leaned in to kiss her good-bye. Phylicia quickly turned her cheek to him, then retreated up the stairs. He'd been home for a week, but she still would not allow him to kiss her or do anything remotely intimate. He watched her walk up the stairs, then said a silent prayer for strength before leaving the house.

That evening, they all enjoyed a warm family dinner with Pharrah, followed by several movies and popcorn. Eva fell asleep on the couch, and Gary carried her to her room after saying good night to everyone else as they headed upstairs to bed. Without waiting for her husband, Phylicia went to her bedroom, undressed, then took a long, hot shower. As she walked out of the bathroom almost an hour later wrapped in only a towel, she was startled to see Gary seated on their bed, as if waiting for her. Ignoring him, she walked past him to the dresser and retrieved her pajamas. Feeling his eyes on her body, she retreated to her closet to get dressed. She'd just dropped her towel onto the floor when she suddenly realized he was behind her.

It had been more than a month since they'd made love. Phylicia could not bear the thought of him touching her knowing that he'd been with her sister. Each night since he'd returned home, she climbed into bed and moved as far away from her husband as she could in their king-sized bed. When he came to bed, he would reach for her, feel her protest, then kiss her gently on the back of her shoulders before saying, "I love you, Phyllie," then he'd turn over and go to sleep. She never answered. She only lay there in the darkness fighting the tears.

Now he was standing behind her, seeing her naked body for the first time in weeks. She knew it was irrational, but Phylicia felt fear. A crippling fear of what he'd do to her and of what she'd allow herself to do with him. Standing as still as a statue, she froze as he moved closer and wrapped his arms around her from behind.

"Phyllie, I need you. Please don't pull away from me," he whispered into her ear, then filled it with kisses.

He pressed his body close to her, and she could feel his manhood growing inside his pajamas as it pressed against her behind. Her body betrayed her, and she instinctively leaned into him as he began to grind against her and kiss her neck and shoulders. She felt his hands loosen their grip around her waist and find their way to her breasts. Gently, he began to caress them, feeling her finally respond to his touch.

"Let's go to bed, Phyllie," he said, then reached for her hand.

Cautiously, she placed it into his and slowly followed him out of the closet and to the bed. He sat down then pulled her to him in a passionate kiss. As they kissed, he leaned back onto the bed, pulling her down on top of him. Gently, he shifted her weight and rolled their bodies until he was on top. Slowly and sensually, he smothered her mouth with kisses before he stopped, stood up, and began to remove his pajamas.

"Gary, stop! I can't do this," Phylicia said abruptly as she jumped from the bed, pulling the quilt around her to cover her nakedness.

Dejected, he sat down on the bed and stared at her. "Why, Phyllie? Why won't you let me touch you?"

She pulled the quilt tighter around her. "I just can't. I keep seeing you with Phoebe and it makes me sick. How could you do that to me? How could you do that to us?"

"Phyllie, I'm sorry. How many times do I have to say I'm sorry? I wish I could take back what happened between Phoebe and me, but I can't. I never wanted to sleep with your sister. You are the only woman I have ever wanted in my whole life. Why can't you believe that? I never ever meant to hurt you."

"My pain doesn't know that you didn't intend for it to be here, all it knows is it is."

"I want to erase that pain, if you'll just let me."

"How? By doing to me what you did to my sister on Mom's couch?"

"This is not about sex. You are my wife, and of course I want to make love to you, but you've taken away the intimacy of our marriage. You won't let me kiss you, or hug you, or even cuddle with you while we sleep. I need that. I need you. Phyllie, I love you!"

"I'm going to get dressed. Please don't follow me this time," she said as she turned toward the closet.

Without answering, Gary put on his robe and walked in the opposite direction toward the door. "Where are you going?" she asked.

"I'm going to sleep downstairs in Mom's old room until you are ready to allow me to really come home. I can't take lying next to you night after night treating me like a stranger," he said, then quietly closed the door.

When he was downstairs, he walked toward the bedroom then changed his mind, and instead went into the family room. He slumped into the couch and flipped on the television. He flipped from channel to channel before finally settling on an infomercial for a new blender. He sat in silence, staring at the screen.

"Dad, what are you doing up?"

"Pharrah, honey, did I wake you with the TV? I'm sorry. I'll turn it off," he said, reaching for the remote.

"No, you didn't wake me. I'm a night owl. I was coming down for a snack. Can I get you something?"

"Uhm . . . no, I just started watching this movie. I've never seen it before."

"Are you okay?"

"Huh?"

"I said, are you okay?"

"No, I'm not hungry."

Pharrah reached for the remote and turned off the TV, then sat down on the couch next to Gary. "What's going on, Dad?" she asked, reaching for his hand.

"Nothing's going on. Why do you ask?"

"Because I was talking to you and you were spaced out."

"I'm sorry. I was just into the TV and not listening."

"Really? Is Eddie Murphy in that movie you were watching?"

"Uhm . . . I don't know, maybe."

Pharrah laughed. "Dad, you weren't even watching a movie. Something's wrong. I wish you would tell me what. I'm nineteen years old. Just tell me what's going on. Maybe I can help."

Gary sighed. "I don't want you to worry about me. Your Aunt Phylicia and I are still struggling, but it's going to work out."

"I'm sorry that my coming here has caused you so much trouble. I never meant for that to happen."

"It's not your fault at all, Pharrah, and don't you for one minute blame yourself."

"But if I hadn't come here the weekend of Grandma's funeral, you and Aunt Phylicia would be getting along fine. Your family wouldn't be torn apart. She and my mom would probably still be speaking."

"Pharrah, listen to me. My family is not torn apart. You are a welcome addition to it. You didn't mess up anything."

"I ruined your relationship with Aunt Phylicia, and her relationship with Mom."

"No, you didn't do either of those things. The truth had to come out, and sometimes people have a difficult time dealing with truth. But I promise you, God brought you to us for a reason. This family is going to be stronger because of it. Don't worry about me and Phylicia. We'll work it out."

"How can you be so sure?"

"It's called faith, honey. God will take care of it. Now, what were you saying about a snack? I think there's some leftover banana pudding in the fridge." He got up and pulled her to the kitchen with him.

Phylicia stood near the stairs, watching and listening to them laughing and talking happily as they ate their snack, before she finally returned to her bedroom and closed the door.

Chapter Thirteen

Phoebe ran into the tiny motel bathroom screaming at the top of her lungs. Maurice ran behind her and pounded on the door, trying to get her to come out, but she only screamed louder. He finally stopped pounding and began laughing at her. "Phoebe, come out. It's gone now," he said.

"No. You are just saying that."

"Phoebe, come out and quit acting stupid."

"That thing was huge. Call the manager. I won't come out until I know it's gone." Phoebe sat on the porcelain commode, trembling from cold and fear. She'd just gotten out of bed and was on her way to the bathroom to wash up when it scurried across her foot. Maurice called it a mouse, but she knew a rat when she saw one. It was hairy and fat and it had bared its fangs at Phoebe before rushing off to the other side of the room. As if it weren't bad enough that the room had roaches as big as quarters, an air conditioner that creaked and groaned all night but barely pumped any cool air, a bed that had a valley running down the middle, and sheets that were so dingy they looked brownish-grey, now she had to contend with rodents as well. Phoebe was furious with herself that she'd allowed Maurice back into her life to drag her down once again.

"You are gonna be late for your meeting if you don't get of out there, girl," he yelled. "You lived in New York City for all these years and you are afraid of mice. I can't believe that."

Unenthusiastically, Phoebe stood up and peeped out of the bathroom door, then allowed her eyes to roam around the room. "No, I'm not afraid of mice. I'm afraid of cat-sized rats. Hand me my clothes. I'll get dressed in here."

Maurice laughed again, as he reached for her pants and blouse. "You know we wouldn't have to live like this if you'd just listen to me. All you'd need to make is one drop and we could have enough to go back to the Marriott."

"Forget it, Maurice. I'm not running any drugs for you," she said as she took her clothes, then closed the bathroom door. She dressed quickly in the minuscule space, bumping her elbow twice on the sink while trying to maneuver around. Maurice cackled loudly as she screamed and cursed in pain. When she was done, she pulled the door open just a crack again. "Can you hand me my makeup case, please?"

"You are gonna have to come out to leave, Phoebe. Quit being ridiculous."

"It's on the dresser. Maurice, please, you are going to make me late."

Maurice walked over to the dresser and picked up the makeup case, then he tossed it in the general direction of the bathroom, scattering the contents all over the floor.

"Dang, Maurice, what is wrong with you?" she said, finally coming out of the bathroom. She looked around the room quickly for the rodent before kneeling to pick up her makeup. Just as she'd put the last lipstick into the case, she noticed the rat peering at her from under the bed. His beady little red eyes were poised directly on her. Screaming another blood-curdling scream, she ran back into the bathroom, slamming the door behind her as Maurice doubled over on the bed, laughing at her again.

Forget him. After I meet with Phyllie this afternoon and pick up my check, I'm putting him in the wind anyway. Phoebe ignored his cackling and carefully applied her makeup. When she was done, she pulled the scarf off of her weave and stared at the roots in the mirror. She had almost three inches of new growth coming in, and the weave was starting to look tattered and worn. She folded the scarf and retied it, covering the edges of her hair. *I need to get my hair done as soon as the check is cashed.* Finally satisfied with the way she looked, she took a deep breath and tentatively stepped out of the bathroom. "Has that thing come out again?" she asked, looking around.

"I haven't noticed. It's probably just hungry, and I promise you, girl, it ain't gonna try to eat you."

"Very funny. Did you call the manager and see if he could set a trap or something?"

"No, but I will." Maurice turned from the television and looked at her. She was dressed in her red silk Prada pantsuit with matching pumps. It was one of the last she still owned. She kept it for meetings and special occasions. Maurice let out a long whistle. "Maybe that rat will try to eat you, 'cause you look good enough to eat. Girl, you cleaner than a Safeway chitlin," he said as he leered at her.

"For someone from New York, you say some country stuff," she answered.

"I told you, my daddy is from North Carolina, so what

of it? You act like this hick town is not the country. I try giving you a compliment and all you do is complain."

"Yeah, whatever. Thanks, Maurice. Did you call for the cab yet?" She walked to the other side of the room, avoiding his stare.

"You got money to pay for a cab?"

"You said you were going to pay for me to get to my meeting."

"I did?"

"Yes, you did. You said it last night when we . . . When we were in bed you said you'd pay for it."

"Naw, I believe what I said was I'd make sure you got there. I never said nothing about paying for no freakin' cab. The bus stop is on the corner. I'll go with you and pay for it."

Phoebe was livid. After having to move in with him and staying for several weeks, she'd been making excuse after excuse to avoid being intimate with him. Unable to run anymore, she'd finally given in to sex with Maurice the night before. But she only did it to get him to pay for her cab to meet Phylicia and Gary at the lawyer's office. The last thing she wanted to do was arrive on the bus with Maurice following a few steps behind.

He thought she was meeting her sister to go over her mother's estate. She didn't bother to tell him that she would be getting a check for her half of the value of the house. When Phylicia called and told her she was going to buy her out, she insisted that they hire an appraiser whom she approved. With the additions as well as the location, the house had appraised at $275,000. Her cut, minus the lawyer's fees, was $130,000. She'd almost fainted when she'd read the letter and seen the amount. All she had to do was meet them, sign away her rights to the house, pick up her check, and be on her merry way.

Or, at least, she thought that was all. Now she had to find a way to get there and shake Maurice at the same time.

She tried desperately to think quickly. "I don't think you coming with me is such a good idea. You broke into my sister's house, remember? You should just stay here and wait for me to come back."

"I'm not gonna let you ride that bus alone, looking like you do. Those perverts would have you sized up and robbed before you got three blocks. I won't go inside, so your sis won't even know I'm there."

But I'll know. "No, it's too risky. It would violate your terms of release, getting so close to them, and you could end up back in jail." *Oh, how I wish that would happen,* she mused. "I think I'll call Pharrah. Maybe she can come pick me up."

"Since you calling the house, why not ask your sister to pick you up?" he smirked.

"I thought I already explained all of that to you. Her husband is Pharrah's father and she didn't know we'd had an affair. I am not on my sister's 'favorite person' list right now," she said as she reached for the phone.

It took her several moments of convincing, but finally Pharrah had agreed to borrow Gary's car and pick her up for the meeting. She hung up the phone feeling satisfied.

"What time will she be here?" Maurice asked his wife.

"Half an hour or so."

"Good. I have time to get dressed. I'm going with you."

"Maurice, we've already discussed this. Why do you insist on going with me?"

"This is why." He held up a piece of paper. Phoebe instantly recognized it as the letter from the lawyer outlining how much money she would be getting. She froze when she saw it.

"Wha . . . what are you doing with that?" she stammered.

"Does it matter? Did you think you were going to go over there, get paid, and not give me a dime? Were you even planning on coming back here at all, Phoebe?"

"I don't owe you anything. That house belonged to my parents."

"You are an ungrateful wench. I took you in when you had nowhere else to go. Now that you are about to get paid, all of a sudden I'm not good enough to share the wealth. You already cheated me out of that insurance policy money."

"I told you I couldn't get any of that money. My mother fixed the policy so that it would all go directly to Pharrah for her education." Phoebe was positive about that because she'd actually tried cashing in the policy, but the stipulations were very strict.

"Whatever, Phoebe. You've been living off of me for weeks and don't even want to give me a li'l trim as a thank you. You owe me, girl."

"I'll give you some of the money. But only if you stay here until I get back."

"No way; if I let you out of my sight, I won't ever see you or a penny of that money."

"No, Maurice, you are not coming with me and that's final!"

With her back turned, she never saw him coming. She only felt the sudden excruciating pain and fear as Maurice grabbed her arm and twisted it, spinning her around to face him. Then he slapped her across the face. She fell backwards onto the bed, and he immediately pulled her up and slapped her again, knocking her across the room. Each time she fell, he picked her up again, then violently punched or slapped her until her face was bloody and swollen. Finally, he threw her listless body like a crash dummy onto the bed. Phoebe moaned in agony as she heard him leaving.

"Let's see you make that meeting now," he said as he walked out.

"I knew she would be late. This is so typical of Phoebe," Phylicia said, staring at her watch.

"Calm down, honey. Pharrah went to pick her up. I'm sure she'll rush her along. Besides, she's not that late."

"The meeting was scheduled to start half an hour ago. This is ridiculous. I'm giving her ten more minutes and then I'm gone. I'm not waiting all day."

"What good will that do? We'll just have to come back another day and start all over. Just be patient, sweetheart." He turned to his attorney. "Can you give us a few more minutes?" Will Nash was a family friend, a member of their congregation, and one of the best estate attorneys in the business.

"I'm sorry, but your wife is right. I have another appointment that will be here shortly. Maybe we should just reschedule."

Gary sighed loudly. "I suppose we don't have a choice, but I really wanted this to be over and done with. The sooner we sign everything, the sooner we can move forward."

"Well, I tell you what, since you are practically family, I'll bend the rules a little bit for you. Your wife can go ahead and sign everything we need from her, then I'll just need your sister-in-law's signature. You don't all have to be present at once as long as she agrees to the terms already outlined. There's no need for mediation, just signatures."

"Phoebe is greedy," Phylicia replied. "All she'll see is dollar signs. Besides, we are giving her the most valuable asset, which is Mom's car. Mom only drove it a few weeks before she got sick, and it's completely paid for. She'll agree. Just show me where to sign."

"Have you told her about the other assets? She is entitled to know about your mother's jewelry," Will said.

"It's all in the paperwork. Trust me, once she finds out she's getting all this money and a new car, she'll think she just won on a game show. Besides, it's nothing more than some costume pieces and her wedding rings. Phoebe doesn't care about the things with sentimental value, only those things she can put a price on," Phylicia responded, reaching for the pen Will had in his hand.

Once the papers were signed and they were inside her car on their way home, Phylicia breathed a loud sigh of relief.

"What's that for?" Gary inquired.

"Now that the estate is settled, I don't ever have to see my sister again. Will said he'd deliver the car to her. I'm actually glad she never showed up."

"You don't really mean that, do you, Phyllie?"

Phylicia turned swiftly in her seat and stared at him. "Of course I mean it. She's been nothing but trouble since she got back to town. Why would I want to see her?"

"I don't know, maybe because she's your sister."

"Hmph. If you are about to start defending her, then we can just ride home in silence."

"I was only going to say that—"

Phylicia held up her hand in his face to silence him, then leaned back in her seat, staring straight ahead, just as Gary's cell phone began to ring. He pulled it from the clip on his hip and flipped it open. "Hello . . . Pharrah, where are you? Phyllie and I have already left the lawyer's office . . . The hospital? Oh my God! What happened? Yes, we are on our way."

"What's going on? Is Pharrah okay?" Phylicia said, suddenly sitting up and turning to him.

"She's fine. It's Phoebe. She's been beaten badly. Pharrah found her when she went to the motel to pick her up. She thinks her husband did it to her."

"Oh, that figures. After the way he broke into our house, it's obvious he's crazy and violent. She should never have gone back to him. What are you doing?" she asked, noticing Gary trying to make a U-turn in the road.

"The hospital is in the opposite direction. I have to turn around."

"Take me home," Phylicia said, then leaned back in her seat once again, staring straight ahead.

"Did you just hear what I said? Your sister is in the hospital."

"You can go and give Pharrah some comfort and support but I want to go home. I no longer have a sister."

Gary stared at the woman sitting next to him. She looked like his wife. She had his wife's voice when she spoke. But surely this was not the woman he'd married. His wife was kind, generous, and forgiving. He did not recognize the woman who was now riding with him, filled with such anger and hatred. Staring at her, searching for signs of identification, he finally spoke. "Fine, I'll drop you at the house."

As soon as he pulled into the driveway, she opened the door, got out, and stalked away without even saying good-bye to him. Gary sighed loudly. *Lord, I need you for this one. Please soften Phyllie's heart*, he silently prayed, then looked down as his cell phone rang again. He answered; Pharrah was on the line.

"Hey, Dad, it's me. I hope I caught you in time."

"In time for what? Is your mother okay?"

"Not really, but we'll be leaving the hospital soon. The doctors say the bruises and swelling should heal in a few days."

"Thank God she's okay. Do you want me to come? I was just leaving the house."

"What are you doing back there?"

"Phyllie wanted to be dropped off. She still doesn't want to see your mother."

"Well, I guess I don't need to ask what I was going to ask."

"And what was that?"

"Well, Mom won't stay at the hospital, and I can't take her back to that motel. She won't admit it, but I know Maurice did this to her. I was hoping she could come back there for a few days, but I'm sure Aunt Phylicia won't like that. Do you think you could loan me a few dollars so I could get her a hotel room? It doesn't have to be the Marriott again, just some place clean."

"To be perfectly honest, honey, your aunt and I had to liquidate quite a few assets to meet your mother's demands about the house. Phyllie would have a fit if I spent more money on her."

"Make it a loan to me, Dad. I'll pay you back, I promise."

"I know you would, honey, but I don't want you having that responsibility. You don't have a job and school should be your priority."

"I don't know what to do. She has nowhere else to go. I suggested calling one of her cousins, but you know Momma and her foolish pride. She'd never let them see her like this."

"Hold on a sec, I think I may have an answer for you." He clicked the phone over and dialed another number. A few moments later, Gary clicked back over to Pharrah. "Great news, honey, I spoke with Mrs. Farmer. Your mother can stay with her until she gets the check from the lawyer. It should only be until she's feeling better and can sign the papers. It shouldn't be more than a couple of days."

"Are you sure about that, Dad? Why would Mom want to stay with your secretary?"

"She's not just my secretary. She's a trusted family friend. Besides, your mother shouldn't be alone in a hotel room, and Mrs. Farmer will enjoy having someone to take care of. Do you know how to get to her house from the hospital?"

"Sure, Dad, I remember where she lives. Brown Bottom isn't big enough to get lost in. I'll see you at home after I get Mom settled in."

"Okay, honey."

"Thanks for looking out for my mom. I love you."

It was the first time she'd said those words since they'd met, and Gary felt his heart growing in size like in *How the Grinch stole Christmas!* "I love you too, Pharrah," he said as he slowly hung up the phone.

Chapter Fourteen

"Where are you taking me? I told you to ask Gary for money for a hotel. I know he has it." Phoebe sat in the passenger seat trying not to wince in pain each time she spoke. Her lip was swollen and her jaws ached when she moved them.

"Dad spoke with Mrs. Farmer and she agreed to let you stay there. I'm sure she'll make you comfortable."

"I barely know that old woman. Take me to a hotel."

"I don't have any money to pay for a hotel."

"I told you to ask your father. If he cared, he would."

"Listen, Mom, he does care. He cares a lot. He didn't have to ask Mrs. Farmer to let you stay with her. He could have let you go back to Maurice or fend for yourself. He and Aunt Phylicia had to cash in some CDs and close out some savings accounts to get you the money you wanted for their house. They gave you half with no consideration for all the money they've spent on it. You've taken more than enough from him. You've taken enough from both of them."

"I raised you all by myself and I never asked him for

child support or anything. He got off easier than most men."

"I can't believe you, Mom. It's like since you came to Brown Bottom you've turned into this selfish, spoiled, conniving woman whom I don't even recognize. Where is the woman who raised me to care about people and have compassion? He didn't pay you child support because you lied and told him I didn't exist. You lied and slept with your sister's boyfriend. You lied to me about who my real father was. And I'm guessing you lied to Maurice about the money and that's why he beat you. If you'd just stop lying, maybe things wouldn't turn out so horrible."

Phoebe sat staring at her daughter in awe, unable to believe what she'd just heard, as Pharrah pulled into Mrs. Farmer's driveway and put the car in park. "She's expecting you. I'll be back tomorrow to see how you are doing."

"Aren't you going to come in with me?"

"No, I have to go now. I want to have dinner . . . with my family."

Reluctantly, Phoebe reached for the car door, opened it, and slowly got out. She meticulously took her time and emphasized the pain in each movement, hoping to garner some sympathy. Pharrah kept her hands on the wheel, staring straight ahead. Realizing she was unable to draw out the moment any longer, Phoebe finally closed the car door and walked toward Mrs. Farmer's front door.

Her legs felt like lead pipes as she put one in front of the other, so she stopped halfway up the walkway and watched Pharrah drive away. She tried to fight it, but the memory of the last time she'd been there hovered over her like a cloud, then came raining down on top of her head, stopping her from going any further.

Phoebe looked up into the mud-colored face of the young boy holding the basketball tightly under his left arm. He looked down at her, his eyes traveling across the mountainous caverns of her bosom, straining to be freed from the tight halter barely covering them. As she stood there, his eyes lowered, outlining the curves of her wide hips and thighs squeezed tightly into a pair of denim shorts. She placed one hand on her hip and struck a pose before speaking. "Hey, is Tino here?"

"What you want with him when I'm standing right here, babygirl?"

"I wanna talk to him."

The young boy shifted his weight and the basketball to his other side as he devoured her with his eyes. His hormones raged as he stared at her, trying not to become visibly aroused. "What you need to talk to Tino about?"

"That's my business. Where he at?"

"He just left with his girl, but you can hang out with me if you wanna wait, beautiful."

"What girl?"

"He left with Sonya. That's the flavor of the week. Oh no, don't tell me you been cut from the team and didn't get the memo." He covered his mouth with his fist as he laughed heartily at her.

"It's not even like that. I . . . I just wanted to tell him something, that's all. When will he be back?"

"Who knows, girl? Look, if you and Tino ain't like that, how about me and you hooking up? That's my car parked over there. Just let me finish beating these fools in b-ball and then we can go for a ride." He leered at her as he held out the "i" in "ride" for several syllables.

"No, thank you. Can I leave a message for him?"

"I'm not Tino's personal secretary. But hey, if you tell me your name, I'll be sure to let him know that you brought your sexy, thick self by." He licked his lips.

"It's Phoebe. Just tell him Phoebe came by, and uhm, ask him to call me." She turned to walk away, then felt his hand on her arm.

"What's your number? I mean, so I can give it to him."

"He has it," she said, then gently but firmly pulled herself from his grasp and began walking back down the street toward her house.

"Well, the name's Wayne, baby. If you change your mind, I'll be right here waiting," she heard him yell after her before returning to his game of basketball.

She sat by the phone for the rest of that night waiting for Tino to call, but he never did. She never spoke to Tino or Wayne again.

"Phoebe, girl, get in this house. I'm not gonna stand out here waiting on you all night. Phoebe?" The sound of Mrs. Farmer's voice brought her back to the present. She began walking again as she noticed the woman waiting on the front steps. "What were you doing just standing out there in the yard?"

"I'm sorry. The doctor gave me some pain pills. I was just a little disoriented."

"My goodness, child, let's get you into the bedroom so you can lie down. Why didn't your daughter stay and help you in the house?"

"I told her to go on. I thought . . . I thought I was fine," she said as Mrs. Farmer led her down the hallway and into a small bedroom in the back. She looked around at the bunk beds stacked in one corner and a matching twin in the other corner of the little room. Curtains hung on the windows with cowboys chasing Indians across them, and the three twin-sized bedspreads all matched their design.

"This was my boys' room," Mrs. Farmer said. "I know I should have redecorated years ago, after Wayne and

Jarvis got married, but I just never got around to it. Now my grandsons use it when they come to visit. But it's clean, the sheets are fresh. You go ahead and take the twin bed, honey."

Phoebe stood still, staring at the bed. "Uhm, I don't mean to sound rude or ungrateful, Mrs. Farmer, but is this the bed Tino slept in?"

"You knew Tino?"

"Uhm . . . not very well. I just heard about what happened to him."

"Don't tell me you're afraid of ghosts, child."

"Well, no, ma'am. It's just that . . . I mean, if this was his bed, I'd just rather sleep in another one, that's all."

"If you must know, right after he died, my husband and I got rid of his bed. There used to be four bunks in here. The boys always seemed to have a friend sleeping over, so we added an extra bed for company. The bed Tino slept in is long gone," she said with a far-off look in her eyes.

"I'm sorry, Mrs. Farmer. I didn't mean—"

"Hush, child. It's okay. I loved my baby boy, but he's been gone a long time. Now, where is your suitcase? I'll help you get settled in for the night."

"I don't have one. I mean . . . well, my husband . . . soon-to-be ex-husband . . . Well, I left everything at the motel. Pharrah only brought my purse," she stammered.

"There's no need to feel embarrassed. Reverend Gary filled me in on what happened. Don't worry about your things. We can try to get them later. I'm sure I have an old T-shirt and a pair of sweat pants you can sleep in. I used to be about your size before I lost my figure," she said with a smile, then left the room.

When she returned a few moments later, she gave Phoebe the clothes, a clean toothbrush, and a washcloth, then led her to the bathroom. Once she'd changed, Mrs. Farmer helped her into bed and brought her dinner on a tray. Phoebe ate a few bites, then declined more as she winced in pain each time her mouth moved. Instead, she opted to take her pain medication and turn in early. Just as she dozed off, her daughter's words echoed in her ears: *"If you'd just stop lying . . . stop lying . . . lying."*

Part II

Nine months later

Chapter Fifteen

Reverend Gary Morgan smiled contently to himself as he watched the soloist step to the microphone. He'd specially requested that the choir sing this song, and was pleased with what he'd overheard during their rehearsal. As the soloist opened her mouth and the words of praise floated out, Gary closed his eyes, allowing himself to succumb to God and worship Him totally.

He praised God from his seat until he could no longer contain himself, then he and a majority of his congregation stood clapping, stomping, and singing along with the choir. By the time they'd reached the song's climactic ending, the ushers were filling the aisles fanning those who'd been filled with the Holy Ghost. Gary waited patiently for the fervor in the crowd to decrease to a low rumble before stepping up to the podium to begin his sermon. His morning's text was the same as the title of the song the choir sang.

"Church, through the midst of the turmoil, when your life seems out of control, God sent me by to tell ya this morning that you gots to praise Him anyway," he began as shouts of "Amen" and "Hallelujah, Pastor" rang out from the crowd. He quickly gave his scriptural reference, then waited for his parishioners to find the chapter and verse to read along with him.

"Psalms 111:1—'Praise ye the Lord. I will praise the Lord with my whole heart, in the assembly of the upright, and in the congregation,' He read aloud. "Now, I know what you're thinking. You're saying, 'Pastor, I sure do praise the Lord, 'cause He helped me get a new job and He healed me when I was sick. I praise Him 'cause he's been mighty good to me.' But that's not what God sent me by to tell you 'bout this morning, church. He told me you gots to praise Him even when you lose that new job and can't pay none of your bills. You gots to praise Him even when you so sick you can't hardly move out of your sickbed. You gots to keep right on praising Him when the world is tumbling down around you and you don't know which a-way to turn. That's when you gots to send the praises up. God doesn't just want you to praise Him for all that He's done for you. But, church, you gots to praise Him for who He is. God told me to tell ya this morning, church, you been praying to Him, now stop praying and start praising."

Gary paused dramatically as he heard applause and rumblings of agreement flowing throughout the congregation. He wiped his brow, then continued. "You gots to praise Him, church, no matter what the situation is. When praises go up . . ." He paused as his congregation shouted out in unison, "Blessings come down."

"That's right, church, blessings come down. So you gots to praise Him anyway for all He's done for you and all He's gonna do for you. You got to praise Him. Praise ye the Lord!"

Gary's sermon continued for twenty minutes before he finally reached the culmination and took his seat behind the podium. Breathing heavily with excitement, he wiped his brow as his associate minister led the call to the altar.

He knew he'd preached that day's sermon as much for himself as anyone. His personal life was not going the way it should, and he wasn't happy, but he continued to praise God anyway for what he was gonna do. Gary realized there was nothing more that he could do.

"That was a beautiful sermon this morning, honey," Phylicia said as she set the dirty rice she'd prepared for dinner on the table.

"I'm glad you enjoyed it," he replied as he, Li'l G, and Eva took their seats around the dining room table.

Phylicia returned to the kitchen to bring out the rest of the meal as he chatted with the children. Lately, their conversation was the most he enjoyed. He and Phylicia spoke in polite tones and sentences, but the tension between them was building from a small, smoldering brush fire into a blazing inferno. Gary wasn't sure how much longer they could last before it erupted into a full-scale meltdown of their marriage.

He'd been sleeping in his late mother-in-law's room for almost a year, as Phylicia didn't seem to want him back in their bed.

After spending the summer with them, Pharrah returned to Southern University to complete her senior year. In just a few weeks, the family would be traveling to Baton Rouge to see her graduate with honors. As a family unit, their time together was straight out of an episode of *The Cosby Show*. The three kids bonded and enjoyed their time with each other.

Eva no longer felt threatened, as she began to idolize her older sister, wanting to be just like her. Li'l G used Pharrah as a sounding board as he'd begun to date; having an older sister made him feel as if he understood women just a little bit more than his friends. Phylicia had formed a quick bond with Pharrah and took a genuine interest in her and her well-being. Gary had taken the podium one Sunday and admitted his teenaged mistake to his congregation, and they welcomed Pharrah with open arms. They'd spent family nights laughing and playing games, taken a four-day excursion to the beach, worshipped each Sunday morning at Freedom Inspiration, praying together, and it seemed as if Pharrah had always been a part of their lives.

However, once the lights were out and everyone returned to their respective beds for slumber, Phylicia and Gary said their prayers in separate rooms and continued to sleep in separate beds.

As they ate dinner, the whole family talked, laughed, and enjoyed each other's company. Gary noticed that when the kids were around, Phylicia seemed to lighten up, and he could see the fire in her that he'd fallen in love with. Each time it happened, he got lost in her eyes, searching and hoping that there was an opening for him to find his way back inside her warmth.

However, as soon as the dishes were cleared and the children were upstairs enjoying their video games and toys, Phylicia returned to the cold, stone face she'd reserved for him.

Bored with flipping channels on the television, he went into the kitchen and immediately felt his nature rise as he found Phylicia bent over the dishwasher putting dishes inside. "Would you like some help?" he asked the moment she noticed him staring at her voluptuous behind.

"I'm almost done. Thanks anyway."

For the umpteenth time, he tried to reach out to her. "Your favorite movie is on tonight. Would you like me to pop some popcorn and we can watch it together?"

"Sure, I'll call the kids down," she said as she closed the washer.

"No, don't do that. I just thought maybe the two of us could watch it together."

She looked at him, realizing he had more than movies and popcorn on his mind.

"You know, I'm sorry. I just remembered that Mrs. Farmer gave me a large stack of papers to go over. We still haven't chosen a speaker for this year's Women's Conference. I really need to go upstairs and read through all of it."

He hated the fact that she always made excuses, rarely saying no to him outright. It exasperated him to no end. How could they solve the problem if she continued to pretend there wasn't a problem? Instead, she chose to avoid him and any moments of intimacy at all costs.

"The Women's Conference isn't for several months. You can take care of that tomorrow." He stepped closer and reached for her hand. "Come on, Phyllie. I'd like to spend some time with my wife."

"You've been with me all day. We went to church together this morning, then we had ice cream with the kids afterwards and we just spent a lovely dinner together." She pulled her hand away and turned her back to him. She pretended to busy herself wiping down an already spotless countertop.

Gary sighed loudly. "I don't know how much longer I can take this, Phyllie."

She spun around and looked at him. "Take what? What is your problem, Gary?"

"I don't have a problem, but we do. Our marriage has a serious problem, and until we face it, we can't move on."

Phylicia threw the sponge into the sink and folded her arms. "Oh, yeah, and what is the problem as you see it? Exactly what is wrong now? I cook for you. I clean for you. I take care of this house and the kids for you. I'm active in the church for you. What else do you want?"

"I want you, Phyllie. I want the woman I married. The woman I fell in love with."

"What are you talking about? I'm right here."

"No, you're not. From the moment you let me move back in here, you moved out. Your body is here, but your heart and your spirit, the flair that I fell in love with, is gone. I miss that Phyllie. I want my wife back."

"I'm not going to have this conversation again. I told you when you moved back in that I needed some time. You promised me that you'd give me that."

"It's been months. Months and months and you won't let me touch your hand or even caress your cheek. It's been months since I held you in my arms and kissed your lips. It's been almost a year since we made love. Don't you understand, Phylicia, I need you!" he said, pleading with her with his eyes.

"So that's what this is about, sex? You want sex? Gary, statistically speaking, most married couples our age are not having sex. Many of them sleep in separate beds and separate rooms. It's not a big deal."

"We are not most married couples our age, and it is a big deal to me. It's a very big deal if my wife doesn't want to share intimacy with me. It's not just about sex and you know it. Sometimes you treat me like a complete outsider."

"After a certain age, Gary, sometimes those desires just fade away. It's perfectly normal."

"So are you saying you no longer have a desire for me? Is that it, Phyllie? You don't want me anymore?"

She bit her bottom lip as she stared at him. At thirty-nine years old, he still had the muscular build of the college basketball player he once was. Phylicia desired him. She desired him so much that it ached. But she wouldn't allow her body to rule her. Her heart and her mind made her refuse him. "I didn't say that, Gary."

"Then what are you saying?"

"I don't want to discuss this. Why can't you just leave me alone?" she said, not realizing she'd raised her voice. Suddenly she noticed the look of pain on his face.

"All right, Phyllie. If you want me to move out, just say so. I don't want to, but I will leave if that's what you want."

Phylicia stared at him for several moments without answering. Finally she spoke. "Get Li'l G to watch the movie with you. I'm going upstairs."

She walked briskly past him without another word and trotted swiftly upstairs. In the privacy of her bedroom, she slumped against the wall, slowly slid down to the floor, then buried her head in her knees as she began to sob.

Chapter Sixteen

"I'm sorry, ma'am, but your card has been declined."

"There's must be some mistake. Try it again."

"I'm sorry, ma'am, we've tried it three times. I'll need another form of payment for your dinner, please?"

Phoebe stared at the tall, thin Caucasian waiter as he patiently waited for her to figure out a way to pay for her lobster and shrimp meal. She knew there had to be some kind of mistake. *The restaurant's machine must be malfunctioning,* she thought as she reluctantly dug inside her purse and retrieved her last twenty dollar bill. She handed it to the waiter.

"Your bill was seventeen dollars and fifty cents; do you require change, ma'am?"

"Of course I do. I'll leave your tip on the table."

When he returned, Phoebe took her change, laid twenty-five cents on the table for the waiter as punishment for informing her that her card was declined, and walked out to her car. She checked her weave in the rearview mirror, then slowly pulled out into the traffic, humming casually. Within a few moments she pulled into the driveway of her luxurious townhouse. She hopped out, checked her mailbox, and went inside as she flipped through the envelopes.

A large white envelope bearing the name, "William K. Nash: Attorney at Law" caught her attention. She turned it over and ran her fingernail under the flap, freeing the letter. Her mouth dropped open as she read its contents. A smile spread across her face from ear to ear, and she hugged the envelope tightly as if it were a long-lost lover.

"Free at last! Free at last! Thank God a'mighty, I'm free at last," she squealed loudly.

The official-looking letter said that her divorce from Maurice was final. She breathed a sigh of relief, realizing she was liberated from him forever.

During her brief stay with Mrs. Farmer, she had convinced Phoebe that calling the police and having him arrested was in the best interest of everyone. She'd driven Phoebe to the police station early one morning to file a report, and Maurice was back in jail by early afternoon. When he arrived in court a few weeks later, he stood trial for resisting arrest, shooting the police officer, aggravated assault for attacking Phoebe, and burglary, since Phylicia and Gary had decided to press charges after all. His public defender chose not to fight extradition, and he was sent back to New York on violation of probation charges. He would be spending the next twenty years in lockdown at Sing Sing Correctional Facility.

It couldn't have happened to a nicer guy, Phoebe thought as she carefully laid the envelope that contained her emancipation on the coffee table.

Then she noticed a second letter also from the attorney's office. Gleefully, she ripped it open, anxious for more good news. She read it slowly.

Dear Mrs. Cox,

This will be our firm's last correspondence with you. On the 3rd of this month, you withdrew the final install-ment of your settlement from our governing account, in the amount of $250.00. Therefore, at this time, as we have no further business regarding your mother's estate, we will be closing your file. If you need our services in the fu-ture, please do not hesitate to give us a call.

Sincerely,

William K. Nash, Esq.

Phoebe reread the letter three times, believing that if she reread it, somehow the news would change. "How could I have spent it all so quickly?" she wondered aloud.

That question was easy to answer as she looked around her townhouse at the leather living room set, glass-and-brass dinette table with posh matching chairs, and the exquisitely tasteful and expensive art on the walls. Men-tally, she pictured her master bedroom with the four-poster sleigh bed and Evan Picone comforter set. Inside her walk-in closet, every designer name that Brown Bot-tom's small mall carried was either draped over a hanger or standing inside a shoe box neatly stacked on the floor. Although she really only needed one bedroom, she'd rented and furnished a three-bedroom townhouse on the pretense that maybe Pharrah would want to stay with her occasionally. That never happened as Pharrah was con-tent to stay with Phylicia and Gary, only stopping by to see her mother for brief visits.

When Phoebe first arrived at the lawyer's office the previous year following her recovery, Will Nash handed her a cashier's check for the full amount of $130,000 and the keys to her mother's Toyota Camry. She placed them in her purse and was about to leave when she decided to ask Will if he handled divorces. Maurice had torn up the previous papers she'd sent him, and her moving into the motel meant they were no longer legally separated. She would have to start the process all over again.

"It's not my forte, but I'm sure I can help you," Will answered.

Phoebe carefully explained to him the situation with Maurice, starting from the day they met. "I've never loved him, and now I just want to be rid of him as quickly as possible," she said after she'd given him the gory details of their last encounter.

"Are there any children involved?"

"No. I mean I have a daughter, but she's not his."

"Well, then it should be a pretty easy process since the only property you seem to possess is the car and the money." Will took out a piece of paper and began taking notes.

"I'm not giving him one thin dime of this money. You can believe that."

Will stopped writing and looked at her. "Mrs. Cox, as your husband, he may be entitled. Louisiana is a community property state, and I have seen cases where money acquired during the marriage was considered an asset, and thusly split during the divorce."

"That's crazy. Listen, if I hire you as my lawyer, isn't there something you could do?"

Will looked at her for several moments, sizing her up. He noticed the knockoff purse, faux fur coat in seventy degree weather, and tattered weave. It only took him a moment to realize she was an easy mark. "Okay, what I can do is, instead of you leaving with that check, give it back to me. I can set up a trust account for you that will be in the firm's name. Whenever you need money, simply stop by the office or call and request small amounts that you can then deposit into your own checking account. There won't be any paper trail of large transactions of money, and no judge will be able to connect it to you. Since you are a family member of the Morgans, we'd only require a twenty-five percent fee to set this up." He leaned back in his chair and grinned at her.

Phoebe was intent on Maurice not having any of her money, and the only time 25 percent meant anything to her was during a designer sale, so she quickly agreed. Along with the fees for the divorce, Will managed to walk away with more than fifty grand of her money without Phoebe even realizing it was gone.

In exchange, he'd had his secretary open an interest-bearing savings account with the money, and each time Phoebe made a request, the secretary went to the bank and made a withdrawal for her. Will had the interest transferred to his own personal account each month, resulting in an even bigger profit for him. It was the easiest money he'd ever made.

After picking up her latest installment from Will's secretary, she deposited the entire $250 into her checking account and went shopping the same afternoon. Tossing the letter aside, Phoebe rushed to the kitchen and picked up the phone, then punched in numbers. A computerized voice gave her instructions that she followed, tapping her long, red nails against the keys. She stopped momentarily, said a silent prayer, then pressed the last four digits the voice requested. She held her breath as she listened: *"Your available balance is seven dollars and eighty-two cents."* Dejected, Phoebe placed the phone back into its cradle and slumped down into her kitchen chair. She couldn't believe that once again she was completely broke.

Chapter Seventeen

Sitting at her desk in the dorm, Pharrah rubbed her temples gently, willing the headache that had plagued her for three days to go away. The throbbing nauseated her and she'd thrown up breakfast and lunch. Unable to concentrate any longer on the numbers floating across the pages of her calculus book, she laid her head down on the desk for what seemed like seconds. An hour later her roommate woke her from a deep slumber.

"Pharrah . . . wake up. Pharrah, you okay?"

Sitting up, Pharrah pried open her eyes and stared at Kelli. "Yeah, I'm fine. I just can't seem to shake this awful headache. Do you have any ibuprofen?"

"Didn't I give you four already? You're pre-med, girl. You know that you don't need to take any more today. Maybe you should stop by student health or something."

"I don't have time. I have to study for my calculus exam. It's my last one and then I'm done. Just give me one, to ease this pain enough for me to concentrate, okay?"

"I will if you make me a promise."

"What is it?"

"If you are not feeling better, that you'll go see the nurse at student health tomorrow. You don't look good."

"I promise. I'm just stressed out. I'm trying to get through finals, take the last board exams for medical school, and find lodging for my family to come here next week for graduation. It's just a hectic time. That's all."

"Tell you what. My parents have already made their reservations for graduation weekend. Do you want me to take care of your arrangements for you? That will at least lighten part of the load."

"That would be awesome," Pharrah answered as she took the pill Kelli handed her and popped it into her mouth. She picked up her bottle of water and took a long, slow swig.

"No problem. So I need to get a suite for your aunt and dad with an adjoining room for your little brother and sister, and a separate room for your mom, is that right?"

"Right, and if possible, could you tell them to make sure my mom is on another floor? The last thing I need is an altercation during graduation."

"I thought your mom and aunt were speaking again."

"Well, they are. I mean, they did. We all spent Thanksgiving and Christmas together at my dad's house, but you could have cut the tension in the air with a butter knife. I know my dad spent weeks convincing Aunt Phylicia to even allow Mom into the house. No one would have dared to act out in front of Eva or Li'l G, but it was all very surreal."

"What about your dad's marriage? Is that back on track yet?"

"I'm not sure. He won't really talk about it when he calls. He still doesn't know I saw him sneaking in and out of Grandma's old room each night so that we kids wouldn't know they aren't sleeping together."

"Are you sure about putting them in a suite together?

Maybe I should get an extra room, you know, just in case."

"No, don't do that. I want them together whether they like it or not. I love Aunt Phylicia and I want my dad and her to work this out. He told me to just keep praying about it and I am, but there's no way I'm getting them two rooms."

"Okay, you're the boss. I'll get on it right away."

Pharrah watched her roommate walk out, then turned her attention back to her calculus book. The ibuprofen was beginning to work, and the pain eased down the scale from a ten to an eight-and-a-half. She tried to concentrate, but it was no use. Instead, she put the book aside and crawled into bed.

Several hours later she awakened, realizing that the pain had again risen to category ten and was steadily increasing. She tried to sit up, then fell back down as the whole room spun around her. She lay still, willing her body to obey her commands. After several attempts, she was finally able to sit up again. Frantically, she grabbed the bottle of ibuprofen and gobbled down three more pills without the benefit of water. She curled into a ball and waited for sleep to return.

Suddenly, she felt her whole body shaking. She sat upright, wondering when Baton Rouge started having earthquakes. Startled, she looked into Kelli's worried face. She was standing over her and had shaken her awake. She shielded her eyes from the glare of sunlight streaming into her dorm windows, wondering how long she'd been asleep.

"Pharrah, your mom's on the phone. Are you okay?"

"What time is it?" Pharrah moved her head, trying to shake loose the cobwebs of sleep.

"It's nine-thirty."

"It's daylight. How could it be nine-thirty?"

"Uhm, it's nine-thirty AM. Are you sure you're okay?"

"It's morning? How long have I been asleep?" Pharrah frantically jumped from the bed.

"I don't know. When I got in last night you were asleep. I just covered you up and went to bed. Calm down. You have plenty of time to get to calculus. Your mother is holding on the phone."

"I have time, but I didn't finish studying. I'll have to do some cramming." Pharrah sat down at her desk and pulled out her book. She quickly buried her head in the numbers.

"Pharrah, your mom."

"What about her?"

"I said she's on the phone. What is wrong with you?"

"Nothing. I'm sorry, I just didn't mean to fall asleep last night, that's all. But at least my headache is gone." She grabbed the phone. "Hey, Mom, what's up?"

"Is everything all right over there? I've been holding for a while."

"Yes. I just overslept this morning. How are things with you?"

"Well, as the saying goes, I have good news and bad news."

Pharrah rolled her eyes. Her mother never ceased to have a dramatic style about her. Growing up, it had been fun. Her mom was the life of the party, and everyone was fascinated by her sparkling wit and charming demeanor. But as she got older, it began to annoy Pharrah, and, at this moment, she was in no mood for it. "Give me the bad news first," she said, sighing.

"I'm sorry, baby, but I can't make graduation next week. Something's come up."

"Mom, what could possibly come up that would cause you to miss this day?"

"Well, that's part of the good news. My divorce from

Maurice is about to be finalized. I have to go to New York to sign some last minute paperwork and then I'll be free. I wish it could be rescheduled, but it can't."

"I thought you filed for divorce in Brown Bottom with the same lawyer who handled Grandma's estate. Why do you need to go to New York?"

"Well, I did but, uhm . . . Well, it's complicated."

"You're lying again. What's really going on? Mom, I know how much you sacrificed to even get me into college. You waited tables for years just to send me a few dollars of spending money. If it wasn't for Grandma's insurance policy, I would not be going to med school and probably could not have even afforded this semester. How can you sit here and tell me you aren't coming? Why? I don't understand you anymore. What's happened to you, Mom?" Pharrah's voice cracked as she began to cry.

"I'm sorry, baby. Pharrah, please don't cry. I wish I could be there. I really do. It's just that . . ."

"Just what? This is the biggest day of my whole life and you are sitting here, giving me some excuse about that jerk Maurice. What did he ever do for either of us? Who cares if your divorce is final or not? Let him rot in that jail. You have to be here! You just have to!"

"Honey, please just listen to me."

"No! If you aren't coming to my graduation, we have nothing else to say to each other."

Phoebe heard a loud thud as Pharrah threw the phone across the room. She heard mumbled voices for several minutes, then finally someone picked up the line again. "Hello?"

"Pharrah? Honey, listen."

"No, Ms. Phoebe, it's me, Kelli. Uhm, Pharrah left the room. I'm sorry, she's pretty upset."

"Yes, I know."

"It's not my business, Ms. Phoebe, but she really wants you at her graduation. I mean, if you haven't already realized it, it's extremely important to her."

"I just thought since she's gotten so close with her dad and his family this past year that as long as one parent was there she'd be fine with it."

"She loves them very much, but you're her mother. You are the one who gave birth to her. You are the one who kept her out of foster care and took her when her adoptive mom died. You are the one who's raised her and made her the woman she is today."

"I know all that, Kelli, but you don't understand."

"Did you know she told me you sat up with her for hours on end filling out college applications and scholarship forms? She says you promised her that no matter what, she'd get the college education you missed out on. I know things have been a li'l tense since she found out about her real father. But she loves you very much, Ms. Phoebe. It's just my opinion, but I think you need to find a way to be here."

Wiping away a tear, Phoebe clutched the phone tightly. "When she gets back, tell her I'll be there. I promise I'll be there." Quietly, she hung up the phone.

She'd spent hours thinking up the lie to tell to Pharrah about not attending her graduation. The truth was, she couldn't afford to be there. It had only been a few days since she'd learned she was broke, but she knew it wouldn't be long before the creditors were calling and knocking on her door. Her original plan had been to drive to Baton Rouge for the ceremony. Pharrah told them all at spring break she'd reserve and pay for the hotel rooms for her family. But now with gas prices being so unpredictable, Phoebe knew it was virtually impossible. Gary, Phylicia, and the children would be driving down in Phylicia's new Escalade Gary had given her as a Christmas

present. Phoebe realized she'd have to come up with an
excuse and ask them for a ride.

Lately, talking to Phylicia was like speaking to one of
those recorded voices on the telephone. Every word was
stilted and rehearsed. Asking her was out of the question. At Thanksgiving and Christmas she'd put the bug
in Pharrah's ear about her coming for dinner, then allowed her daughter to work her charms on Gary, but this
time she couldn't use her. Reluctantly, she grabbed her
purse and her keys from the table and headed for the church
office. She knew she was going to have to ask Gary herself.

Pharrah walked out of the mathematics building with
a knot in her stomach and a cannon going off in her head.
She hated that her mother had called only a few minutes
before her final with devastating news.

Throughout the exam she could barely concentrate.
She'd never been so upset, angry, and disappointed in
her mother than at that moment. The fact that she could
just casually blow off graduation for Maurice was infuri-
ating, but what bothered her most was that Pharrah did
not believe her. There was some other reason she wasn't
coming, and knowing her mother, it was probably an all-
day sale at Macy's.

She'd managed to get in a few moments of studying at
the library between tears before her final, but the pain in
her head returned almost as soon as she sat down at her
desk. She felt nauseated, and the words and numbers
started floating off the pages and dancing around in front
of her eyes once again. She closed her eyes and tried to
bring the last semester's worth of tables and formulas
back to the front of her brain, while pushing the intense
pain closer to the back. They collided midway and the
pain fought to gain control of the space between her ears.

Pharrah bowed her head and rubbed both temples in slow, easy circles, freeing the formulas from the pain's chokehold. Slowly and methodically, she picked up her pencil and began to fill in the answers on her paper. After what seemed like only a few moments later, her professor tapped her on the shoulder, advising that time was up. Pharrah looked around and realized she was the only one left in the classroom. Reluctantly, she handed over her exam paper and silently prayed that the markings she'd managed to make were the correct answers to the test.

As she walked across the quad on her way back to her dorm, the throbbing in her head demanded attention. Ignoring it was useless as it grew in intensity and became a serious force to be reckoned with. Remembering her promise to Kelli, she took a detour behind the physics building and then a shortcut near the cafeteria. *Student health is only a hundred yards. If I can just make it, maybe they can give me something stronger than ibuprofen*, she thought.

Pharrah's breathing suddenly slowed and she struggled to take each breathe. Her legs turned into jelly and wobbled underneath her. Pounding on the inside of her chest, her heart felt as if it were trying to break free. She gasped for air and screamed for help, but no sound came out of her mouth. Everyone and everything around her suddenly began to move in slow motion and she wondered if she was even moving at all. Her heartbeat swelled into her ears, deafening her.

All was quiet, then blackness engulfed her. Two feet from the student health building, Pharrah collapsed in a muddled mass onto the ground.

Chapter Eighteen

"What are your thoughts on Reverend Sheila Rivers? She's a good speaker, virtuous woman of God, and our church family loves her," Mrs. Farmer asked Phylicia as they sat in her dining room going over candidates in search of the main speaker for their church's annual women's conference.

"Yes, the church family loves her because she's been on panel at every conference for the past four years. I think we need to get some new blood."

Mrs. Farmer sighed. Phylicia had shot down every suggestion she'd made. The first one was too young, the next too old, another was too controversial, then another too conservative. The last one was an unknown and couldn't draw a crowd, and now this one wasn't new enough. Exasperated, she closed her folder and looked at her. "Phylicia, what's going on with you? We've planned these conferences together for years. We've never had this type of problem. Even last year right after your mother passed you were more focused, and last year's conference turned out to be wonderful."

Phylicia looked at Mrs. Farmer and sighed loudly. "I'm fine. Let's take a look at the next candidate."

They went back and forth over choices for the next several minutes, until Li'l G came sauntering in after school. He enjoyed the fact that the high school was only two blocks from their home. "Hey, Mom. Hey, Mrs. Farmer," he said, kissing them both on the cheek before heading to the kitchen for a snack.

"I swear that boy looks more like his father every day. He's gonna be a heartbreaker. If I were fifty years younger, I'd have to be your daughter-in-law." Mrs. Farmer laughed loudly at her own joke before realizing Phylicia was not laughing along. "What is it, child?" She reached over and held her hand.

Phylicia waited until Li'l G had left the kitchen and climbed the stairs to his room before finally speaking. "I think my marriage is over. I think Gary's planning to move out," she said softly.

"Why would you think that? I thought the two of you were working things out."

"He's wanted to, but I've been pushing him away. I don't even know why. I just do it." Phylicia paused and sniffed before continuing. "He's been sleeping in Mom's old room for months now. I can't tell you how many times I've come downstairs at night to ask him to come back to our room, but I end up going back up without saying a word. There's something inside me that won't let me fix this. I want to, I know that I need to, but I don't know how."

Mrs. Farmer let go of Phylicia's hand and reached for her Bible. She flipped through several pages before settling on a verse in the sixth chapter of Matthew. She read it aloud very slowly.

And forgive us our debts, as we forgive our debtors. For if ye forgive men their trespasses, your heavenly Fa-

ther will also forgive you. But if ye forgive not men their trespasses, neither will your Father forgive your trespasses.

She waited for Phylicia to respond.

"I've forgiven him, but how do I just forget?"

"I'm sorry, Phylicia, but I don't believe you have forgiven him. When God forgives our sins, the slate is wiped clean as if it never happened. If we want that type of forgiveness in our lives, then we have to forgive others in the same manner. Once you forgive your husband, you can get your marriage on track."

Phylicia stood up and walked toward the fireplace. She studied the pictures on the mantel before picking up one of her niece. "When I look at her, I wonder how something so beautiful, sweet, and pure came out of something so revolting. I wonder how the essence that is her life has totally seemed to ruin mine. What her mother did was unspeakable, yet a beautiful life was formed from it."

"Have you ever wondered why this happened?"

"I ask myself that every day." She placed the photo back onto the mantle.

"Have you asked God?"

Phylicia turned to look at her with a puzzled look on her face. "What do you mean? It's not my place to question God."

"Don't question Him, honey, talk to Him. I did. Why do you think I let your sister stay in my house? Because God told me she needed to be there. God needs you in your sister's life. She's lost, Phylicia. She is completely without a relationship with God, but He wants to help her. You are the link between your sister and God. While you are forgiving people, you need to forgive her, too."

"You don't understand, Mrs. Farmer. I tried to talk to

her. I tried to understand why she did this to me. Instead of explaining and apologizing, she was hurtful and insulting. I pray for my sister daily, but that's all she'll get from me."

"Well, I know I'm just an old busybody, but I have to tell you that until you find a way to forgive them both, you are not going to find any peace of your own. Carrying unforgiveness in your heart is like carrying around a sack of raw potatoes. After a while, it begins to stink. " Mrs. Farmer gathered up her purse and her Bible and walked to the front door with Phylicia following her. "I'm gonna go because your mind is not really on this business right now. We'll finish it some other time." Before leaving, she leaned in and gave Phylicia a long hug. "Forgiveness is the only way, child," she said before turning to walk away.

Phylicia sat down in the plush chair in her living room and stared at the sofa. It wasn't the same one they'd had when she was in high school, but it sat in the same spot. The same spot her sister had seduced her husband. The same spot that each time she walked by, demons from the past seemed to rise up through the floorboards just to taunt and laugh at her. She jumped up quickly. "Li'l G, get down here!" she yelled up the stairs.

After several minutes, he strolled his lean frame downstairs. "What's up? Mrs. Farmer gone already?"

"Yes, she is. I need you to do something for me."

"Sure, Mom."

"Help me move this couch. I want it on the other side of the room, then I want the chairs over here, and that table moved," she said, pointing.

"You wanna rearrange the whole living room? Maybe we should wait for Dad to help us."

"No, I want it done before your father gets home. Come on, help me."

Once the couch was removed from its spot and sitting in the middle of the floor, Li'l G proceeded toward the chairs.

"Wait. I need to do something first." Phylicia rushed to the kitchen and came back carrying a bottle of olive oil. She opened it and carefully let three drops fall to the carpet in the space where the sofa previously sat. "One for the Father, one for the Son, and one for the Holy Ghost," she recited after each drop fell.

"Is that holy oil?" Li'l G asked with a puzzled look on his face.

"The power is not in the oil, son, it's in your faith. You can go ahead and move the chairs now."

Li'l G worked quickly, and by the time Eva arrived home a short time later, the entire living room had been transformed. Phylicia was kneeling in front of one of the chairs praying, and did not notice her as she entered the living room.

"Mommy?" she whispered, realizing her mother was praying.

Phylicia opened her eyes and looked at her. She smiled. "Hello, sweetheart."

"I'm sorry to interrupt, but can I have a cookie?"

"I just filled the cookie jar this morning. Help yourself." Phylicia watched her bounce into the kitchen, then she slowly stood. As she did, a sudden feeling of calmness took over, as if a huge weight had finally been lifted from her shoulders. "I forgive you, Gary. I forgive you, Phoebe," she said before joining Eva in the kitchen.

Chapter Nineteen

Gary looked at the clock hanging on his office wall. It was almost four-fifteen. During the course of the day he had stacked and re-stacked all of the papers on his desk, stared at his computer screen, and played on-line games. He knew he should concentrate on church business or start writing his sermon for the week, but he couldn't. All he could think about was Phylicia and his marriage crumbling right before his eyes. In just a few moments, his day would end and it would be time to go home. For the first time in his entire marriage, he dreaded going.

Each time he saw Phylicia, his heart ached for the closeness they once shared. Since his best friend, Tino, had died while they were in college, he found it hard to get close to another man in his life. He had casual acquaintances and some he truly considered friends, but no one with whom he was really close. His parents were deceased, and he had no siblings. Phylicia was much more than just his wife. She had become his best friend.

He sat at his desk thinking of all the nights they'd lain

awake in bed planning their future together. He remembered his joy the night she told him she was carrying Li'l G, and his panic when she went into labor three weeks early. He relived the day Eva was born and how beautiful his wife looked holding her for the first time. He wandered to Disney World, Myrtle Beach, New Orleans, and the Grand Canyon as he relived every family vacation. He reminisced about his and Phylicia's first honeymoon spent at a cheap motel in Shreveport, Louisiana because that's all he could afford, and their second honeymoon to Jamaica after his ministry began to prosper.

She still blushed when he'd remind her that they made love on the balcony of their hotel room overlooking the crystal clear blue water. It was pretty risqué for the pastor and his wife, but they were crazy in love. He'd felt that way about her since he was a teenager and he knew it would never change, but now he couldn't help wondering if how Phylicia felt had changed.

Gary didn't know how long he'd been daydreaming when he heard a knock at his office door. He wondered where Mrs. Farmer was, before remembering he'd given her the afternoon off to work on the women's conference. "Come in," he yelled.

"Hi, Gary, can we talk?"

Surprised, he looked up at Phoebe standing in his doorway, then cordially offered her a seat on the leather sofa in his office. Moving from behind his desk, he sat down in the chair facing her. "What's on your mind, Phoebe?" he asked as he settled into his chair.

Phoebe swallowed hard trying to regain her courage. She'd left her townhouse on her way to the church hours earlier, but detoured to the mall where she had walked from store to store, stalling for time. Several times she thought she'd come up with the perfect lie to justify needing to ride with them to graduation, but then she'd find a flaw in the plan. She'd driven to the park and watched some kids playing on the swings. One of them reminded her of Pharrah, and she knew there was no way she could let her baby girl down. Reluctantly, she finally made her way to the church. It was almost five and she had hoped he had not left his office yet. She was grateful to find that Mrs. Farmer was out, and she could speak with him privately.

"I was wondering if I could ride with you and Phyllie to the graduation ceremony next week. My car is making a ticking sound and I don't want to make the drive."

"Have you taken it to a mechanic? That car is barely a year old and it's still under warranty."

"I don't know any mechanics. Brown Bottom may be my hometown but I'm still like a stranger here. Besides, they could tell me anything and I really wouldn't know the difference."

"Maybe you are right. Tell you what. Li'l G is taking auto shop at school. Why don't I send him over on Saturday to take a look at your car? Maybe he can fix it, or if he can't, he can tell you what the problem is before you look for a mechanic."

"Well, that's fine, but what if they can't fix it by graduation? I need to have a backup plan. So let's just plan on me riding with you guys. That Escalade holds eight passengers. I'll ride all the way in the back so Phyllie won't have to look at me. Please, Gary?"

He looked at his sister-in-law strangely. "You came all the way over here to ask me that? Why didn't you just call?"

"Uhm, well I was in the neighborhood, so I just stopped in. So do I have a ride?" she smiled seductively at him.

"I have to talk to Phylicia. I can't make any promises."

Phoebe was unwilling to take "maybe" for an answer.

She needed a yes so that she could call Pharrah back and tell her she would definitely be there. She crossed her legs sexily and eased her skirt up a few inches. "Oh, that's right. Phyllie wears the pants in your house. I forgot. Do you have to have her permission to do everything, Gary? Does she cut up your meat for you, too?"

"I don't need her permission to do anything, and she doesn't need mine. We discuss things before jointly reaching a decision." Gary shifted in his chair. Phoebe's perfume was intoxicating, and her move to reveal more of her thighs wasn't lost on him.

Phoebe noticed how uncomfortable he was becoming in her presence. She scooted forward on the couch to get closer to him, and fixed her face into one of an innocent damsel in distress. "I guess that's what being in a good marriage is all about, huh? I never had that with Maurice. I've never had it with anyone. Phyllie is really lucky to have you, Gary," she said, batting her long eyelashes.

"Thanks, Phoebe." He shifted again in his seat.

"Oh, no thanks needed. I'm only telling the truth. You are a very desirable man."

"Yeah, well, your sister doesn't seem to think so." Gary wasn't sure why he'd said it. For the past year, he'd kept his problems with Phyllie between him and God, but suddenly the words just fell from his lips.

"Are you and Phyllie still having problems?" Phoebe asked with a bit too much joy in her tone. Over the past several months she'd thought she felt some tension, but Phylicia never allowed her to get close enough to them to find anything out. Perhaps this was her chance; not only to get a ride to graduation, but to finally get Gary all to herself. She felt her sister never really knew how to handle a real man anyway. At least, not the way Phoebe believed that she could.

"It's nothing that we can't handle," he answered.

"Listen, we're family. I mean, I know we've had our differences, but you and I share a child, Gary. Talk to me, I'm a great listener. Maybe I can help."

He felt her sliding closer to him, then her hand rested on his muscular thigh. He knew he should make her move it, but at that point, he was so starved for affection he allowed it to remain. "I really don't think there's anything you could do to help, Phoebe. This is something Phyllie and I have to work out on our own."

"Let me guess. She's still upset about you and me?" Phoebe used her index finger to make tiny circles on Gary's thigh. "She's upset that we made love, isn't she? After all these years my sister is upset about our little tryst."

Gary looked into her face, and although they were identical twins, he realized he'd never paid much attention to how much she looked like Phylicia. Sitting this close to her, feeling her hands on his leg for a few moments, he imagined that she was. He imagined that he could put his arms around her and hold her closely, and she'd feel just like Phylicia. He imagined he could lean in and kiss her, and she wouldn't pull away or protest. There would be no excuses. She'd welcome his advances. He fantasized that if he laid her down on his couch and removed all of their clothing, he could finally release the swelling inside his pants that had been suppressed and dormant for close to a year. That for a few moments, he could find that place inside her that always made Phylicia whimper and moan his name. He imagined how wonderful it would be and he smiled.

The phone ringing loudly on his desk suddenly brought him back to his office, and back to reality; the reality that the woman sitting in front of him was not his wife. She was his sister-in-law. The woman his indiscretion with had hurt his wife so deeply. Moving quickly away from her, he reached for the phone. "Reverend Morgan's office."

He listened closely for several minutes as Phoebe watched his face wash over with a look of horror, and the color drain completely from it. "How . . . how is she? Is she going to be all right?"

"I don't know, Reverend Morgan. I had a late class, and when I got back, there was a note on the door from someone who'd seen her taken away by ambulance. I rushed over to the hospital, but I'm not family, so they won't let me see her or tell me anything. I tried to call her mom, but there's no answer. You gotta get here as soon as you can."

"Okay, Kelli, just calm down. I know where Pharrah's mother is. She, my wife, and I will take the next flight out. Call me if anything changes."

Chapter Twenty

As they sat on the plane en route to Baton Rouge, Gary looked down at his and Phylicia's hands tightly entwined. He wasn't sure if it was the tragedy they were facing, but for the first time since he'd found out about Pharrah, he felt he had his wife back. He'd called her from his car with the news. According to Kelli, Pharrah had been experiencing headaches for several days and suddenly collapsed outside the student health building. She'd been taken, unconscious, to the nearest hospital. By the time he'd gotten to the house, Phylicia had called the hospital and spoken with a doctor. Pharrah was in intensive care and not breathing on her own, but they couldn't release any other details over the phone.

After that, she'd called the airport, booked three seats, packed their bags, called Mrs. Farmer to pick up Li'l G and Eva, and was waiting by the door ready to go when he rushed in. She immediately wrapped her arms around him, and for the first time since he received the call, he let the tears flow. Gently, she kissed them away, and then kissed his lips, holding the kiss for several seconds. When their lips finally parted, she spoke softly. The monotone was gone and he heard love in her words. "Everything's taken care of. Let's pick up Phoebe and get to the airport. I booked us on the next flight out."

When they arrived at Phoebe's townhouse, Phoebe was a complete mess. She was racing around like a chicken with her head cut off, crying and incoherent. She couldn't find her suitcase, purse, or keys, all of which were right in front of her. Gary watched in stunned silence as Phylicia pulled her sister to her in a loving embrace, and gently stroked her back. She whispered things that he could not hear, but that obviously calmed Phoebe down. Phylicia helped her finish packing, gathered her things, and then led her by the hand to the car.

On the way to the airport, as Gary drove Phylicia prayed with him and Phoebe, and offered them reassurance that their daughter would be fine. Each of them held their own grief, but Phylicia, although saddened, was the rock. Now, sitting calmly next to her on the plane, Gary pulled Phylicia's hand to his lips and kissed it gently. She looked over at him and smiled reassuringly.

This was the woman he'd fallen in love with and married. This was the woman with whom he'd shared a lifetime of hopes, dreams, and even disappointments. She was loving, thoughtful, virtuous, and kind. He said a prayer of thanksgiving that she was finally back.

After several delays in the airport and a struggle with the rental car agency, the three of them finally arrived at the hospital shortly before midnight. A weeping Kelli met them at the intensive care wing. Gary immediately went to the desk to ask for a doctor, to find out Pharrah's condition. Half an hour later, someone finally approached them in the waiting area. "Are you the family of Pharrah

Carson?" They all looked up at the doctor, anxious for news.

"Yes, I'm her father, and this is her mother and aunt." Gary motioned toward the women.

"I'm Dr. Jeremiah Richards, the attending neurosurgeon assigned to your daughter. I can only talk to immediate family," he said, looking at Kelli.

"That's her best friend and roommate. She's family. Just tell us what's going on with our daughter," Gary answered.

The doctor gave an unsympathetic look and then opened his chart. "The news is not very good. Your daughter is very ill. Right now we have her on a ventilator to assist with her breathing."

"What happened? Why can't she breathe on her own?" Phoebe asked.

"Her brain is not functioning at a capacity where it's able to tell her body to breathe."

"Are you . . . are you telling us she's brain dead?" Phylicia asked.

"No. There is significant brain activity. However, there is a major blockage in her brain that is hindering the functions of the rest of her body. Without signals from the brain, her body doesn't know to breathe, her kidneys don't know to function, her organs will shut down and, eventually, her heart will stop beating."

Phoebe gasped loudly and began wailing. "My baby's dying. She's dying? Oh, God, I'm so sorry. Please don't take my baby. Please don't take my baby!" she screamed. Phylicia and Gary tried unsuccessfully to console her. She screamed and wailed and screamed some more. Over and over she lamented that she was sorry, and begged God not to punish her by taking Pharrah away. Finally, Kelli took her from the waiting room into the adjoining bathroom so that the doctor could continue speaking with Gary and Phylicia.

Sighing loudly, Gary questioned the doctor. "You said there's a blockage in her brain. What kind of blockage?"

"It's called an astrocytoma." Gary and Phylicia stared at him, puzzled. "A brain tumor," he added for clarification.

Gary's heart skipped a beat. Years before, he'd heard the same diagnosis for his best friend, Tino Farmer. He and Phylicia were on a double date with Tino and his date, Sonya. Tino had complained all day of a headache, and stopped their basketball game early to take a nap. Later, he told Gary he still felt woozy, but he'd promised Sonya he'd take her to see *Purple Rain.* She was a huge Prince fan.

Throughout the movie, Gary noticed there was something not quite right about his friend. He didn't laugh at the usual places or cheer during the concert scenes. He didn't seem to even pay attention to the movie. Most unusual of all, he paid very little attention to Sonya, and never even tried to hold her hand. As they left the movie theatre, Gary and Phylicia were walking ahead of the couple when he heard Sonya scream his name. He turned around and ran toward a stumbling Tino, unable to stop him from hitting the ground in a deafening thud. Three days later his best friend was dead. Aside from the loss of his parents, he'd felt that losing him so suddenly was the most excruciating pain he'd ever experienced. He was wrong. His heart crumbled into a thousand pieces now, and Gary buried his face in his hands, overcome with grief.

Phylicia wrapped her arm tightly around him, then turned to the doctor with tears staining her own face. "Is there anything you can do for her?" she asked.

"Well, the mass is extremely aggressive and growing

fast. However, there's a remote possibility that we could remove it with surgery. After that there'd be a period of radiation and chemotherapy. Best-case scenario, she could survive, and with some therapy, eventually lead a normal life again. About two percent of all patients are able to completely recover."

"What's the worst-case scenario?" Phylicia asked.

The doctor hesitated. "Well, we could do the surgery, remove the tumor, and she'd suffer irreparable brain damage. She would be alive, but a vegetable. If you remember the Terri Schiavo case, that would be her mindset and capabilities. She'd need round-the-clock care and would probably end up institutionalized. That's if she survives the surgery. About twenty percent of those who opt for the surgery die on the operating table. I'm sorry, but I can't make any guarantees."

"When can you take her to surgery?" Gary asked, suddenly looking up.

"We could have her prepped and in surgery first thing tomorrow morning. Do you and your family want to discuss it? There are significant risks and many families opt to just have the patient sedated. If we did that, she would succumb within a few days. It would be very peaceful and is considered a humane way to die. Under the circumstances, with her chances for survival so low, I have to ask: are you sure you want to take the risk of going through surgery?"

Gary suddenly stepped closer to the doctor and stared him directly in the eye. "Let me make myself perfectly clear. My daughter is not going to be sedated and left to die. You will do the surgery. God will guide your hands. There's nothing else to discuss."

The doctor slowly backed away from him. "I'll send a nurse in with the paperwork. I'll need the signature of her next of kin." He walked away, slowly shaking his head.

When the nurse returned with the paperwork, absolving the hospital from any responsibility in case the surgery was not successful, she found the group holding hands in a circle fervently praying for Pharrah. She stood quietly to the side until she heard them all join in a chorus of "Amen," then tentatively she stepped forward. "I have the paperwork here for you to sign. Dr. Richards advised that although it's not visiting hours, under the circumstances, he will allow just two visitors for no more than five minutes."

Without any hesitation, Phylicia spoke up. "Gary, you and Phoebe go ahead. I'll wait here with Kelli. Give her a kiss from her auntie. Tell her we all love her very much and can't wait for her to get better."

Gary took Phoebe by the hand and they walked down the corridor following the nurse. She led them into the cubicle they considered a room in the intensive care ward. In front of them, Pharrah lay with her eyes closed. The sounds of the ventilator and monitors echoed in their ears.

Gary went over to her and placed a gentle kiss on her forehead, then leaned down to whisper in her ear. "Daddy's here. Everything's going to be all right. Daddy is here now." He wasn't sure if she heard him, but he'd read somewhere that oftentimes comatose patients were able to hear their surroundings and he wanted to reassure her, just in case. "You're having surgery in the morning. Don't be afraid. They're gonna make you all better. I love you, Pharrah," he said, choking back tears. "We all love you," he concluded. Not wanting to break down, he rushed from the room, leaving Phoebe alone with her.

She stood staring at her daughter and weeping without saying a word, until the nurse arrived and told her it was time to go and that the doctor would not allow anymore visitors tonight. "I'm sorry, Pharrah. Please forgive me. I'm so sorry," she said, then followed the nurse out.

Chapter Twenty One

Mrs. Farmer slowly hung up the phone after speaking with Gary. She stood immobile for several moments, processing his words in her mind. Over and over she heard the words, "brain tumor." It reminded her too much of a phone call she'd received years earlier. By far it had to be the worst phone call a parent could ever receive. It had changed her life forever. Tears began to flow down her pudgy face, ignoring her will not to cry. Behind her she heard footsteps, and quickly dried her tears with her apron before turning around to face Eva and Li'l G, who'd just entered her kitchen. "Good morning," she said, trying to sound cheerful.

"Was that my dad on the phone? How's Pharrah?" Li'l G asked.

"Yes, that was your dad. Sit down, both of you, and I'll explain to you what he said." Li'l G and Eva sat down at Mrs. Farmer's round wooden kitchen table. She'd prepared them a breakfast of eggs, sausage links, cheese grits, and biscuits. Quietly, she served each of them a full plate, then poured their glasses full of orange juice before taking a seat herself. As Eva said grace, she tried to think of a gentle way to break the news. She put on a counterfeit smile before speaking. "Pharrah is in surgery right now. Your father said the procedure could take several hours. He'll call us just as soon as it's over."

"What kind of surgery?" Eva asked, then bit her sausage link.

"Your sister has a . . . a brain tumor. The doctors are operating to try to remove it."

Both children stared at her in silence before Li'l G spoke up. "Did my dad say Pharrah is gonna die? Is that why you were crying?"

"Your father told me that the surgery is very dangerous and risky. The whole church family is praying, your mom and dad are praying, and right after breakfast, you kids and I are gonna pray. It's in God's hands now."

Li'l G nodded his head and the three of them quietly finished their breakfast, then joined hands to pray for Pharrah. When they were done, Mrs. Farmer gathered up the dishes and told the children they could watch TV in her den. She only had a nineteen-inch color TV and no cable or DVD player, but after flipping through the four channels then fumbling with the antenna, Li'l G was finally able to find a football game to watch. Uninterested in the game, Eva sat in a corner reading a book.

After she was finished washing and drying the dishes, Mrs. Farmer went into her bedroom and pulled an old shoe box from under her bed. From inside, she pulled out several folders and read over the material contained in each. On the last page of the stacks of letters she found what she'd been looking for:

> *This type of fast-acting Astrocytoma is extremely rare. Its exact causes are unknown; however, evidence suggests it is hereditary. It is recommended that anyone who is the*

sibling or offspring of someone diagnosed with this type of tumor be seen by a neurosurgeon immediately. If it is detected in the developing stages, these tumors can be removed with minimal risk to the patient. However, once it has matured, this tumor is fast acting and potentially deadly.

As she closed the folder, Mrs. Farmer thought back to the night her son died. She and her husband stood at his bedside as the doctors advised her there was no hope. The tumor was too aggressive and moving so swiftly it would soon overtake his brain. She and her husband refused him being placed on any type of life-sustaining machines, opting instead to allow him to pass on with dignity. He never regained consciousness after blacking out at the movies, and as she and her husband and other two sons stood by his bedside watching, he seemed to just slip away peacefully while sleeping.

She'd gone through the motions of the funeral like a zombie, fully realizing that the worst pain a parent could feel was the loss of a child. Lucas Valentino Farmer was her youngest son, and it was difficult for her to say goodbye.

In her grief she felt she could not move on without answers. Armed with the information listed on his death certificate, she wrote to any expert she could in order to find out what had caused the tumor that killed her son. Finally, one doctor she'd written to had sent her the papers advising her it that was a hereditary disease. He'd also advised her to have her other two sons checked, but Mrs. Farmer knew there was no way they could have inherited it.

During the first few years of their marriage, Mrs. Farmer and her husband, Luke, tried unsuccessfully to have children of their own. After three miscarriages and two stillbirths, they decided that adoption was the best answer for them. They hired an attorney, and over the next five years, they adopted the three boys. Each one came into their home as days-old infants. Only their closest family and friends, and the boys themselves, knew they were adopted. She loved her children as much as if she'd carried them inside her own womb.

After receiving the letter, Mrs. Farmer contacted the attorney who had handled her sons' adoptions. With his assistance, she found that Tino's birth father had succumbed to the same type of tumor during his wife's pregnancy. Being young, black, and extremely poor, the mother had decided to give up her child rather than raise him alone with no father. She never realized the legacy she was passing along of sudden young death.

Sitting on her bed, Mrs. Farmer reached for the phone to call Gary at the hospital. If Pharrah suffered from the same rare tumor disorder, then he had to have the other children checked immediately to make sure they did not have one as well. She wondered if Gary or Phoebe should be checked also in order to figure out which family was the carrier.

She'd just dialed the last number when a shocking bolt of reality shot through her, and she placed the phone back on the receiver before it began ringing on the other end. She'd known the Morgan and Carson families for as long as she could remember. They and their descendants had lived in Brown Bottom since the early nineteenth century. If anyone in either family had ever died from a brain tumor, she would know it. A horrible thought entered her mind and she tried desperately to chase it out, but it refused to leave. *Reverend Gary might not be Pharrah's father.* She shook her head, trying to force the thought to fall out through her ears. It moved and was replaced with another she didn't want to take up residence in her head: *Pharrah's father could be Tino.*

"That's impossible!" she said aloud to no one in particular. She thought back to the months prior to Tino's death and the procession of girlfriends who went in and out of her house. He was with Sonya the night he collapsed, but that year she was at least his twelfth girlfriend. Tino was a star basketball player, slim with a muscular athletic build, cute dimples, and was the first in Brown Bottom to sport a high-top fade. Many noted his resemblance to Michael Jackson before Michael's face became light and distorted. Without even trying, he became a lady's man almost as soon as he entered puberty. She remembered her phone rang incessantly during her sons' dating years, but most of the calls were from young women looking for Tino. Her other sons, Wayne and Jarvis, were popular, but neither one's popularity came close to Tino's. At the funeral she was lost in her own grief, but no one could miss the procession of young women who wailed, screamed, and hollered, "I love you, Tino!" as they filed by his casket. However, Mrs. Farmer could not remember if one of those girls had been Phoebe, or if she even had attended the funeral.

"Mrs. Farmer, may I have a glass of milk?" Eva said, poking her head into the bedroom and interrupting her thoughts.

"Sure, honey. I'll get it for you." Placing the folder carefully back inside the box, then sliding it under her bed, she followed Eva to the kitchen and poured her a tall glass of milk. After politely thanking her, Eva returned to the den to finish her book while she drank.

As she stood in the doorway watching each of the children engrossed in their own activities, Mrs. Farmer came to a decision. She would wait to see the outcome of Pharrah's surgery, then she would speak with the reverend about her suspicions. She realized the family was going through enough and there was no need to worry them further. For now, she'd just allowed the ghosts of the past to rest comfortably where they were.

At the hospital, Phoebe wandered the halls as they waited for Pharrah's surgery to end. She'd tried sitting in the waiting room with Phylicia, Gary, and Kelli, but sitting still made her antsy.

Wandering aimlessly from floor to floor, she soon found herself standing at the seventh floor maternity ward, where she stopped to look at the assortment of newborn babies. She remembered the day she'd stood on the other side of a glass just like this one, staring at Pharrah who was only a few days old. Phoebe was not like the other beaming parents who stood and waved at their babies while planning their futures. Phoebe was saying good-bye. Her aunt was on her way to pick up the baby and Phoebe was returning home that afternoon to Brown Bottom. Philomena promised her she'd keep in touch so that Phoebe would always know her daughter was safe and well cared for; she'd even allowed her to choose her name and promised to send pictures often. Still, she couldn't fight the tears that flowed as she waved good-bye to her.

When Phoebe had returned to Brown Bottom without her daughter, she felt empty. It was as if giving away her child had left a hole inside her that she couldn't fill. She finished high school, and with her parents' insistence, she'd enrolled in community college. The secretarial and business courses she took bored her to tears and she flunked out within the first year. She felt like such a failure when Phylicia brought home straight As and made the dean's list at Brown Bottom State University. She'd managed to do that while holding down a part-time job at McDonald's and planning an elaborate wedding to Gary. Phoebe plastered on a smile long enough to stand beside her as maid of honor, then left the reception early, claiming to have to study for a class.

Instead, she had rushed home to check the mailbox, as her aunt had promised to send a picture of Pharrah who was approaching her first birthday. She'd locked herself in her room for hours staring at the photo and crying uncontrollably before her mother returned from the wedding reception. Supposedly for Phoebe's sake, her mother took the picture and advised Philomena it would not be wise to send more. It was best to allow Phoebe to forget and move on.

As her sister basked in the glow of love, enjoying her honeymoon with her new husband, Phoebe tried urgently to forget the daughter she'd left behind. Desperately wanting to outdo her sister at something and take away her feeling of uselessness, she decided her love of fashion and clothing could lead her into a career she loved: modeling. She'd asked a friend with a thirty-five millimeter camera to take several pictures of her, which she blew up and fashioned into a homemade portfolio. She began sending out her photo to local magazines and department stores, hoping for a chance to appear in one of their ads. She'd landed one job, but turned it down. There was no way she would model for the Chubettes line of clothing. Once again, she was left feeling like a failure while her sister's life soared like a skyrocket.

Her heart ached for her daughter when Phylicia told her she was pregnant with her first child. Envy and jealousy raged in Phoebe's heart as she watched her sister's face shining with the glow of pregnancy. Reluctantly, she sat idly by and tried not to scream while her family shared in Phylicia's pregnancy and threw her a spectacular baby shower surrounded by beautiful gifts. All she could think of was that she'd had no celebration, no congratulations, only shame and guilt when her daughter was born. She didn't even have her mother. Pharrah had been delivered by the on-call doctor with an attending nurse holding Phoebe's hand for support. None of her family was around to even hear Pharrah's first cries.

When her family received the call that her Aunt Philomena had suddenly died, Phoebe begged her father to allow her to make the trip with him to the funeral. It had been eight years since Pharrah had been born, and although her aunt had kept her promise to keep in touch, she felt it best that Phoebe not see or speak to Pharrah. The baby picture had long since been tucked away inside her mother's dresser. She couldn't help but wonder what her daughter looked like, how she behaved, or what kind of person she was becoming. Reluctantly, her father allowed her to accompany him to Florida.

As she looked into the swollen grey eyes of her little girl wearing a starched white dress, long white knee socks, and black patent leather shoes, grieving the only mother she ever knew, Phoebe realized she had to get her back. She couldn't let her fall into the foster care system and never see her again. She told her father that she didn't want to leave Pharrah and that they should take her with them back to Brown Bottom. "We are her only surviving family. We could say Aunt Philomena wanted us to take care of her," she suggested.

Her father flatly refused. "Bringing that child back into our lives at this point could only cause harm and shame," he'd told her as they drove home. "Your sister is married and happy; there's no way you can bring her home and ruin that. I'll make some phone calls and see if we can keep in touch with whoever the foster family is. But you've got to forget about bringing her back to live with you."

His words stung, and once again, the same as she'd

done eight years before, Phoebe mourned the loss of her child. Her father was never able to make the phone calls he'd promised to make, as he died shortly thereafter.

As much as his death broke her heart, Phoebe realized the money he'd left her was her ticket out of Brown Bottom to reclaim her daughter. She packed her bags without letting anyone know what she was planning. She'd grown tired of living in Phylicia's shadow and just wanted to start all over and do something, anything, on her own. She vowed to reclaim Pharrah and build a life for them together by working as a model. She felt if she could just get to New York City, all of her dreams for both her and her daughter could finally come true.

She arrived in Florida with her daughter's birth certificate proving she was her natural mother, and the department of social services immediately turned her over without any fuss. When she picked her up from her foster family, she told her the truth. "I'm your real mother and I want you to live with me," she said.

"Where's my father?" the inquisitive eight-year-old asked.

"He's dead, sweetie. He died before you were born. That's why I sent you to live with Aunt Philomena. But I'm here now, and you and me are gonna be together forever."

As she now, all these years later, wandered away from the maternity ward, Phoebe wondered why, being in Brown Bottom, she'd begun to lie again. It was as if her mouth could not form truthful sentences once she'd stepped inside the city's boundaries.

Still wandering, she soon found herself at the hospital chapel, and went in and knelt down at the petite altar. She couldn't remember the last time she'd been to church or prayed, but she knew it was what she needed to do. "Dear God, I know I haven't done all that I should. I know that I've lied to my family, and to Pharrah. But I beg you. If you let my baby live, if you let her be okay again, I will tell her the truth. I promise to tell everyone the truth." She looked with expectancy upward toward where her parents had always told her God was, then she wiped away a tear and left the chapel.

Chapter Twenty Two

Phylicia, Gary, and Kelli solemnly stood to their feet as Dr. Richards entered the postop waiting area, where they'd waited for more than nine hours for news about the outcome of Pharrah's surgery. They looked at him expectantly, waiting for him to speak. He removed his surgical cap before advising them all to take a seat, then he sat down in front of them. Gary tried desperately to read his face, but realized as a surgeon he'd become quite competent at hiding any personal responses. They waited patiently for his words. "The surgery is over and Pharrah is in recovery. It will be a few more hours before you can see her."

"How is she? How did the surgery go?" Gary asked.

"We were able to remove the entire mass and stop the blockage." The three of them breathed a collective sigh of relief before the doctor continued. "She's not out of the woods yet. The next few days are going to be very critical. The sooner she is conscious again, the better. Then we can determine how successful we were in removing the mass. However, the prognosis is very good. She came through the surgery quite well. Someone will let you know when she's out of recovery so you can see her." Without another word, the doctor stood up, shook hands with each of them, and left the room just as Phoebe returned.

"What's going on? What did he say?" Phoebe asked

"The surgery is over. Pharrah made it through. She's in recovery," Phylicia answered, then hugged her sister tightly. "She's gonna be okay, Phoebe. I just know it. The worst is over. She's gonna be okay."

The four of them huddled in a circle of hugs, then Gary led them in a prayer of thanks and praise.

Li'l G rushed to the kitchen as he heard Mrs. Farmer's phone ringing. He stood by expectantly as she talked, then waited for her to give him the news.

"Reverend Gary, that is wonderful. The children and I have been praying really hard and so has the whole church family." She said excitedly.

"Thank you, Mrs. Farmer. She has a long road of recovery ahead of her, but I know that God brought her this far. My baby will be coming home soon." He smiled through the receiver.

Mrs. Farmer looked at Li'l G watching her every word. She hesitated before continuing. She turned her back and whispered into the phone. "Reverend, you know that we lost Tino to a brain tumor, and because of that I've done some research. I . . . I, uhm, have some information about tumors I think you should take a look at."

"What kind of information? Is it something to help with her treatment?"

"No, it's just something I think you should see."

"Okay, I'd be glad to take a look at it. Give the children my love and let them know their mother and I will be home soon."

"Of course, Reverend, but don't be in a rush. They are fine right here with me."

"Mrs. Farmer, one more thing."

"Yes?"

"Thank you. I don't know what Phyllie and I would do without you in our lives. We love you."

Mrs. Farmer blushed, then grinned. "You know I love the both of you and those kids. I'll go give them the news right now."

Two months later, assisted by her parents and a cane, Pharrah walked out of the hospital. "Your daughter's rapid recovery is nothing short of a miracle," Dr. Richards said as he signed her discharge papers. "I'm not a religious man, but your family's prayers certainly have been answered. Good luck to you all," he said, and smiled at them for the first time since their meeting.

Following their flight from Baton Rouge, they arrived at the house amidst a shower of confetti, balloons, and signs screaming "Welcome Home, Pharrah!" Li'l G, Eva, and Mrs. Farmer had spent two days making the decorations and hanging them around the house.

"Than . . . thank you ssso much," Pharrah managed to say.

She'd been speaking again since her first day awake at the hospital, but her speech was still a bit jumbled and slurred. It took her a few moments to get her thoughts together and her words out. Dr. Richards advised them that it was normal, and the fact she was talking at all was something to celebrate. He'd also advised them that she still had numbness in parts of her left side and would need to walk with a cane for a few months. With the help of physical therapy, she was getting better at walking and her nerves were getting stronger. During the next several months, she'd have to go through more physical rehabilitation and chemotherapy, but overall her surgery was a success. Pharrah was on the road to recovery.

"We fixed up Grandma's old room for you, Pharrah, so you won't have to climb the stairs," Eva said, taking her right hand and helping her into the bedroom. She stood back as Pharrah looked at the room completely decorated in pink and green, her sorority colors. Unable to speak through the tears, she hugged her little sister tightly.

"Okay, now everybody out. It's been a long day and Pharrah needs her rest," Phylicia instructed, shooing them all out.

"I'm going to stay and help her get changed and lie down," Phoebe said.

"N . . . nnno, Mom . . . I can . . . I can do it myself."

"Are you sure, honey? I don't mind staying to help you."

Pharrah nodded her head slowly.

"Phoebe, I think she wants a chance to do things on her own. It will help her regain her independence. Besides, I need to talk with you," Phylicia said.

Phoebe followed her sister back to the living room as the other children went upstairs to their rooms.

"Mrs. Farmer, we need to get over to the church office and get some work done. You've been goofing off long enough," Gary said, teasing her. He kissed his wife good-bye, then the two of them left.

Sitting in her favorite chair, Phoebe didn't feel the usual comfort the chair gave her. She was apprehensive of what her sister had to say. She crossed her arms and listened as Phylicia began to speak. Suddenly she stopped her, stunned by the words.

"What did you say?" she asked, staring at Phylicia in disbelief.

"I said I owe you an apology. I'm sorry, Phoebe."

"You're sorry? What are you apologizing to me for?"

"For everything. I had no right to throw you out of this house when you first arrived. And as angry and as hurt as I was, I should never have said the things I did to you about Gary. But most of all, I'm sorry for the last thirty-seven years of not being your sister. I've been your competitor. I've tried to be your boss. Lately I've been your judge, jury, and executioner. But through all of that, I was never really your sister. I'm sorry, Phoebe. Will you please forgive me?"

"I . . . I don't know what to say. How could you apologize to me after what I've done? I don't deserve it." Phoebe dropped her head.

"What happened between you and Gary hurt me deeply, but it wasn't what drove you and me apart. I let myself believe it, but the wedge between us was set years ago when we were little girls. The truth is, I've never wanted to admit it, but I've been jealous of you for a very long time. "

"You were jealous of me? What on earth for? You were always the good student; you were the one who made Momma and Daddy proud. You kept our room clean. You went to Sunday school without being threatened. You were freaking perfect. I've seen this crap on *Lifetime* movies where the sisters make up and try to flip the script on each other. I'm not buying it. There's no way you could have ever been jealous of me."

"Yes, there certainly was. Phoebe, you had something I never had."

"What's that?"

"Popularity; everybody loved you. Even as a child you could walk into a room and within minutes have everyone enthralled with you and what you were saying. By the time we were teenagers, you had so many boys calling here, I thought Dad would have a coronary. You knew everything there was to know about high fashion and makeup. Just look at you, Phoebe. You are absolutely gorgeous."

Phoebe blushed. Wearing size-sixteen jeans, there were some who thought she and her sister were fat, but she'd always used her voluptuous curves to her advantage, while Phylicia tried to hide her hips under loose fitting clothes. "Thank you, Phyllie," she said, wondering when was the last time either of them had complimented the other. "And I'm sorry too, for everything."

"I accept your apology." Phylicia walked over to the chair and bent down to hug her. "Are you staying for dinner?" she asked after they broke the embrace.

"Uhm, I was just wondering if maybe I could stay longer. I mean, I want to be near Pharrah. Do you think maybe I could spend a few days in the guest room?"

"I don't see any problem with that. I'm going to go ahead and start dinner. Do you want to go pick up your things now or later?"

Phoebe sat quietly for a few seconds not answering. "Phyllie, the truth is," she sighed deeply. "The truth is I can't go back to the townhouse. I haven't paid rent in two months and I'm being evicted."

"Why haven't you been paying your rent?"

"Since Pharrah has been sick, I just let things go. I should have sent the money back home, but I didn't."

"Just call your landlord and explain. I'm sure he'll accept it late."

"I doubt it. I mean, he's so mean . . . He . . . he . . ." Phoebe stopped talking as she noticed the worried look on Phylicia's face. She realized after everything they'd just been through, she couldn't start things off with yet another lie. "I'm sorry. That's a lie. The truth is he would take it, if I had it. I'm broke. I don't have enough to pay the rent."

"You mean you don't have enough in your account,

right? You have it invested, or you just don't have access to it, right?

"No, I mean I don't have any money left. I've spent it all. That's the reason I had to borrow from you in Baton Rouge. My Visa card isn't lost. I maxed it out." Phoebe stared at her feet and waited for Phylicia to light into her. For once in her life, she felt she deserved the lecture that was coming. Without saying a word, Phylicia picked up the newspaper and tossed it in her sister's direction. Phoebe watched it fall into her lap.

"You can stay here until you get back on your feet. But you'll need to get a job."

"What kind of job?"

"Any kind of job, Phoebe, it doesn't matter to me. Pharrah told me you used to wait tables in New York before coming here. How about doing that?"

"No way, I was fine waiting tables in New York. Nobody really knew me there. Besides, a lot of actors, actresses, models, and industry people wait tables until their big break comes in. That was different. I can't come back to Brown Bottom after all of my talk about being a model and end up at Denny's. I just can't do it."

Phylicia sat down in front of her sister. "So how do you expect to support yourself? Give me the paper, there has to be something in here you qualify for."

Reluctantly, Phoebe handed the newspaper back to her sister. She watched her for several moments perusing the ads. "Here's one: 'Front desk receptionist wanted.' It's for a busy real estate office. Phoebe, you'd be perfect for that."

"I've never worked in an office."

"No, but you took secretarial courses in college. I know you flunked out, but it wasn't because you didn't learn the skills. It was because you gave up. Besides, with your personality and style you are exactly the type of people person they are looking for."

"I'm not sure about this." Phoebe wrinkled her brow with doubt.

"Look, Phoebe, Gary and I are here for you, but you've got to do some things on your own. The first step to that is getting a job so that you can save some money and get your own place. We can help you, but we are not going to give you a free ride."

Phoebe took the paper from her sister and circled the ad. "I'll go over first thing tomorrow morning," she said meekly.

Chapter Twenty Three

Gary sat in his office going over his sermon for the week. His associate pastor, Reverend Joyce Sims, had taken over his duties while he had been in Baton Rouge taking care of Pharrah, but now that he was back, it was time for him to get back to business as usual. He was elated that everything in his life finally seemed to be back on track. The night after Pharrah's successful surgery, he and Phylicia had made love again, in their hotel room. They were like newlyweds, and had made love almost nightly since. The resurgence of their sex life was wonderful, but it wasn't the best part for him. He was glad to have the old Phylicia back. He didn't realize how much he'd missed the little things, like her making sure his collar was straight, brushing down his hair with her fingers when a curl got out of place, or picking a piece of lint from his jacket, until she started to do them again.

Over the past year Phylicia had not allowed herself to even get close to him, let alone touch him. Now that things were better, he'd noticed that her hands were always on him. Not in a sexual way, but in the loving, endearing manner he'd fallen in love with. She sat close to him, instead of several feet away. She leaned into him when standing and their hands seemed to be constantly entwined. She'd finally allowed him to reenter her intimate personal space and be close to her.

Although he was elated with the change in demeanor, he had to ask if it was due to Pharrah's illness. Unable to imagine losing her again, he felt he had to know if she was only being nice to him because his daughter was sick, and when Pharrah got better if it would all go away. She'd quietly explained that she'd done some praying and some soul searching. She realized that her marriage meant everything to her and she didn't want to lose him. So she'd finally allowed herself to forgive him, so that they could move on.

Gary leaned back in his chair and sighed. *Thank you, Father.* Things in his life could not be better and he could not imagine being happier. He had his wife back. Pharrah was on the mend and he had two other beautiful children. Phylicia was even making an effort to reconcile completely with her sister. Turning around to his computer, he felt God leading him to write his sermon on the power of forgiveness. He'd finished all but the last page when he heard a knock at his office door. "Come in."

"Reverend Gary, I really need to talk to you, if you are not too busy," Mrs. Farmer asked tentatively.

"Now, Mrs. Farmer, you know I'm never too busy for you. Come on in," he said, offering her a seat. "What's on your mind?"

"Do you remember when you were at the hospital and I told you I'd done some research on tumors?"

"Oh, Mrs. Farmer, I'm sorry. I was so caught up in everything that was going on, I totally forgot to call you back for that information. I'm sure it would have been interesting to read, but Pharrah's better now, so I guess we don't need it. I hope it wasn't any trouble for you to pull it out."

"No, no trouble, Reverend. It's just that, well, the research I have doesn't exactly involve treatment. What I mean is . . . it's something that could affect you and your whole family. I think you should take a look at it." She handed Gary a folder.

"I'd be glad to." He flipped through several pages. "There seems to be a lot of material here. I'm in the middle of writing a sermon, and, as you know, I'm way behind on things, having been away so long. But just as soon as I'm caught up, I promise to read the whole thing."

Mrs. Farmer stood up to leave then sat back down. "Uhm, Reverend, maybe I should just tell you what's in there?"

"Okay, if you'd like. Go ahead."

"Well, as you know, my boy Tino died of a brain tumor."

"Yes, ma'am, I was with him when he collapsed. He was my best friend and I still miss him."

"Yes, Reverend, so do I. There's something about Tino that you didn't know. Well, actually about all my boys. You see, me and Luke, we tried, we tried several times but the Lord didn't see fit to let me carry a baby. So after much prayer we decided to adopt. First we got Jarvis, then Wayne, and finally Tino."

"Adopted? No, ma'am, I never knew that about your boys. They all looked so much alike. Did they know?"

"Yes, of course. We told each of them when they were old enough to understand. But we emphasized that it didn't mean we loved them any less."

"No, of course it didn't. I'm sorry, I don't understand. What does that have to do with the brain tumor and all of this paperwork?"

"I'm getting to that, Reverend. I'm sorry, it's just difficult for me to even think what I'm thinking, so if you wouldn't mind humoring an old woman while I try to say it." Gary nodded his head and waited patiently for her to continue. "So anyway, when Tino died, it hurt me deeply. I know you understand, 'cause you were hurt too. But as his mother, it was like I lost a part of myself. I must have asked God a million times why my baby had to die so young. He was only a week short of his twentieth birthday. It just didn't seem right or fair."

"Sometimes we don't understand death or who gets to live or die, Mrs. Farmer. It's okay to wonder. We'll understand it better by and by."

"I didn't come in here for a sermon, Reverend. I realized a long time ago that Tino's death is a mystery that I won't understand in this lifetime. Please, just let me finish."

"I'm sorry to interrupt. Please continue."

"Well, when I was looking for answers I started writing letters. I wrote to the hospital. I wrote to his doctor's office. I wrote to the medical university. I just kept writing letters to every expert I could think of. I needed to know what caused that tumor. Some people wrote me back with form letters offering condolences. Some ignored my letters all together, but many sent me information on what they believed was the cause. That's all the paperwork I gave you. It's all the letters I wrote and the answers I got back."

Gary looked down at the folder again and opened it. He flipped through it once again, reading excerpts of each letter. "Most of these don't say much of anything. The doctors told us with Pharrah that sometimes they are unable to detect a cause. It could be diet, stress, or just plain old bad luck."

"Read the last letter, Reverend."

Gary flipped through the pages to the last letter, read it slowly, then re-read it. "Mrs. Farmer, if the tumor Tino had was hereditary, don't you think you would have known that when you adopted him? I mean, don't they research hereditary diseases before they hand over a baby?"

"They do now, but back then it didn't always happen. Besides that, me and my husband didn't go through a regular adoption agency. We used a private lawyer."

"Why would you do that?"

"I guess this is 'Mrs. Farmer, reveal all your family secrets' day," she said with a slight nervous chuckle. "The truth is, before my husband and I married, he had some trouble with the law and spent five years in jail on an armed robbery charge. Luke was young and out of control. We met while I was doing prison ministry and a lot of folks couldn't understand what I saw in him. I didn't see a wild, untamable animal that needed to be locked away. I saw a lost soul who needed the Lord. So I reached out to him. He accepted Christ while in that jail and we found love. That's why I married him. He put all of that behind him once he was released, and you knew him, Reverend; he was a good man and a good father to our boys."

"Yes, ma'am, he certainly was. I never would've guessed he had such things in his past."

"So you see, Reverend, we couldn't go through an agency. They would have never given us a child because of his background. It doesn't matter to them what kind of person he really was or how good of a husband he'd been to me. They only saw his past and nothing more."

"Yes, ma'am, I understand your point."

"Instead of going through that, we hired a lawyer who basically found young women in trouble and offered them an option. We paid their medical bills and sometimes even gave them a little extra cash, and they signed the babies over to us, no questions asked."

"So you have no idea who your son's parents were?"

"Well, at first we didn't really care. As far as we were concerned they were our children and nobody else's. But after Tino died, and I found this out, we realized that the birth connection is important. We went back to the lawyer for information." Mrs. Farmer paused before continuing. "Jarvis has met his birth parents. Wayne's birth mother is dead and his birth father is incarcerated, but they correspond by mail. Of course, it was too late for Tino. His father died from the same type of tumor that killed him. His mother lives in Lafayette. She has remarried and has two other children. From what she told me, Tino's father had an uncle and a sister who also died from brain tumors. It ran pretty rampant in that family and no one ever tried to find out why."

Gary slowly closed the folder and handed it back to Mrs. Farmer. "Thank you. I appreciate you showing me this and sharing your family information, but no one in mine or Phoebe's family has ever died of a brain tumor, so Pharrah's had to be a different type."

"Well, there is another possibility, Reverend. Maybe she didn't get it from you or Phoebe."

"I'm not sure what you mean." He looked at Mrs. Farmer strangely. "I'm married to Phoebe's sister, remember. I know her family medical history pretty well. They actually do have a history of heart disease, diabetes, and a few cases of breast cancer, but no brain tumors."

"Maybe you should keep this folder anyway. You might need it when you talk to Phoebe."

"Talk to Phoebe about what?"

"About this," she said, pointing to the folder. "The tumor Pharrah had is hereditary, and if she didn't get it from you or Phoebe, then there has to be more to it."

"You don't know that for sure. It was a rare tumor and the doctors told us its cause may never be determined conclusively. Besides that, she is making a full recovery. It's nothing short of miraculous. I appreciate your concern for me and my family, but there's no link here. It's just an awful coincidence."

"Well, you may be right, Reverend, but let me ask you this: you were Tino's best friend; tell me, did he ever date Phoebe?"

"No, ma'am, I can assure you beyond a shadow of a doubt that Tino never went on a date with Phoebe."

"Are you positive about that?"

"Like you just said, he was my best friend. We knew everything about each other."

Mrs. Farmer stood up from her chair and walked toward the door. She stopped just before opening it. "I didn't want to say this, Reverend, and please understand why I feel that I have to, but don't you want to at least ask Phoebe? Aren't you the slightest bit concerned that Pharrah may not be your daughter?"

Gary suddenly stood up from behind his desk. "She is my daughter. There is nothing you, that folder, or anyone can say that will change that. Do you hear me, Mrs. Farmer? Pharrah is my daughter!" he yelled.

"Reverend, what is wrong with you? I've never heard you raise your voice, and at me no less. Please calm down and just listen to me."

"No, I don't have to listen to any more of this. I love you like my own mother, but you've officially crossed the line. This conversation is over." He pointed toward the door. "Now, I'm sure you have some work to do at your desk or you can go on home for the day. Either way, close the door on your way out."

Mrs. Farmer stared at him in disbelief. "But, Reverend—"

"Close the door, Mrs. Farmer! I have work to do." He sat down in his chair and spun around, turning his back to her.

She stood there staring at him for several moments, then quietly she closed the door behind her.

As she did, Gary's mind wandered back to his college days and his best friend.

"Hey man, did you see Phoebe? Did she give you the handkerchief?" he breathlessly asked Tino as he strolled into the dorm room whistling.

"G, man, you been holding out on me. That girl was fly! Where you been hiding her?"

"What are you talking about?"

"I'm talking about Phoebe. All this time your girl-friend had this brick house for a sister and you never both-ered to tell me about it. We could have been double dating."

"Didn't you tell me you were not into any girl over a size six? You called me a chubby chaser."

"No offense man, I was talking about Phylicia. I mean she's a nice girl and all but she is kinda thick."

"So why would I think you wanted to meet her twin?"

" 'Cause you didn't tell me that the twin was all that."

"All what?"

"She is the definition of voluptuous. She reminded me of Jackée and you know how I love Jackée. Tino drew an hourglass shape in the air with his hands.

"She and Phyllie are the same size. You trippin'," Gary said, tossing a dirty towel across the room at him.

"I don't know, man. I ain't never seen Phylicia's booty look like that. Your girl dresses like an old lady. But this chick put it all on the table for me to enjoy."

"Phylicia dresses respectfully. What's wrong with that?"

"Nothing, man. That's a good thing. You know when

I'm ready to settle down and get married; I want a woman just like her. But right now while I'm young and sowing my wild oats, I want a woman just like her sister. That girl did things to me that are probably illegal in Louisiana," he said, laughing.

"Please tell me you didn't sleep with Phoebe."

"I didn't sleep with Phoebe," he answered flatly.

"Good." Gary breathed a sigh of relief.

"I'm going to sleep after I take a shower, but I did the wild thang with Phoebe." He grinned mischievously.

"Tino, I sent you over there to get my handkerchief back, not to have sex with Phoebe."

"I know, man. The sex was my idea. Well, actually it was hers. Man, she had it all laid out for you. She was wearing a sexy, tight dress showing all her curves. The lights were low and she had candles lit all around the room. She intended to put it on you tonight, dude. Now, aren't you glad I saved you from that? You gonna be a preacher, we can't have that girl corrupting you again."

Gary shook his head. *"So she set a seduction trap for me? I knew she'd try something like that. Phoebe is crazy. She has no respect for me and her sister's relationship."*

"Yeah, man, I gotta agree with ya there. When I walked in she was on the couch ready to be taken. The thing is, when she realized it was me and not you, she only hesitated for a moment. I didn't even have to pull out any of my lines. She opened up very freely. Those twins are like night and day. One is an angel and the other is definitely a devil. You better watch her, man."

"What do you mean?"

"Well, I gave her what she wanted tonight, but that only satisfied part of her appetite. She won't be happy until she has you, Gary Morgan, all to herself."

"That's never gonna happen. She tricked me once, but I will never fall for one of Phoebe's games ever again."

"But her games are so much fun!" Tino said, laughing loudly again.

"Shut up, man! After all of that, did you at least get the handkerchief back? Phyllie has been bugging me about it for over a month now."

"Naw, G. She said she'd only give that to you. I can try again if you want me to," Tino said with a wink.

Tino saw Phoebe several times over the next few weeks in between dates with other women. They always met at her house or his dorm room and had sex. Gary wasn't sure, but he figured it was probably still going on when Tino died. Gary did not exactly lie to Mrs. Farmer. Tino had a sexual relationship with Phoebe, but, truthfully, he had never *dated* Phoebe. He suddenly wondered why, when he'd found out about Pharrah, the possibility of her being Tino's daughter never occurred to him. He felt like such a fool.

Gary stood up from his desk and retrieved his suit jacket from the coat rack near the office door, then he grabbed the folder of information Mrs. Farmer had left sitting in his office. He walked to the outer office where Mrs. Farmer was sitting behind her desk slowly sipping on a cup of tea, apparently lost deep in thought. He stopped briefly. "I apologize for raising my voice. I won't be back today. I have some things to take care of." He left the church without another word.

Chapter Twenty-Four

The sun beamed brightly through the windows, filling the Morgan household. It was abuzz with activity as the ladies prepared to leave for the church's annual women's conference. Due to Pharrah's illness, Mrs. Farmer and Reverend Sims were assigned the task of pulling it all together, without Phylicia. It was the first time she wasn't directly involved in planning the women's conference. The previous year, during her problems with Gary, she focused her attention away from him and on planning that year's conference. Despite her personal troubles, it had been a huge success. Each year, Phylicia strived to make sure it was better and better. When she had returned from Baton Rouge she sat in on only the last few meetings, but she was pleased with what was done. It was strange not being involved, but she was anxious to hear the guest speaker.

Mrs. Farmer and Reverend Sims had chosen a minister who'd been displaced by the hurricane tragedy in New Orleans. Everyone across the country had been touched in some way by Hurricane Katrina, and they felt that what she'd been through and survived could be an inspiration to the women of Brown Bottom. Reverend Cassandra Nicholas was pastor of a small nondenominational congregation in New Orleans and had lost her home, her church, and her elderly parents in the storm.

Reverend Nicholas was in Los Angeles attending her husband's family reunion when the storm had hit. She'd tried to convince her parents to leave, but they'd ridden out hurricanes many times in their historical home and felt confident they could do it again. Hours before Hurricane Katrina came ashore; Reverend Nicholas spoke to her father for the last time. He assured her that he had the windows boarded up and they were just going to go to bed while the storm rode in.

Unbeknownst to them and a vast majority of the residents, the hurricane wasn't the only danger. Weakened by the storm, the levees gave way, putting a majority of New Orleans under water. A week went by as she made frantic phone calls to government agencies, neighbors, and friends. She literally spent hours upon hours on the phone, receiving little comfort and no news. She'd even considered going back to New Orleans to search for her family, but entry into the city was impossible. Nine days after Hurricane Katrina hit, her mother's body was found inside her home. She had drowned in her first-floor bedroom. Her father's body was discovered in the attic. He'd died of heat stroke while waiting for help to arrive.

Eva walked into her mother's bedroom and sat down on the edge of the bed. "Why can't I go? I'm a woman too," she whined.

Phylicia looked down at her little brown face and chuckled. "Honey, I understand that you feel like a woman, but this is for women over eighteen. I'm sorry."

"It's not fair. I have to stay here with Daddy and Li'l G while all of you get to go be ladies together."

Pharrah sat in a chair a few feet away. "Aunt Phyl . . . Phylicia. Maybe next year you could add another dimen . . . dimension . . . You could add the young women to the conference."

"Do you mean women as young as Eva?" Phylicia responded.

"It's diffi . . . it's hard for me as a young woman to . . . to relate to a woman who is married and old enough to be my mother. I'm sure she can give me some . . . something. But I'd feel better listening to someone closer to my own age."

Phylicia smiled at Pharrah, amazed at how much better her speaking was becoming. She'd been home only a few weeks and was growing stronger by the day. "You know, I never thought of that, but you are right. Our younger ladies need direction at these conferences as well. Next year we'll look into adding a youth division for the conference."

Pharrah beamed as her aunt walked over and hugged her, then returned to her mirror. "See, li'l sis. You can come with us next year," Pharrah said, and winked at Eva.

"Can I go over to Jayla's? There's nothing to do here," Eva said, still pouting.

Phylicia put an earring into her left ear then turned to her daughter. "I don't know. Can you?" she teased.

"May I go over to Jayla's? Please, Mommy."

"Yes, just be back by dinnertime. The conference will be over and I'll be home by then." Phylicia stepped into her leather pumps, then kissed her daughter good-bye. She turned back to the mirror and put on her towering peach-colored hat, then straightened it.

"Can't have the first lady with a crooked hat, now can

we?" Phoebe said, suddenly walking into her bedroom behind her.

Phylicia smiled at her in the mirror, then quickly spun around to face her. "Is that what you are wearing?"

Phoebe was dressed in a pair of tan silk pants with a matching silk tank top. Her pedicured toes were slipped into a pair of shimmering gold sandals with three-inch heels. On each wrist she wore at least five bangle bracelets and an assortment of bling around her neck and on her ears. Her face was heavily made up with three coats of lipstick, blush, eyeliner, and enough foundation to build a small apartment building.

"Yes, what's wrong with it?" Phoebe looked down at herself.

Phylicia chose her words carefully. "It's a bit flamboyant, don't you think?" she said cautiously.

"That's me. I'm flamboyant. You know that."

"Yes, I know, but for this conference could I suggest a little less bling, and maybe a tad bit less makeup?"

Phoebe looked at Pharrah, who nodded her head in agreement with her aunt. She sighed heavily, then took off three of the bracelets and one of the necklaces laying them on the dresser. Then she removed the multiple earrings and left only one tasteful pair of diamonds in her ears. She pulled a few tissues from the box on the dresser, then blotted her lipstick and wiped off a layer of her makeup, leaving just a hint of color where needed. "Is that better?" she said when she was done.

"Yes, you still look nice, just not as flashy." Phylicia smiled at her.

"Okay, now it's your turn."

"My turn for what?" Phylicia looked surprised.

"If I can tone my look down, you can at least perk yours up. I mean come on, Phyllie, it's ninety-five degrees out. Are you really gonna wear a long-sleeved jacket with a blouse underneath, pantyhose, and closed shoes? You are going to suffocate."

Phylicia looked in the mirror at the outfit she'd chosen for the conference. It was a double-breasted peach skirt suit. The skirt was ankle-length, and the jacket was long-sleeved. Underneath, she wore a white button-up blouse that was also long-sleeved. Her pantyhose were flesh colored and her shoes were dyed to exactly match her dress. "Phoebe, I'm the first lady. There is a certain way I should look."

"Come on, Phyllie. Does being the first lady mean looking like you just stepped out of the Sears winter catalog?" Phoebe walked to her sister's closet and pulled out several items. "Here, wear this dress." It was a simple, royal blue, sleeveless A-line dress with a moderate hem. Phylicia slowly changed as her sister organized the rest of the items. When she was done, Phoebe took one of her sister's large, colorful scarves and draped it around her for a shawl, then secured it on her shoulder with an ornate butterfly pin. Next, she handed Phylicia a pair of open-toed black pumps. "Lose the pantyhose, Phyllie," she ordered.

"I need the control top . . . for support," she said reluctantly.

Phoebe dug into her sister's dresser drawer until she found a panty girdle, then she handed it to her. "This will hold in that tummy."

"I only wear that with pants."

"It works with dresses, too, Phyllie," Phoebe said, laughing.

When she was completely changed, Phylicia twirled around, checking herself in the mirror.

"You look beautiful, Aunt Phylicia." Pharrah gave her the thumbs-up.

"Wait, there's just one more thing." Phoebe ran from

the room and came back moments later with her makeup case.

Phylicia shook her head, and held up her hands in front of her. "Oh, no, you are not gonna paint my face like some streetwalker. The outfit is fine, but that's taking it too far."

"Look, Phyllie, I'm not going to paint your face. I just want to give you a little bit of enhancement. I promise if it's too much you can wash it right off." Phoebe flashed an innocent smile.

Still a bit unsure, Phylicia sat down at her vanity and allowed her sister to put mascara, blush, and a small amount of lipstick on her face. Without asking permission, Phoebe reached behind her head and pulled the pins from Phylicia's bun, letting her hair fall luxuriously onto her shoulders. "Phyllie, why do you hide your hair? It's beautiful. I wish I'd never cut mine. I wouldn't have to spend so much money on weaves."

"I just prefer a more conservative look." She examined herself in the mirror, then turned to Pharrah for approval. "What do you think?"

"Beautiful." Pharrah smiled.

Phylicia took a longer look at herself. She hated to admit it, but she approved also. "All right, ladies. Let's go. We don't want to be late," she said.

As they descended the staircase, Li'l G and Gary teased them with catcalls and whistles of approval. Phylicia was used to her husband saying that she was beautiful no matter what she looked like, but today she actually felt he meant it. She thanked them for the compliments as they left.

Once the women arrived at the church auditorium, Phylicia was surprised at the looks and stares the three of them received. Out of the corner of her eye, she noticed several of the women pointing and whispering. She was ready to retreat and rush back home to change her clothes when Mrs. Farmer approached them. "You three look absolutely beautiful," she said.

"Mrs. Farmer, thank you. But you're just saying that," Phylicia answered.

"Now, you know me. I'd tell ya if you had a tear in your drawers and not think twice about it. I'm honest and I don't put on no airs. You three really look wonderful."

"Thank you," they all said in unison.

"I can't get over it. The last time I saw Pharrah she was just leaving the hospital and, to be honest, she looked like it." They all laughed. "But now she looks healthy and happy."

"I am feeling . . . much . . . better, Mrs. Farmer," Pharrah responded slowly.

"I'm so glad to hear that, sweetheart." Mrs. Farmer reached over and gave Pharrah a hug. "And you two look more like twins today than I've ever seen you."

"We do? Why do you think so, Mrs. Farmer?" Phoebe asked.

"Well, in the past the differences in your looks were always obvious. Like I said, I'm gonna tell you the truth. Phoebe, you were trying too hard, with all the pomp and circumstance. Your look was way overdone. And Phylicia, I know you are the first lady and all, but sometimes you dressed like you were an old lady. You were not trying hard enough. But today it looks like you both found the right place in the middle, and it works."

They all laughed at her refreshing honesty before thanking her for the compliments again.

Phylicia knew that it was more than the way they looked. She and her sister had found their middle ground and they both were better women because of it. "Thank you, Mrs. Farmer. I think we are going in to find our seats now."

Phylicia put her right arm around her sister and her left around her niece as they walked in.

"Foul, foul!" Li'l G screamed as his dad reached around him in a game of basketball in their yard.

"Okay, your point." Gary moved to the other end of the driveway and got into a guarding stance. Li'l G tucked the ball under his arm and watched him, not moving. "What's wrong?" Gary asked.

"You tell me, Dad. What's wrong with you?"

"Nothing's wrong with me."

"C'mon, Dad, you didn't foul me. Why are you letting me win?"

Gary grinned. " 'Cause I don't wanna embarrass you by getting beat by ya old man, that's why. Now come on, check the ball."

Li'l G put the ball down on the ground and sat on it. "Really, Dad, you haven't been yourself for a couple of weeks now. I mean, things were great when Pharrah first got home, but now they've changed again."

Gary looked at his son, then he walked over and grabbed a bottle of water from the side of the driveway. As he opened the twist cap, he sat down on the ground near Li'l G. "Changed? How do you think they've changed?" He took a swig of water and wiped his sweat with the hem of his T-shirt.

"Well, at first it was a good change. You and Mom were acting like you liked each other again. Auntie Phoebe moved in and nobody was fighting. I mean, we really seemed happy again. It was just like before Grandma died, only better since Aunt Phoebe and Pharrah are here now. But then one night you came home from work, you went to Pharrah's room, and spent an hour talking to her. When you came out, you were just different. I can't explain it."

"Well, son, I have to say you are very observant. If you

must know, I had a long talk with Pharrah about her illness."

"Why? I thought she was better. I thought the doctors said they got the whole tumor."

"Yes, they did. There's nothing for you to worry about. But you know some of her memories from the illness are gone, and I wanted to discuss with her what had happened to her."

"So, she is getting better? You wouldn't lie to me, would you, Dad?"

"Of course I wouldn't. She's getting much better."

"Then what's wrong? And don't say nothing again, because I know it's something. I'm almost eighteen years old. You can confide in me."

Gary looked over at his son, whom he knew would shortly be a man, offering a shoulder for him to lean on. Without hesitation, he allowed himself to reach out and take it. "Do you remember my friend Tino I told you about who died when we were in college? He was Mrs. Farmer's youngest son."

"Yeah, his picture is in the trophy case at school. He scored the most points in a single game of anyone ever in the history of Brown Bottom High School basketball. They retired his jersey number. He could've been as great as Michael Jordan."

"Yes, he was a great athlete and a very special friend. He died of a brain tumor, just like the one that almost killed Pharrah."

"Wow. I never knew that."

"Mrs. Farmer thinks . . . well there's a slight possibility that his death and Pharrah's illness may somehow be connected."

"I don't understand."

"Well, son, it's actually possible that I'm not Pharrah's dad. There's a really good chance that Tino was."

Li'l G looked at his dad in stunned silence for several minutes. "Is that what you talked to Pharrah about?"

"No, I didn't want to tell her unless I was sure. I just needed to spend some time with her."

"Are you sure now?"

"No. God and I have been doing some talking, and I'm just trying to find the best way to deal with this whole situation. That's why I've been different, sadder. I love Pharrah. I would hate to think that she's not really mine." Gary took another long swig of his water, then stared at the concrete driveway.

"Dad, you once told me that families come in all different shapes and sizes. Even if you are not her dad, you can still love her like you are. I mean, if it turns out that Tino is her father, I know she won't love you any less."

Gary looked over at his son, feeling humbly amazed at his simple wisdom.

"Well, if that's the case and she's the daughter of a basketball legend, then you better get up and practice your skills before she gets better, or she's gonna beat you as bad I am."

Li'l G stood up and grabbed the ball. "Oh, yeah, you think so?" He dribbled around the driveway. Within minutes, he saw his father's old demeanor return and they had a rousing game of basketball, with Li'l G winning by a mere two points.

"C'mon, loser, I'll buy you a soda," he said as he hugged his dad around the neck, and they walked inside the house.

Chapter Twenty-Five

The next several years seemed to pass quickly for Gary Morgan, and before he knew it, he was proudly holding Pharrah by the arm and walking his little girl down the aisle on her wedding day. She was dressed elegantly in a long, flowing white gown with a five-foot train extending behind it. Her little sister, Eva, stood next to Kelli as bridesmaids, while Li'l G had donned a tuxedo as an usher. Gary looked at his children and swelled with pride as they slowly descended the aisle of Freedom Inspiration. Pharrah beamed at her groom waiting for her at the altar. Sam McNeil was a young man she'd met in medical school, and they'd fallen quickly and deeply in love.

As he held tightly to her arm, Gary could hardly believe the miracle that was his little girl. She'd recovered completely from the brain tumor with barely any side effects. Her speech had returned to normal, and she'd been able to walk without a cane only a few months after coming home. With physical therapy and constant workouts, she was regaining her muscle control and athletic build.

Since she'd collapsed only days before graduation but
had earned the grades, Southern University had allowed
her to participate in graduation ceremonies a year later.
She received her degree with honors as her family
cheered from the stands.

Determined not to allow her illness to defeat her, Pharrah immediately began attending medical school the following fall. It was difficult for her at first, so she'd hired a
tutor named Sam. Within a few short months, the two of
them were madly in love. Even with their hectic sched-
ules, as Sam studied to be a surgeon and she to be a pediatrician, they managed to find time for each other.

Then one fateful afternoon, Pharrah came home in
tears telling Gary, Phoebe, and Phylicia that she'd found
out she was pregnant. She didn't want to leave school,
but she had no other choice. Phoebe suggested an abortion, but Gary and Phylicia quickly vetoed that idea,
with Pharrah's agreement.

"Well, you are not going to send her away in embarrassment and shame like Momma and Daddy did to
me," Phoebe wailed.

Trying to remain calm and be the voice of reason, Gary
asked how Sam felt about becoming a father.

"Oh, he's ecstatic, Daddy. He can hardly wait," Pharrah replied.

"Then I think the best thing is for the two of you to get
married."

"Gary, are you crazy. She's still in medical school. How
is she going to finish if she's married? Who's going to
care for the baby when she has long hours and studying
to do? No, Pharrah, don't throw away your life so young.
I'm not ready to be a grandma," Phoebe protested.

"Gary and I, and Eva and Li'l G, will pitch in. We can
help her; she's family. There are enough hands around
here to take care of one little baby," Phylicia offered.

"Then there's no need to get married. She barely knows this boy," Phoebe retorted.

Pharrah stood between her mother and aunt. "Mom, I do too know him. And I love him."

"You are too young to get married, Pharrah. You can raise your child on your own like I raised you."

"Being a single mother in medical school is not a great idea. Besides, Pharrah, if you and Sam are sleeping together, marriage is the right thing. It's the Christian thing to do," Gary said, interrupting them both.

The arguing back and forth continued into the night, before Gary was finally able to convince everyone that marriage was the best option. "I promise you, honey, your mother, aunt, and I will make sure that your baby has the best of everything. We will help you get through this."

Now, as he gave her hand in matrimony, Gary kissed Pharrah on her cheek and brushed a tear away with his handkerchief. He sat between Phylicia and Phoebe as they watched the two of them take their vows.

"I can't believe she's such a beautiful bride," he said to Phylicia hours later as they both waved good-bye to the car with tin cans clinking in the rear.

"You are a proud father. Of course she's beautiful to you," she teased.

"Do you think we made the right decision?"

"It wasn't our decision to make. I'm just glad that Pharrah and Sam made the right decision."

"I know you're right, but I feel like I pushed her hand. Maybe she thought she had to get married since she's the preacher's daughter. She still has another year of medical school. Maybe I don't know, maybe she should not have kept the baby."

"Gary, don't be ridiculous. Pharrah and Sam are very happy. Stop worrying, Grandpa. Those two, I mean those three, are going to be just fine."

A few months later, as he stood outside the hospital nursery with his video camera shooting photos of his first grandchild, Gary was filled with joy. He stood beaming and waving at his new grandson, Carson Gary McNeil. He'd never been more proud of his daughter than at that moment.

As he filmed, he felt a tapping on his shoulder and slowly he turned around. He smiled at her, but she didn't smile back. "Mrs. Farmer, isn't my grandson beautiful?" he asked, turning the camera back to the window.

"Reverend Gary, say good-bye to him now. It will make it much easier." She stood there with a blank look on her face.

"What do you mean? Easier than what?" He lowered his camera to his side and stared at her.

"Easier than watching him laugh, play, grow up, and die before he's twenty-one years old."

"No, he's healthy. The doctors told me so. He's a healthy baby boy."

"Just like my baby boy. Say good-bye, Reverend."

Gary stared at Mrs. Farmer as she turned and walked slowly down the hospital corridor, then disappeared into the darkness. *What if he carries the gene? What if little Carson Gary McNeil has a tumor growing inside him right now? I should have told Pharrah years ago. How could I keep her legacy from her?*

He turned around to face the glass and pointed his camera at the bassinette, but it was empty. The baby was gone. "Where is he? What happened to my grandson?" he screamed. He tapped on the glass trying to alert the nurses, but no one answered.

Gary dropped his camera and ran down the hallway, frantically searching for help. When he could find no one, he began opening doors hoping his grandson was behind one of them. He opened every door in the long hallway and each room was empty. Nervously, he reached the final door and tried to open it. It was heavy, as if made of stone. He pushed and pushed until it finally opened.

Gary found his grandson dead on the floor, and a man's body lying next to him. "Who are you? What have you done to my grandson?" He rushed over to the man and turned his body over. Shocked, he looked down into the man's face. "Tino?" Backing away, Gary began to scream hysterically at the top of his lungs.

"Gary . . . Gary, wake up. You're dreaming. Honey, wake up!" Phylicia shook her husband several times before he sat straight up in the bed with sweat pouring down his brow. He was breathing heavily, as if he'd just run a marathon. "Honey, are you all right?"

"Pharrah, where's Pharrah?" he said, looking around.

"She's downstairs in her room. You were screaming. Are you okay?"

Gary looked around his bedroom, confused. He struggled to focus on what year it was before his mind finally brought him back to reality. It suddenly dawned on him that Pharrah had not yet graduated college, started medical school, or gotten married. She was still recovering from her illness. Sam McNeil didn't exist, and Gary realized that he didn't have a beautiful grandson whom he'd just found lying dead. It wasn't several years in the future. He was back in the present. It was all a dream, a horrible dream. He took in several gulps of air before answering his wife. "I just had a nightmare, that's all. I'm fine." He continued to breathe heavily, taking strenuous breaths.

"Are you sure? Can I get you anything? Let me get you some water or something."

Phylicia peeled back the covers to get up as he slowly shook his head, then lay back down, pulling her into his arms. "No, don't leave. I'm fine now. I'm fine."

"Do you wanna talk about it?" She waited as her question hung in the darkness for several unanswered seconds.

"It's nothing, honey. Probably that chili dog the kids and I had for dinner. I know better than to eat spicy foods."

"I'm sorry the women's conference lasted longer than I expected. I planned to get home and cook dinner, but it didn't work out that way."

"No, it's not your fault. I made the choice." He pulled her to him and kissed her forehead, then snuggled her closer under him. Within a few moments Phylicia had drifted off to sleep, while Gary remained awake, staring into the darkness.

Chapter Twenty-Six

"Good afternoon, Mrs. Farmer. Is Gary in?"

Surprised, Mrs. Farmer looked up from her desk at Phoebe standing over her.

"Yes, he is, but he has an appointment at two o'clock. Maybe I can give him a message or you can see him later at home."

"I am his two o'clock appointment, Mrs. Farmer. Could you please tell him I'm here? I'm on my lunch hour; I haven't eaten and I need to get back to work."

Mrs. Farmer looked Phoebe up and down. She wasn't as demure and put-together as she'd been at the women's conference the previous weekend. In Mrs. Farmer's opinion, her skirt was too short and her blouse cut too low. It was a cute ensemble with a pink skirt, and matching white blouse with pink polka dots. As usual, her feet were perfectly pedicured, and she wore pink sandal slides with a high heel. She did, however, look nice; too nice to be talking alone with the pastor as far as Mrs. Farmer was concerned.

"Oh, yes, Phylicia told me you'd found a job. How are you enjoying that?"

"Actually, it's a lot of fun. I got a job on my first interview at a real estate office. I answer the phones, make coffee, and greet clients. Whenever one of my agents has an appointment, I make sure to tell them right away so as not to keep the person waiting." Phoebe plastered on a fake smile, hoping Mrs. Farmer took the hint.

Mrs. Farmer looked her over once more, then finally picked up her desk phone and dialed Gary's office. She spoke softly so that Phoebe could not hear, and within a few seconds, she hung up. "He's expecting you, go right in," she said half-heartedly.

Phoebe sauntered into Gary's office, swaying her hips. Once inside, she turned around and gave Mrs. Farmer a satisfied "I told you so" look, and closed the door. "Hi, Gary!" she said, smiling.

"Hello, Phoebe. Please have a seat. There's something I need to discuss with you."

She sat down on the couch and sexily crossed her legs. It had been months since she had last been alone with him in his office, and although they had been interrupted with the phone call regarding Pharrah, she was convinced that she felt something between them. There was a spark, a look in his eye that made her believe he wanted her.

On the drive over, she'd wondered why he called her at work and asked her to meet him at his office. It wasn't like she didn't see him every evening at the house. As she thought about it, she remembered that several times over the last few days she'd noticed him staring at her across the table. When she'd catch him, he'd avert his eyes, but she saw what was there. She just knew that Gary was longing for her.

She'd debated with herself about meeting him, but

then realized she'd waited more than twenty years to hear the words he was going to say. From the first moment she'd laid eyes on him she knew that one day Gary Morgan would desperately want to be with her.

It would be a bittersweet victory due to the fact that Phoebe no longer had any interest in Gary. Living with him and Phylicia, she'd found him boring and predictable, just like her sister. The two of them enjoyed spending evenings at home playing board games or watching movies with the kids. In the month since they'd returned from Baton Rouge with a recuperating Pharrah, and Phoebe had moved in with them, Phylicia and Gary had gone out to dinner only once; they were home before ten. Gary Morgan may have been gorgeous on the outside, but in her opinion, he was like an empty soda can. If you popped the top, there was nothing inside.

Phylicia and Gary belonged together as far as she was concerned. He would never be able to keep up with Phoebe. She'd also met a young, sexy real estate agent, who hadn't cared that she was twelve years his senior when he asked her to dinner for that weekend. Nevertheless, she couldn't help but feel elated that her prophecy seemed finally to be coming true. Phoebe put on a sexy smile and waited patiently to break Gary's heart. "Go ahead, Gary. Say whatever you feel," she said, almost bursting with anticipation.

"I'm not going to beat around the bush with you, Phoebe. Let me get straight to the point. Who is Pharrah's father?"

Phoebe's face cracked into a million pieces and tumbled to the ground. She watched the pieces scattering all over the impeccably waxed hardwood floor of Gary's office before finally picking it up, putting it back on, and speaking again. "What did you just say?" she asked incredulously.

"I think you heard me. Who is Pharrah's father? I have a pretty good idea, but I want you to tell me."

Phoebe suddenly felt hot all over. She picked up a piece of paper from the edge of Gary's desk and folded it. She uncrossed her legs as she began to fan herself. "Where's this coming from? I don't understand."

"So you are gonna keep playing games. I can't believe you, Phoebe." He opened his desk drawer and pulled out the folder Mrs. Farmer had given him. "Read the last page, then answer my question."

Phoebe put down her homemade fan and took the folder. She opened it slowly, and after several moments, finally flipped to the last page. Gary was sure she'd read it all, but she still stared at the page, not speaking. "What is all this? What is this supposed to mean?" she finally asked.

"I got that from Mrs. Farmer. It means that Tino died of a hereditary brain tumor."

"That's impossible. If it was hereditary, where did Tino get it?"

"If you must know, Tino was adopted. His natural father died of the same type of brain tumor that he had. It's also the same fast acting type that Pharrah had. Now I'm going to ask you again, Phoebe, who is Pharrah's father?"

Phoebe looked at Gary, then dropped her head in shame. He noticed tears begin to drop down her face and land on the folder. Quietly, he handed her a tissue. "So my suspicions are right. Tino was Pharrah's father. You were pregnant when he died, weren't you?"

Phoebe slowly nodded her head. "I wanted to tell him. I went to the dorm and to his house to tell him, but he wasn't there. Then I went home and I sat by the phone for hours waiting for him to call me, but he didn't. When

Phyllie came home that night she told me what happened to him. Before I could think or do anything, he was dead. He was already dead." Phoebe sniffed and wiped away her tears as more replaced them.

"So you decided to lay the blame on me? The negative test you had after we were together was accurate, but you still lied to me. How could you be so spiteful?"

"No, you don't understand. I never intended to blame you. Not ever."

"What do you mean not ever? What exactly did you intend?"

"I didn't know what to do. Tino was dead, and I was pregnant and nobody even knew about us. I was scared and confused. For a long time I didn't do anything. I was in denial hoping that maybe if I ignored it, it wouldn't be true."

"But why blame me, Phoebe? Tino was dead, but you could have told your family or his family. You could have come up with a solution that didn't involve me. I don't understand why you didn't just tell the truth."

"I wanted to, but I never got the chance."

"That doesn't make any sense at all."

"It was about three months after Tino died. You and Phyllie were happy together and planning your wedding. By this time I was close to five months pregnant, but because of my size, it was easy to hide under clothes. I'd been depressed for months because I'd lost Tino and because I didn't know what to do. I barely came out of my room. Momma thought I was moping over you and jealous of Phyllie, so she decided to do something special for me. She came into my room and told me to get showered and changed so that we could go shopping and to lunch, just the two of us. I'd just gotten out of the shower and dropped my towel, when Momma walked in to ask me if I wanted to wear lavender since she was wearing lavender. There was nowhere for me to run to or any place to hide. She could see that I was pregnant."

"That still doesn't explain—"

Phoebe held up her hand. "Just let me finish. I didn't tell any lies about you. Momma assumed. She started crying and screaming about the test being wrong and why didn't I say something sooner. Since she and Daddy knew about me and you, she just assumed that you were the father. I never once told her that, because she never bothered to ask. We still went out to lunch, and over lunch she decided that since you and Phyllie were engaged, there was no use in telling you or her about the baby. She said she'd come up with a solution that would be best for everybody. Later that evening she talked to Daddy and Aunt Philomena, and they came up with the plan to cart me off to Florida. At that point I didn't care what they did. I went along with the arrangement."

"So you went to Florida and had the baby without ever trying to correct their assumptions. Pharrah told me my name is on her birth certificate. Why did you do that?"

"I tried to stop Momma from doing that. I really did. I told her to just leave it blank or something. But she overruled me and that was that. I mean, I was barely seventeen, and confused and alone. I know it was wrong, but at the time I saw no harm in any of it. I left Pharrah and those secrets in Florida. I never thought I'd see her again until Aunt Philomena died."

"So that's why you left town and never came to visit. You wanted to hide your lies and keep anyone from knowing your secret."

"I left town so that I could keep my daughter. Momma and Daddy wouldn't allow me to bring her back to Brown

Bottom. After I saw her at the funeral, I knew I couldn't give her up a second time. I just couldn't."

"That was the perfect time to start telling the truth, Phoebe. You could have told your parents the whole truth."

"No, I couldn't. It was bad enough I'd slept with you; the last thing they wanted to hear was I'd slept with someone else, too. Do you have any idea how much that would have embarrassed them? Daddy was head of the deacon board and Momma was president of the ladies society. They didn't just send me away because it was your baby. It would not have mattered who Pharrah's father was. They sent me away to keep me from embarrassing and shaming the Carson name. Even if Pharrah had to end up in foster care, they were not about to let anyone know their daughter was an unwed mother. No, it was better for me to just leave."

"How could continuing to lie be better?"

"It was what was best for me and Pharrah. Besides, I never told her you were her father. From the moment I picked her up in Florida, I told her the truth. I told her that her father was named Lucas Valentino Farmer and that he was dead. That's all she ever heard from me. Whenever she asked I told her everything that I knew about him: what he looked like, the way he walked with just a bit of a pimp stroll, that he had a crooked smile that made him seem like a mischievous kid. I told her how he was a basketball star and I told her that if he'd known about her, he would have loved her very much."

"Well, I will give you that. Tino probably would have loved her."

"Oh, no, there's no probably to it. If he'd known, he would have loved her as much as he loved me."

Gary looked at Phoebe with pity in his eyes as she

wiped the tears from her face. He wondered if he should tell her how Tino really felt about her. He took a deep breath and spoke. "Phoebe, I don't want to cloud your memory of him, but Tino had other girlfriends. You'd only been seeing him a short time and he didn't even consider you his girlfriend. When he died it was Sonya. He was my best friend, and trust me, he wasn't in love with you."

"You think you know everything, don't you, Gary Morgan? Well, there was something you didn't know about me and Tino. I know he was with Sonya that night. He intended to break up with her but he never got a chance to." She reached into her purse and pulled out a blue velvet ring box. "Tino gave me this about a week be-fore he . . . before he . . . well, before he passed." She opened the box to reveal a gorgeous one carat engage-ment ring. Gary recognized it immediately. He had been with Tino when he bought it, but he'd always assumed it was for Sonya. He had no idea what had happened to it after his friend died.

"Where did you get that?"

"I just told you, Tino gave it to me. We were engaged to be married, Gary. As soon as I was out of high school we were going to be married. Just like Phyllie, I was going to have a husband who loved me, too. He would have been ecstatic to know I was pregnant. I just never got a chance to tell him."

"That's crazy. He said he'd found the right girl and was gonna pop the question, but I know it wasn't you. I don't want to hurt your feelings, honestly, but he never talked that way about you."

"How could he? You hated me for what I did. He knew that. And even though you were his best friend, he didn't know how to tell you that he'd fallen in love with me. I know it wasn't supposed to happen that way. He was just supposed to get the handkerchief back, but fate intervened. How could he tell the person who hated me so much what he truly felt?"

"I never hated you, Phoebe. I just never understood you. I still don't. Sometimes you are kind, generous, and warm. Then it seems when you want something, you push all of that to the side and a lying, vindictive woman comes out. It's like instead of twins there are triplets: Phyllie and the two sides of you."

Phoebe looked down at her hands, then wiped away another tear before placing the ring box back inside her purse. "This ring and his letters were all I had of Tino after he was gone. Carrying it with me feels almost like he's still with me. I know it's odd, but I keep the ring with me all the time, as a reminder of what we had." Phoebe sniffed. "No matter how hard times got, I've never parted with it and I've never shown it to anyone but Pharrah, not even Maurice. Pharrah believed he was her father until she found that birth certificate and talked to Momma. That's all that mattered to me."

"Then you came here and confirmed what Mom told her."

"Did I, Gary? Or did I just go along with the plan once again? Did you ever hear me utter the words you are Pharrah's father?"

"Don't waste my time with semantics. You knew full well what you were doing. You were telling and living a huge lie, one that almost cost Pharrah her life. It doesn't matter if you said the words directly to me or not. You allowed me to believe and wanted me to believe that I was her father."

"She wanted a father so badly growing up. She loved the stories about Tino, but there was no way a few words and letters could be a father to her. When I married Maurice I thought I'd found her that father she longed for, but that was a huge mistake. The two of them never got along or bonded." She paused and sniffed loudly. "I didn't come here to tell lies. I came to visit my sick mother. Everything was happening so fast, first with Maurice following me to town, then Pharrah. So when I found out she believed you were her father and wanted you to be her father, you believed it and you wanted it, too. I . . . I just . . ."

"You just what?"

"I gave her the one thing I'd never been able to: a good father. At that point I wished it were true. So, yes, I went along with it."

"You came into my home and almost tore my marriage apart to give your daughter a good father? This is exactly what I mean, Phoebe. When you want something there is nothing too sacred to stop you from receiving it."

"What do you want me to say, Gary, that I'm sorry? Well, I won't say it because I'm not sorry I let her believe you are her father. The only thing I regret is hurting Phyllie, but she got over it. Your marriage is back on track. She and I are getting along better than we have since we were kids. Pharrah is growing stronger every day. This last year with you has made her a better person, a more confident woman. No, I'm not sorry at all."

"Well, sorry or not, you have to tell Pharrah the truth. You can't keep living this lie."

"Are you crazy? There is no reason for her to know the truth. Look, I admitted it to you, isn't that enough? She's happy. She loves having siblings. She loves you, Gary. Why would you want to take all of that away from her?"

"None of that is going away. I love Pharrah very much, and after this past year-and-a-half there is no way you could ever keep me from being a part of her life. But she has to know the truth. That tumor was hereditary and she could pass the same gene along to her children. She has to know."

"So we'll tell her if and when she's pregnant. There's no reason to tell her now."

"Phoebe, you are being ridiculous. She has a right to know the truth."

"What about Phyllie? This is going to hurt her. Things are back on track for the whole family. I see no reason to rock the boat now."

"I told Phylicia about my suspicions last night. She and I agree that you should be the one to tell Pharrah."

Phoebe looked at him, stunned. "She knows? That figures. I guess she's celebrating now that she knows Pharrah is not really your child."

"You know Phylicia better than that. We are both hurt that Pharrah is not my daughter, but we also both want what's best for her. Besides, Phyllie wasn't hurt because I had a child so much as she was hurt that I had one with you. The fact that you and I shared a night together hasn't changed. But Phyllie is a strong woman and she's forgiven us both."

"So you and Phyl have this all figured out, huh? The good reverend gets his halo back. He doesn't have an illegitimate daughter after all. His dutiful wife can now say she's the only mother of his children, and all is well with the world. Is that it? What if I don't go along with it? What if I refuse to tell Pharrah, then what?"

"Pharrah told me about your phone call the day she got sick. You really disappointed and hurt her. Yet she's forgiven you. From speaking with her I realize that over the years, disappointments and forgiveness has been a huge part of your relationship with her. You promised her a big Christmas surprise only for her to wake up with one gift. You promised her a new daddy only to bring Maurice home. Her whole life has been a series of big buildups, lies, and disappointments. She loves you, Phoebe, and she just wishes you'd be honest with her so that she can learn to trust you again. Now, I will tell Pharrah if you don't, but I wanted to give you the opportunity. After all, she is your daughter."

"I never disappointed her on purpose. I always did the best I could for Pharrah."

"I know that. Don't you see that telling her the truth now is the best you can do for her? Why do you want to keep hiding behind a lie?"

"You don't understand at all. It wasn't easy living in Phylicia's shadow. If Tino had just lived I'd have had a big wedding, a big baby shower, and Momma and Daddy would have been proud of me, too. Pharrah is all I have. This will tear us apart. Why do you insist on putting me through it?"

"Phoebe, you can't let Pharrah keep believing I'm her father when it's not true. It's going to be hurtful, but you have to tell her. You have to stop lying."

Phoebe pulled out a fresh tissue and blew her nose. She remembered Pharrah saying almost identical words to her more than a year before. She dramatically blew her nose again before speaking. "I'll tell her, just give me a few days, okay?"

"You have one week, Phoebe."

Chapter Twenty-Seven

After leaving Gary's office, Phoebe decided against going back to work that afternoon. She called her boss and told him that she'd gotten sick over lunch and needed to go home. The first part was true, as her talk with Gary had sickened her to her stomach. But the last place Phoebe wanted to be at that moment was home. Pharrah was there and she wasn't ready to talk to her yet. Phylicia was also there and she'd probably be looking at her in a condescending manner, and Phoebe couldn't take it.

Instead, she got in her car and began driving around. After traveling aimlessly for more than thirty minutes and ending up back almost where she started, she cursed Brown Bottom for being so small. *Shoot, this hick town is nothing but a big circle,* she thought.

She checked her gas gauge, then pulled onto the interstate. Due to the devastation done to her home state by the recent hurricanes, she knew better than to head south, so she began driving north. She drove about twenty-five miles, then pulled off the interstate onto a lonely country road that seemed to stretch into forever. Solitude was just what she needed.

Turning up the radio, she pressed her foot onto the gas pedal, speeding forward. As she drove, the miles of fields and trees to her right and her left whizzed by with barely a glance. She turned off the air conditioner and rolled down her windows to get some fresh air, then she reached down to change the station on the radio.

I hate when they mix gospel in with my regular jams. Phoebe fiddled and played with the radio for a few moments, then just as she looked up, a brown-and-white speckled cow seemed to appear out of nowhere in the middle of the road. Phoebe screamed, then hit her brakes, but the cow was too close. She swerved, throwing her car off the road. Her back wheels spun, turning the car out of control for several moments before finally coming to rest in a nearby ditch. The airbag popped out, smashing Phoebe in her face. She slumped over it as the car stopped moving.

Phoebe lifted her head and looked around, unsure of how long she'd been sitting with her head resting on the now deflated airbag. The cow was a few feet away in a pasture, munching happily on some grass. Or, at least, she thought it was the same cow. She was so disoriented she wasn't sure.

"Hello, Phoebe."

Startled at hearing a voice inside the car with her, she jumped and looked in the direction the voice came from. "Tino?" she said, staring at the young man suddenly sitting next to her in her car. She had to admit that it looked like him, but there was no way it could be him.

"Hey, baby."

Phoebe screamed. "Oh, my God, I'm seeing dead people. I must be dead too." She screamed again, startling the cows standing in the nearby field.

"Calm down, Phoebe. Stop screaming. You are not dead."

"I'm not? Then what's going on?"

"So you have forgotten about me? You told our daughter I wasn't her father and now you want to forget I ever existed."

"No, it's not that."

"What happened to all the beautiful memories of us you used to tell her? Why have they been replaced with lies about her and G?"

"I did it for her. Pharrah needed a father."

"I am her father."

"She needed a live father."

"No, she didn't, Phoebe. Pharrah is a beautiful young woman and you've done a wonderful job with her. She didn't need you to erase me and add in G."

"But this past year, with her being around him and having a man in her life, has been so wonderful for her. She's never known what it was like to have a positive male figure in her life."

"She could have had all that without the lies. Gary is her uncle and he would have loved her no matter what."

"An uncle is not the same as a father."

"Don't you mean a brother-in-law is not the same as a husband?"

Phoebe slammed her hands against the airbag in the steering wheel. "No, of course not. What are you talking about?"

"Isn't that the real reason you did this? You wanted Gary? You needed Gary in your life and you tried to use Pharrah to get to him."

"Gary Morgan is boring. He's not my type."

"Oh, sure, now he's not. But when you came back to Brown Bottom with nothing but your suitcases, being with Gary was mighty appealing. I know that you never stopped loving him. You took my ring, but you secretly wished it was from Gary."

"Tino, I did love you but—"

"No, you didn't, Phoebe. You loved the idea of getting married and having what your sister had. That's why you lied, so that you could have what your sister has. Look what you've done to our daughter, Phoebe. You've built up a false family that now you have to tear down."

"I love Pharrah. I would do anything for her."

"That sounds like what you said at the hospital. You'd do anything to save her life. You'd even tell the truth. Her life has been saved. Why are you still lying? Why did you break your promise to God?"

"I don't know. I was scared. I would have said anything at that point."

"Poor little scared Phoebe. If it meant you could have Gary, you'd say anything. You'd even destroy my memory with our child."

"I never meant to do that."

"You never mean to do anything, do you? You never got over him. No matter how many years had passed, you still wanted him. You let everyone believe Gary was Pharrah's father, not for Pharrah's sake, but for your own selfishness."

Phoebe turned to him and swung her fist, wanting to punch him in the face, in the arm, or anywhere. She swung and swung, and each time her hands landed on the car seat leather. "What are you? Why are you here?" she wailed.

"I'm not here, Phoebe. Not like you think."

"What are you saying?"

"I'm in your head, not in the car. I'm only saying to you what you already know but refuse to admit."

Phoebe laid her arms on the steering wheel and put

her head on top of them. She began to sob uncontrollably. "I know I was wrong. I'm so sorry."

"Don't tell me. Go home and tell Pharrah."

"Ma'am, are you okay?" Phoebe raised her head and looked around the car. Tino was gone, and peering into her driver's side window was a man who she could have sworn was Jed Clampett. He was dressed in dirty denim overalls with a red checkered shirt and straw hat. She jumped backward in the car as he startled her. "I'm sorry my cow Lizzie ran you off the road. I called 911 for ya already. Are you okay?"

"I . . . I think so," she answered as she took one last look around her empty car.

Several hours later, a disheveled Phoebe arrived on her sister's doorstep escorted by a police officer. She rang the doorbell, unsure of where she'd left her house keys.

Li'l G answered the door. "Mom! Dad! Come quick. It's the police with Aunt Phoebe!" he yelled. Then he assisted the officer with getting Phoebe inside the house and seated on the sofa.

"Phoebe, are you all right? What happened?" Phylicia asked, rushing to her sister.

"Officer, is my sister-in-law in some kind of trouble?" Gary inquired.

"No, sir. She just had a minor accident and wasn't able to drive her car. I agreed to make sure she got home safely. She's a little shook up, that's all."

"Thank you, we certainly appreciate that," Gary answered.

"Mrs. Cox, your car has been towed to a local garage. Here's their card. You can call them tomorrow about getting it repaired." He handed Phoebe the card. "You folks have a good evening."

Gary shook the officer's hand and walked him to the front door, then said good-bye. Once the officer was gone, he returned to the others who were hovering over Phoebe.

"Are you okay? Can I get you something? What about some water? Are you thirsty, Phoebe?" Phylicia inquired.

Phoebe shook her head. "I'm fine. Stop fussing over me. Where's Pharrah?"

"She's in her room."

"Go get her, Phyllie. I need to talk to her. I need to talk to you, too."

"Uhm, you don't have to do that right now. Maybe you should take a shower and get some rest first," Phylicia suggested.

"No. I've put it off long enough. She needs to hear the truth and she needs to hear it now."

"Li'l G, go get Pharrah and then go up to your room and finish your homework," Gary instructed.

A few minutes later, Pharrah came out of her room and joined them in the living room. She immediately rushed to make sure Phoebe was okay, and sat down next to her on the sofa. Gary grabbed Phylicia by the hand and motioned toward the stairs. "We'll just go upstairs and leave you two alone to talk."

"No, Gary, I want you and Phyllie to stay. There are some things I need to say to the both of you, as well. Please sit down."

Slowly, Gary and Phylicia sat down in chairs close to Phoebe. They waited patiently for her to begin.

"Pharrah, there's no easy way to say this, so I'll just be quick with it. Gary is not your natural father. I lied to you. Tino Farmer is your father. Everything I've told you since you were a little girl is the truth. It wasn't until you came to Brown Bottom that I began to lie to you," Phoebe admitted.

"Mom . . . I—"

"Please don't interrupt. I need to get this all out. When

I came here to see Mom I was so jealous of your aunt Phylicia and her family. I was jealous of her beautiful home, but most of all I was jealous of her husband. I spent my whole life chasing dreams and I believed that you'd suffered because of it. A part of me wanted to give you what you never had by making Gary your father. But the biggest part hoped that by lying I could break up their marriage and he would be with me. I was wrong, Pharrah, so wrong."

"I'm confused. His name is on my birth certificate and Grandma told me he's my father."

"Your grandmother believed that. Since I was giving you up for adoption anyway, I didn't see any reason to tell her the whole truth. So I let her believe that Gary was your father all these years."

"You let her believe a lie?" Pharrah looked puzzled.

"Let me explain. Everything I told you about me and Tino being in love and planning to marry was true."

"So the part about you growing up in Georgia and him playing basketball for Georgia Tech was a lie?" Pharrah asked.

Phoebe looked at Pharrah, stunned that her anger seemed to clear her speech, and nodded her head.

"So I came here to find out the truth and you just pile on more lies. Are you even telling me the truth now?"

Gary leaned forward in his chair, closer to them. "Pharrah, Mrs. Farmer gave me some information from a doctor. Tino died of a brain tumor just like the one that you had. She told me that those types of rare tumors are hereditary, but she didn't know until after he was dead. Tino inherited the tumor from his father and you inherited it from him."

"What does Mrs. Farmer have to do with this?" Pharrah asked.

"She's Tino's mother. Mrs. Farmer and her husband

adopted him after his natural father died while his birth mother was carrying him. You mean you didn't realize the connection?" Gary answered.

"When I found out about you, I thought Mom made Tino up. I assumed he was a fictional character created in her mind."

"No, honey. He was very real. He and I were best friends growing up. Yes, he loved basketball, but he played for Brown Bottom State University, not Georgia Tech. We were teammates."

"Pharrah, everything I told you about Tino was real except for where I met him. I knew my mom still thought Gary was your father and I was afraid of you finding her. That's why I lied about my hometown and her being alive. I just wanted to start over with just the two of us."

Phoebe reached for Pharrah's hand, but she pulled it away and turned to Gary. "So, you really are not my father?"

"No, honey, I'm not," he said solemnly.

"Pharrah, I didn't mean for everything to get so out of hand. I'm so sorry. Please forgive me," Phoebe pleaded.

"Forgive you?" Pharrah paused as she tried to gather her words. "Right now, I . . . I don't even want to look at you!" She got up abruptly from the sofa, grabbed her cane, and walked swiftly toward her room.

"Pharrah, wait." Phoebe stood to rush after her.

"Let her go, Phoebe. She needs some time," Phylicia said, grabbing her sister's arm.

Phoebe glared at Phylicia and Gary. "I hope you two are satisfied. I told her. Now she hates me. That's exactly what the two of you wanted, isn't it?"

"Phoebe, you know that's not true. Surely you are not trying to blame me and Gary for this mess," her sister answered.

Plopping down on the sofa again, Phoebe buried her face in her hands. "She's all I have. I can't lose my baby girl. I just can't," she sobbed.

Phylicia sat beside her and wrapped her arms around her. "You are not going to lose her. She's upset. That's understandable. But she loves you very much and she will forgive you. Just give her some time."

"How do you know that? I've hurt her so deeply."

"I know because I forgave you. Gary and I both have. It's going to be okay. You've made the first step by being completely honest with her. Once she gets over the initial shock and hurt, she'll come around. Come on. You've been through a lot today. Why don't you come upstairs and take a long, hot bath?"

Phoebe stared in the direction Pharrah had gone before finally following her sister upstairs. Gary sat still for several moments, lost in his own pain, before he got up, tiptoed to Pharrah's room and slipped quietly inside. He found Pharrah lying on her bed, consumed with tears. He sat down next to her and gently rubbed her back. "It's okay, honey. Don't cry. Daddy's here."

Pharrah sat up and wrapped her arms around him. "You're not my . . . my dad. I wish you were, but you're not," she sobbed.

"I may not be your natural father, but there is nothing stopping me from being your dad." She sat back and stared at him. "I love you as much as if you were my own flesh and blood, and that won't ever change."

"You don't have to say that. You don't have to pretend."

"Pharrah, you know me better than that. I'm not pretending. A dad is more than the person whose genes created you. He's the person who cares for you, and is there for you no matter what. He offers advice, encouragement, and even discipline, if needed. I've been those things to you for more than a year, and I will continue to be your dad for the rest of your life."

"What about this Tino person? I don't know who he was, but his blood runs through my veins. I can't just act as if it doesn't."

"I would never want you to. Like I told you earlier, Tino was my best friend, and I promise that I will always keep his memory alive in your life. I believe if he'd known about you, he'd approve of me stepping in to be your Dad in his place."

"Was he a good person? Would he have been a good father to me, if he'd lived?"

"He would've been the best. He was a good student. He was also a great friend and quite a character. He loved to make jokes, and kept everyone who knew him in stitches laughing all the time. Most importantly, he loved your mother. I was with him when he bought the ring. He was going to marry her. If nothing else, Pharrah, you now know that your conception was not part of a trick, but you were conceived in love."

"That's what Mom always told me when I was little. I never had any reason to doubt her."

"If you don't believe anything your mother says, you can believe that she loves you very much. As selfish as it was, I think she really wanted to do what was best for you."

"I know she did. As angry as I am about the lies, I know that she thought she was helping me. I just didn't want to lose my new family. Being a part of a real family here with you has been the best time of my whole life. I couldn't believe she was taking all of that away from me now."

"We are not going anywhere, Pharrah. You are still a part of this family. But now you also are going to get to be a part of another family. Mrs. Farmer is so anxious to welcome you. She has two other sons, your Uncle Jarvis and Uncle Wayne, and you have a bunch of cousins, too. So you are gaining a lot more family." Gary reached into his back pocket and pulled out his wallet. "Have you ever seen a picture of Tino?"

"No, Mom said she didn't have any."

Gary handed Pharrah a worn and tattered snapshot of himself with Tino in their college basketball uniforms. "You know, you actually have his smile."

She stared at the photo for several minutes, then Pharrah wrapped her arms tightly around Gary. "Thank you. I love you so much," she whispered.

"I love you too." He held tightly to her before finally letting her go and wiping the tears from her face. "Don't stop calling me Dad."

Three weeks later, Phoebe stood at the front door with her suitcases in hand, preparing to move out. She wasn't able to get another place as nice as her townhouse, but she'd managed to find a comfortable one-bedroom apartment only a few miles away. Even though Pharrah still was barely speaking to her, Phoebe wanted to be close to her. Earlier that morning, Li'l G and Gary moved what was left of her furniture from the storage building into the cramped space. A yard sale she had held the weekend before had netted her a nice profit and allowed her to get rid of the extra items that would not fit. Leaving the suitcases by the front door, she walked over and tapped on Pharrah's door. She waited patiently until she heard her yell, "Come in."

"Pharrah, I hope I'm not interrupting anything."

"Oh, it's you. What do you want?" she said icily, turning her attention back to the book she was reading.

"I just came to say good-bye. I'm moving out today."

"See ya!" Pharrah said with a wave of her hand.

"How many times do I have to apologize before you forgive me?"

Pharrah slowly put down the book she was reading and turned to look at her mother. "That's a good question, Mom. How many times? How many times are you going to lie to me and apologize and expect me to just get over it? For that matter, how many times are you going to lie to everyone who loves you and cares for you and then expect them to just get over it? My dad says . . . I mean Uncle Gary says that in the Bible it says we are to forgive seventy times seven. Mom, you are running dangerously close to topping out that number."

Phoebe dropped her head and stared at the carpet, unable to find a response to what Pharrah said. She knew she was right, but her pride would not allow her to admit it. Instead, she used her usual tactic of helplessness as a defense. "Well, I really am sorry. I guess I'll just go now since you obviously don't want to have anything else to do with me." She hung her head even lower and sniffed loudly.

"Before you go, I have something I want you to have." Pharrah stood up from her bed and went to her desk drawer. She opened it and pulled out a pamphlet, then handed it to her mother.

"What's this?"

"It's something . . . Uncle Gary gave me. It's all about forgiveness. He felt I needed to read it in order to be able to forgive you. I think you need to read it, too. Good-bye, Mom. Please close the door when you leave."

Phoebe stuffed the pamphlet deep inside her purse, then slowly walked out.

Chapter Twenty-Eight

Phylicia laid the phone back in the receiver as Gary walked out of the closet. Seeing the look of concern on her face, he stopped straightening his shirt collar and turned to her. "What's wrong, Phyllie?"

"I don't know, maybe nothing. I just tried to call Phoebe to invite her to homecoming service this morning but there's no answer."

"Honey, why didn't you call her sooner? You know Phoebe, she's probably sleeping late and has the ringer turned off."

"I tried to. I've called several times this week, and each time she's told me she was in the middle of something and would call back, but she never does. Honestly, I'm really worried about her."

"Worried? What on earth for?" Gary said as he wrapped his tie around his shirt collar and began tying it.

"I can't explain it. Maybe it's a twin thing. My sister is very unhappy right now. I feel like I need to do something to help her."

"Something like what?"

Phylicia walked over and finished tying her husband's tie, then straightened it for him before answering. "I wish I knew. Besides praying for her, I don't know what else I can do."

"Prayer is what Phoebe needs most right now. Just keep praying for her, we all will."

"I just wish Pharrah would forgive her. I think it would make her feel better."

"You know Pharrah; she's not one to hold a grudge. I'm sure she has forgiven her. She's just not ready to deal with her yet. Besides, that's not the answer for Phoebe." Gary sat down on the bed and reached for his shoes.

"What do you mean?"

"You've forgiven Phoebe, I've forgiven Phoebe, and Pharrah has forgiven Phoebe. But it's not our forgiveness that is going to turn Phoebe's life around. Even if she and Pharrah make up, until Phoebe asks God for forgiveness and truly means it, she is just going to keep making the same mistakes over and over."

"That's why I wanted her in church today. When we were girls, Momma and Daddy always made such a big deal over homecoming service."

"Really?" Gary asked.

"Yes. Our church always had a huge picnic on the grounds right after morning service. Former members and present members would come 'home' from wherever they were. There was always lots of singing, praising, and celebrating. Sometimes it went on well into the evening." Phylicia paused and stared dreamily into the air. "Daddy said it symbolized coming home to Christ for those who may have been backsliding or lost. Phoebe needs to come home."

Gary smiled at his wife's memory. "Why don't you try her again? Maybe she's awake by now."

* * *

"Hey, Phoebe, this is Phyllie. It's homecoming Sunday this morning at church. I was hoping you'd join us. After service we're having dinner in the social hall. There will be plenty of good Southern cooking. I know things are tense with you and Pharrah, but we all really want you to come. Service begins at eleven thirty. I hope to see you there."

Phoebe stared at the answering machine until her sister's voice was gone, then she turned back to the empty pill bottle resting in her lap.

After moving from Gary and Phylicia's home more than a week before, Phoebe felt herself spiraling downward deeper into depression. She felt that she'd lost her daughter for a third time and this time she couldn't get her back. Worse of all, she realized it was all her fault.

When she'd had to give Pharrah away as an infant, she'd blamed her parents for not allowing her to be a good mother. When she'd left her following Philomena's funeral, she was again able to shift the blame squarely off her shoulders. Even during the past year-and-a-half while living the lie of her being Gary's daughter, she'd blamed Pharrah for snooping and Gary for wanting to be involved. None of it had anything to do with her.

However, her first night alone in her small apartment, as she had stared into her bathroom mirror at the woman who looked back at and mocked her, she realized that this time she had driven her away. She believed that Pharrah no longer loved her or wanted her in her life, and for that reason, Phoebe sincerely wanted to die.

She'd called into work on Monday morning claiming to have the flu, and she'd partially convinced her body that she was sick. She did nothing but sleep off and on for three days, waking only to answer the phone and make up an excuse not to talk to Phylicia, drink a small amount of water, nibble on leftovers from the weekend, and then crawl back into hibernation. By the fourth day, she had decided that she wanted to sleep forever. She went into her medicine cabinet to search for the pain pills that her doctor prescribed following her car accident. Inside the bottle she found only two pills, so she called her pharmacist for a refill. After hanging up, she had downed the two pills available and returned to her bed for another two days.

When she awakened late Saturday evening she felt listless, woozy, and empty inside. She missed Pharrah and wanted to call her, but she knew she wouldn't want to talk to her. Instead, she climbed into her car and drove to the pharmacy, picked up more pain pills, and returned to her apartment.

Feeling alone, distraught, and confused, she sat on her floor Sunday morning staring at the pills. Slowly, she'd opened the bottle and poured them all into her hand just as the phone began ringing. She listened to Phylicia's message, then turned back to the task at hand.

Realizing she couldn't swallow that many pills without liquid, she laid them down on the coffee table and trudged to the kitchen for a glass of water. As she returned to the living room to sit down, she noticed him on the sofa. She shook her head for clarity before sitting on the floor and sighing in exasperation. "Not you again. Tino, leave me alone. You've been dead for twenty years and now all of sudden every time I look up there you are. Go away! This is all your fault!"

"There you go again. Blaming someone else for the mistakes you made. Why do you always do that?"

"You made me tell her. You, Gary, and Phylicia made me tell her the truth and what good did it do me? I've lost my daughter. I've lost her for good. Just go away!"

"I didn't make you do anything, Phoebe. I can't make

you do anything. My actions are inside your head. When you are ready for me to leave, I'll go."

"Then go now!" she screamed, but he just sat staring at her with a look of disappointment on his face. Phoebe put her head on her knees and began sobbing. "I love Pharrah. I love her more than anyone else in this world," she wailed.

"I think I know someone you love even more than Pharrah."

She raised her head swiftly and stared at him. "If you mean Gary, you're wrong. That was infatuation, it was never really love. I don't love anybody more than my baby."

"There you go again. You know things have gotten bad when you not only lie to others but you lie to yourself as well."

"I'm not lying! Everything I've done has been so that things could be better for Pharrah."

"Sure, Phoebe, you lied to her about who her father was so that you could break up your sister's marriage and end up with Gary. You knew just how happy that would make Pharrah. I know you love her, but you don't love anybody more than you love yourself."

"Shut up! Why don't you just shut up!" she screamed. She reached for a pillow on the couch and threw it at him. It bounced off of the cushions and landed on the coffee table, spilling the pills and the contents of her purse all over the floor.

Phoebe knelt down on the floor, crawling around like a junkie scrambling after each pill. As her fingers grasped the last one on the floor, Phoebe noticed that it was lying on top of a pamphlet; the one regarding forgiveness that Pharrah gave her the night she had moved out. Phoebe had never even bothered to read it, but suddenly it became the most interesting thing in the world to her. She laid the pills aside, picked it up, and began reading. As she silently perused the small writing, her eyes immediately dropped to a scripture that Pharrah had highlighted with a large yellow marker.

Acts 8:22—Repent therefore of this thy wickedness, and pray God, if perhaps the thought of thine heart may be forgiven thee.

Phylicia sat between Pharrah and Eva, with Li'l G on the opposite side of her, listening as the choir sang. Gary had just completed his sermon and the choir took over with a rousing song of praise. She allowed her foot to tap and nodded her head, but she was not at all involved in the music. Her mind could not let go of her sister. She'd called her again from the car, then from the church vestibule before entering service. As she'd sat through the morning's service, she'd hoped and prayed that Phoebe would get her message and join them. Throughout service, each time a new parishioner entered and walked down the aisle, she looked backward hoping it was Phoebe.

As the choir's song came to a close and they began to hum softly, Gary stepped forward to offer anyone who needed it a hand of fellowship or the opportunity to accept Christ as their personal savior. It was then that Phylicia decided she would not remain at the church for dinner. As soon as it was over and they'd greeted the parishioners, she was going to drive straight to Phoebe's apartment to check on her.

She closed her eyes, praying silently as she listened to Gary give the call. "Salvation is offered to all who will but come up here with me and take it. Jesus says, 'Come unto me, all ye that labour and are heavy laden, and I will give you rest.' The call is given, will you please come? Will you please come?" he said.

Phylicia prayed fervently along with her husband, but she wasn't giving a call to the congregation. She was calling her sister and praying that somehow, someway, she would be able to hear it.

Chapter Twenty-Nine

"Phoebe, open the door, it's me, Phyllie! Open the door, Phoebe!" Phylicia pounded harder and harder, but there was no answer. She peeped through the front window and saw that the living room was empty and the television was off. Consumed with fear and panic, she rushed to the manager's office to ask for a spare key.

The tired old man who rented the apartments looked at her over his wire-rimmed glasses. "Maybe you should just call her later. She must not be home," he said, not wanting to leave the comfort of his tattered and well-worn easy chair.

"You don't understand. I have called repeatedly. I've pounded on the door. Something is wrong. I need to get inside and get to my sister!"

"Y'all is twins, ain't ya? You sure do look alike," he said, not understanding the urgency of the situation.

"Yes, we are twins. And something is wrong with her. I can feel it. Just please let me into the apartment," she pleaded.

"Let me go find my keys. It won't take but a few minutes." The old man stood, and Phylicia could swear she heard his bones creak. He walked slowly but with purpose into the next room. Several moments later, he walked out jingling a large ring of keys. He held one out from the others. "All right, I think this is the one what fits her door," he said in a slow, easy drawl. "I'm gonna let you take my keys, but you best to brang them right back, ya hear me?"

"Yes, sir. I promise." Phoebe snatched the keys from his wrinkled brown hands and rushed out the door.

Once inside her sister's apartment, Phylicia felt a strange sense of calm overcome her. Quietly, she tiptoed through the living room, noticing how unkempt and disheveled it was. Her sister was a lousy housekeeper, so she felt relieved at the sight of normalcy. Slowly, she crept into Phoebe's bedroom, where she found her lying on her stomach across her bed. She had on her pajamas and socks with the covers thrown back in a jumbled pile. "Phoebe, are you okay? It's me, Phyllie," she called, but her sister did not stir.

Phylicia looked around the room and noticed a Bible lying on her sister's nightstand. She found that odd; she'd never known Phoebe to read the Bible. Right beside the Bible on the nightstand was an empty pill bottle. She rushed to the bed and flipped her sister over, then began shaking her violently. "Phoebe! Oh, my God, Phoebe, what did you do?"

As she shook her, she looked into her face. It was ashen; the color was washed completely from it. Her weave was matted against her head in a complete mess.

As Phylicia stared at her sister's face, continuing to shake her with tears streaming down her own, Phoebe suddenly opened her eyes. "Phyllie, what are you doing here?" she asked groggily.

"What did you do, Phoebe? Did you take all those pills? What did you do?" she screamed, still shaking her.

"Stop shaking me. Stop it!"

"No! Tell me what you did. Did you try to kill yourself? Talk to me, Phoebe."

"Phyllie, let me go!" Phoebe finally screamed while wrenching herself from her sister's grasp. "I only took two so I could get some sleep. I flushed the rest down the toilet," she said, trying to catch her breath from the shaking her sister had just given her.

"What? Why did you flush them?"

"I was afraid of what I'd do to myself if they were here. I thought about it, Phyllie. I really came close, but I realized I don't want to die. Right now I already feel dead. What I want is to feel alive again."

Phylicia reached over and pulled her sister into a hug as they both began to cry. "You will, honey. I promise you. You will."

As they hugged tightly, Phylicia suddenly wrinkled up her nose. "You smell awful. Have you taken a shower today?" she said, holding her sister and her nose firmly.

"I haven't taken a shower all week," Phoebe answered, then began giggling. Within a few seconds they both were laughing hysterically.

As the laughter finally subsided, Phylicia spoke. "Phoebe, what's wrong? Why are you sitting here not bathing or leaving your bed?"

"You know what's wrong. I've lost Pharrah. I don't know what to do to get her to forgive me. I've been so stupid, Phyllie."

"Honey, I know that Pharrah has forgiven you, but that's not all it's going to take to heal this family. Pharrah is afraid that this will happen again. She's afraid that once things are going good, you'll disappoint her again."

"I won't. I swear it. I would do anything for Pharrah. It's just that every time I think things are going on the right track, they suddenly jump off without any warning. Why do these things keep happening to me?"

"I can't answer that one. You have to find that answer for yourself. Come on, let's get you into the shower and then I'll take you out to eat. We can talk over dinner."

Reluctantly, Phoebe got up off the bed and walked into her bathroom to shower. While she waited, Phylicia quickly returned the manager's keys. When she returned, she decided to tidy up her sister's bedroom. She pulled the sheets from the bed, then took them to the laundry area before putting fresh sheets down and remaking the bed. When she was done, she fluffed the pillows and sat down looking around for something else to keep her busy, since she knew her sister would spend quite a while pampering herself after so many days without showering.

Feeling bored, Phylicia ventured into the living room and eventually the kitchen, getting rid of all of the empty take-out containers, paper plates, and cups. Since her sister still was not out of the bathroom, Phylicia pulled out the vacuum cleaner and vacuumed the carpet before finally returning to Phoebe's bedroom to wait for her. She sat down on the bed and once again noticed the Bible on the nightstand. It looked strangely familiar to her, so she decided to pick it up. Opening the front flap, Phylicia was surprised as she read aloud the name inside. "Gertrude Evangeline Carson."

Phylicia remembered searching for her mother's Bible in the days preceding her funeral, but she couldn't find it anywhere in the house. She had asked Gary and he'd told her that he'd taken it to her mother at the hospital. She was too weak to pick it up, so he'd read it to her. Several days after the funeral, Phylicia called the nurses' station to ask about her mother's belongings, and was told her sister picked them up. She wasn't speaking to Phoebe at the time, and after a while the Bible completely skipped her mind.

She flipped through the pages idly until something caught her attention. Inside the Bible she found a letter, and Phylicia suddenly remembered she was supposed to mail it for her mother the day she had become ill. The envelope was yellowed, but otherwise it was in perfect condition: sealed, stamped, and waiting to be delivered. Phylicia pulled it out and held it tightly inside her hands.

"I feel so much better now. Thanks for coming over and getting me up out of that bed. A good hot shower can do wonders for how a person feels," Phoebe said as she emerged from the bathroom, wrapped in her robe and rubbing a towel over her wet hair. She noticed her sister was not answering. "Phyllie, did you hear me?"

"Phoebe, your hair, I mean, your weave. I mean, what happened?" Phylicia asked, staring at her sister's real hair for the first time since she'd returned to Brown Bottom.

"The tracks were all matted to my head. I just went ahead and took them out then washed my hair. That's what took me so long. I'm sorry, I'll be ready to go in a few minutes." Phoebe turned toward the dresser and pulled out her blow dryer. She plugged it in before she noticed her sister staring at her lap and what looked like an envelope. "What's that you're holding?"

"Uhm, it's a letter."

"I can see that. What kind of letter?"

"It's . . . it's a letter from Mom."

"Really?" Phoebe put the dryer down and turned to stare at her sister. "Where'd you get it?"

"Uhm . . . it was inside the Bible."

"Well, don't just sit there with it. Open it up, Phyllie. Let's see what she had to say."

"I can't. I mean, I shouldn't. I mean, this letter is not for me it's for you, Phoebe. Mom wrote this letter to you before she died."

"Are you sure? I don't understand."

"I'm sorry, I forgot all about it. Mom wrote it the afternoon of her heart attack and she asked me to mail it for her. I was out running some errands and shopping for dinner when she called me on my cell phone. She said she wasn't feeling well and was going to take a nap, but before she did she wanted to know if I would mail this letter for her as soon as I got back. I told her to just leave it for me on the dining room table, but she said she didn't feel like leaving her room. Instead she told me she would put it in her Bible, in the fifteenth chapter of Luke. She told me to be sure to look for it there and mail it."

"But you never did?"

"No, when I got home Mom was having chest pains and Gary was on the phone calling for an ambulance. After that everything just happened so fast. Later, she asked me if I'd mailed the letter and I nodded my head to keep her quiet because she was so frail. I planned to do it the next day and didn't want to worry her. When I finally remembered, I couldn't find the Bible."

"I guess I should have told you. The hospital called the hotel while we were having breakfast the morning after she passed. You'd stepped into the bedroom to finish packing so I took the call. You were already doing so much taking care of the funeral arrangements and everything and I just wanted to help. I asked Li'l G to take me by the hospital to pick up her belongings. By the time we got back to the house, it was full of family, and I just put everything inside my suitcases without even looking at it. I had no idea that Pharrah was going to show up and everything was going to get so out of control. I've had the Bible since then, but I had it packed away until I moved here. I never had a chance to get the hat and shoes, so this was my keepsake of Mom. It's just been sitting on my nightstand. I've never even opened it."

"Here, I think you should sit down and read this."

Phylicia handed the letter to her sister, then scooted over on the bed so she could sit next to her. She watched with anticipation as her sister held the envelope in her hands for several moments, staring at it, before she slowly opened it and began to read it out loud:

> *Dear Phoebe,*
> *I know you are surprised to get a letter from your old mother. It's not often that I write letters anymore. It seems everyone has gotten used to communicating with phone calls and such. Your sister bought me a cell phone, but I still have to get my grandkids to help me use it properly. So I decided that an old-fashioned letter was the best way for me to tell you what I need to say.*
> *A little more than two years ago, I got a phone call from a young woman who told me she is your daughter, Pharrah. She called because she was looking for her father, and I told her that Gary Morgan was indeed her father. I know it surprises you that I've known about her living with you this long and never mentioned it, but I felt keeping the skeletons of the past a secret was the best thing for everyone involved. Your sister and her husband have a good, strong marriage, and they are very happy. I was afraid this young woman and the truth about who fathered her could spoil all that, so I kept it to myself.*

Phoebe paused to look at her sister for a moment. Phylicia nodded her head encouraging her to continue reading.

Pharrah and I have continued to talk at least once a week since then, and I must say you've done an amazing job in raising her on your own. She seems to be a very intelligent and put-together young woman. She loves to talk and she tells me practically everything that goes on in her life. I know that you are married now and all about the years she's spent with you. I'm so sorry I've missed so much.

About a month ago while chatting away, Pharrah told me she'd given blood at a drive sponsored by the Red Cross. She went on and on about how glad they were to get a student with AB as her blood type since it's so rare, especially in African Americans. I guess at that point I should have told her that it's so rare that I'd never met anyone with that blood type, not even the man I'd told her was her father. We found out when Gary had gall bladder surgery six years ago that he is O +.

The next time we talked, I asked Pharrah about the man you'd always told her was her real father. As soon as she said his name I immediately remembered the tall, lanky kid who died suddenly while out at the movies. I also remembered how often I came home and found him in my kitchen eating a snack, or sneaking out of my back door. I realized that I was wrong, Phoebe, not just about who Pharrah's father is, but about everything.

Phoebe suddenly stopped reading as she became overcome with tears. She sat weeping for several moments. "I can't finish this. Take it." She tossed the letter in her sister's lap.

"Do you want me to continue for you?" Phylicia asked.

Phoebe nodded her head and waited for her sister to begin reading where she had left off.

While speaking with her, I realized that I'd been a fool-
ish old woman. I guess you could say I was a foolish
young woman, too. I was so intent on protecting Phylicia
that I forgot all about you and your feelings. I'm sorry I
never allowed you to talk or have a say in what we did re-
garding the baby. I'm sorry I didn't ask you what was
wrong when you were moping around the house, instead
of assuming you were jealous of your sister. I'm sorry we
sent you away, but most of all I'm sorry you felt you had
to run away and hide from your family.

It's time for you to come home, Phoebe. It's time for you
to come home and tell everyone the truth. Maybe I should
have told Pharrah the truth myself once I realized it, but I
felt I'd meddled too much already. I want a chance to
know my granddaughter and your sister should know her
niece. I know you ran because you felt you had to, but I
know the truth, Phoebe, and I wish I'd allowed you to tell
it to me so many years ago.

It's not too late for us. You can tell the truth and you
can finally come home.

I love you dearly. Mom

Phylicia slowly closed the letter and placed it back inside the envelope before giving it back to Phoebe. She
reached over to the nightstand and handed her sister a
tissue, then kept a few for herself. They both sat there for
several minutes weeping and wiping their noses. Finally,
Phoebe spoke. "I can't believe Mom knew. In the hospital, that is what she was trying to tell me. That's the truth
she wanted me to tell you about Pharrah. I assumed it
was the truth she'd always believed."

"She thought you'd read the letter. I guess that's why
she kept asking for you every day. She thought you'd
read it and was wondering why you had not come home.

I'm sorry, Phoebe. I should have mailed it like she asked me to."

"No, it's not your fault. With everything that was going on I'm not surprised you forgot. But she was wrong about something. It wasn't just the secrets that made me run, it was the jealousy. Not just over Gary, but over everything. I always felt like Momma and Daddy loved you more. I always felt like I wasn't good enough to be their daughter."

"What made you feel that way? Daddy spoiled us both rotten. There was hardly anything you could ask of him that he'd refuse either of us. Momma was always strict, but we both had the exact same curfew, the same chores. The rules were always the same."

"I know, Phyllie. I realize now it wasn't Momma and Daddy who made the difference; it was me. You kept the rules and I always broke them. So I was always in trouble and you never were. That's why Gary loved you. Because you were what a young woman should be. And it's why Tino loved me, because I was easy and promiscuous. I wanted a righteous man, but I wasn't willing to be a righteous woman."

"Phoebe, you make yourself out to sound so horrible. We all make mistakes."

"I know, but it's time I started facing mine instead of blaming everyone else for them." Phoebe turned to face her sister, then took her hands. "We've been getting along great for a while now, but there's something that I should have said a long, long time ago." Phoebe paused and took a deep breath. "I'm sorry about what I did with Gary. I'm sorry for tricking him and I'm sorry for disrespecting your relationship. I was wrong, Phyllie. Please forgive me?"

"But, Phoebe, you already apologized."

"Not really. I only said I was sorry because you were

apologizing to me. I said I was sorry for everything instead of being truthful and admitting everything I'd done. I didn't even understand what it meant to be truly remorseful. But I do now. I'm so sorry I hurt you. I promise I will never do anything to hurt you again."

Phylicia reached out and hugged her sister. "I forgave you a long time ago, but thank you for saying the words."

"This letter made me realize how blessed I am to have this family. After all of that, Momma still wanted me to come home. She didn't fuss about me not telling the truth. There's no lecture about having sex with Tino. She understood and still loved me. I never believed she would." Phoebe held the letter to her breast and sniffed loudly. "Thank you, Mommy. I love you," she whispered into the air.

Phylicia abruptly got up and reached for the Bible she'd left lying on the bed earlier. She began thumbing through the pages until she again arrived at the fifteenth chapter of Luke. She skimmed down to the eleventh chapter and began to read aloud.

Jesus continued "There was a man who had two sons. The younger one said to his father, 'Father, give me my share of the estate.' So he divided his property between them. Not long after that, the younger son got together all he had, set off for a distant country and there squandered his wealth in wild living. After he had spent everything, there was a severe famine in that whole country, and he began to be in need. So he went and hired himself out to a citizen of that country, who sent him to his fields to feed pigs. He longed to fill his stomach with the pods that the pigs were eating, but no one gave him anything. When he came to his senses, he said, 'How many of my father's hired men have food to spare, and here I am starving to death! I will set out and go back to my father and say to him Father, I have sinned against heaven and against you. I am no longer worthy to be called your son; make me like one of your hired men. So he got up and went to his father. But while he was still a long way off, his father saw him and was filled with compassion for him; he ran to his son, threw his arms around him and kissed him.

The son said to him, 'Father, I have sinned against heaven and against you. I am no longer worthy to be called your son. But the father said to his servants, 'Quick! Bring the best robe and put it on him. Put a ring on his finger and sandals on his feet. Bring the fattened calf and kill it. Let's have a feast and celebrate. For this son of mine was dead and is alive again; he was lost and is found. So they began to celebrate.

Phylicia stopped reading as she began to cry again.

Phoebe sat staring at her, wondering what it all meant before finally responding. "That was me wasn't it? The lost son was me?"

"Yes, it was, but there was another son," Phylicia said, then she took a moment to compose herself before continuing to read the Bible passage.

Meanwhile, the older son was in the field. When he came near the house, he heard music and dancing. So he called one of the servants and asked him what was going on. 'Your brother has come,' he replied, 'and your father has killed the fattened calf because he has him back safe and sound.' The older brother became angry and refused to go in. So his father went out and pleaded with him. But he answered his father, 'Look! All these years I've been slaving for you and never disobeyed your orders. Yet you never gave me even a young goat so I could celebrate with my friends. But when this son of yours who has squandered your property with prostitutes comes home, you kill the fattened calf for him!' 'My son,' the father said, 'you are always with me, and everything I have is yours. But we had to celebrate and be glad, because this brother of yours was dead and is alive again; he was lost and is found.

Phylicia stopped reading as her tears took her voice away. Phoebe reached over and hugged her sister tightly. "I'm not lost anymore, Phyllie. I'm home," she said, trying to comfort her.

"You don't understand. This letter wasn't just for you. It was for me, too. Mom didn't just randomly pick the fifteenth chapter of Luke to place the letter in. She wanted me to find it there. This part was for me. You were the lost son, and I was the son who couldn't welcome you home." Phylicia paused and wiped at her tears. "Mom knew I wouldn't be glad to see you. She knew I would have a hard time accepting your presence in my life again. So she asked me to mail the letter, and she placed it into the Bible at the exact verse I would need in order to cope with the situation."

"I don't understand, Phyllie."

"Even before I found out about Pharrah, I wasn't happy to see you. We were fighting almost from the moment you walked in the door. I was jealous that Mom kept asking for you to come home after all the years you'd been gone. Then after she died and I found that life insurance policy, I was so angry and hurt. I thought Mom had forgotten all about me and rewarded you. She knew, Phoebe; she knew exactly what we both needed to hear."

"She really did seem to know exactly who we both are."

"I wish we'd found this letter a long time ago. I think it could have made everything we've been through so much easier."

"No, Phyllie. I think today was the day. It was the exact day, time, and place that we both needed to see it," she answered, and pulled her sister into a long hug. "Everyone has forgiven me. First Momma, then you and Gary, even Pharrah has, but I don't think that's enough."

"What do you mean, Phoebe?"

"Listening to you read those verses, I realized that it's not just about a father and his lost sons or our mother and her lost daughters. It's about a lost soul finding her way back to God. It's about me finding my way back to God."

Phylicia stared at her sister, stunned by her words.

"Yeah, I know, you didn't think I was listening all those years in Sunday School, did you?" They both laughed before Phoebe continued. "I haven't asked God to forgive me, Phyllie. I know that I should have, but I was afraid."

"Afraid of what?"

Phoebe shrugged her shoulders. "I don't know." She stared down at the floor. "I was just afraid."

Phylicia got up off the bed and knelt down on the floor, then she reached out her hand, inviting her sister to join her. "I'm right here with you. There's nothing to be afraid of. We'll ask him together, okay?"

Slowly, Phoebe stood up then knelt beside her sister. "Should I close my eyes? Are we going to pray?" she asked.

"We are going to talk to God, and you can close your eyes if you feel more comfortable that way, but you don't have to."

"Okay." Phoebe closed her eyes and waited. She knelt with them closed for several seconds before peeping out at her sister. "Go ahead, aren't you going to start praying?"

"If you want me to, I can start." She gently squeezed Phoebe's hand.

"Heavenly Father, my sister and I come to you with heavy hearts. We come to ask for your forgiveness. We come to ask you to forgive the sin of jealousy we've felt in our hearts. We ask you to forgive us of all of our sins. We thank you for your son Jesus Christ who died on the cross for us." Phylicia nudged her sister.

"I don't know what to say," she whispered.

"Confess your sins."

"Uh, I confess my sins."

"Now ask for forgiveness for them."

"Just ask? That's all I have to do? I don't have to say a bunch of Father Gods and Oh Heavenly Fathers first?"

"If you are earnest and sincere, Phoebe, that's all you have to do."

"Uhm, I confess my sins and I ask your forgiveness," Phoebe said as she felt her sister give her hand another reassuring squeeze, urging her to keep going.

"Uhm . . . I'm not really sure what to say next, God, except that I truly am sorry for everything that I've said and done, and I thank you. I thank you for saving Pharrah's life and for bringing me back home to my sister and my family. Uhm . . . I'm going to do my best to do things the way you want me to from now on. I'm going to need some help, but I promise you I will be trying. Thank you for listening, God."

"Amen," Phylicia whispered.

Epilogue

Graduation Day

Pharrah turned to look at herself in the mirror after putting on her long, black robe. She adjusted the hanging gold tassels that denoted her as an honors graduate, then stepped into her low-heeled black pumps. She no longer needed a cane for walking, but she wasn't taking any chances with high heels on such a special day. After four years of college and another year of grueling rehabilitation and chemotherapy following her brain tumor, she was finally on her way to her college graduation.

As she reached for her cap, she heard a light tapping at her hotel room door. "It's open," she yelled.

"Wow, you look great!"

Pharrah turned to see Li'l G standing in her doorway. He was hardly little anymore, standing six feet four inches tall only a few months after his eighteenth birthday.

"Thanks. Where is everybody else?"

"They've already left for the stadium. I have been assigned as your driver and escort," he answered. Li'l G did a mock English bow, then he crooked his arm for her to link into it.

"I'm ready. Will you carry my cap for me? I don't want to put it on until I'm in line with the other graduates." Pharrah linked her arm into Li'l G's, and followed him out to the car.

The roar of the crowd was almost deafening when Pharrah and her classmates stood to their feet as the dean of students announced their department. Pharrah's entire family stood, waving signs and cheering so loudly they seemed to take over the boisterous crowd. She was overwhelmed that in the stands were not only her mom, Aunt Phylicia, and Uncle Gary, along with Li'l G and Eva, but also her grandmother, Mrs. Farmer, and her uncles Jarvis and Wayne. Jarvis brought along his wife and three kids to add to the cheering section, while the recently divorced Wayne had his two sons in tow. She was overwhelmed that when she began college she was an only child with just a mom; now she had a huge extended family.

Following the ceremony, Li'l G was standing by the stadium gates waiting to take Pharrah back to the hotel, when she emerged. "Now, where is everybody?" she asked again.

"I don't know." He shrugged. "Dad just told me to make sure you had a ride back. Is something wrong?"

"Well, not really, I just thought they'd all want to greet me or something," she said as she looked around at her other classmates' families hugging and congratulating them.

Li'l G shrugged his broad shoulders again. "Well, I'm here, big sis," he said with a wink and a smile, and then bent down to hug her tightly. "I'm real proud of you." She hugged him back, grateful that after everything they'd been through, Li'l G and Eva still considered her their sister. She looked around at the other graduates and their families again before following Li'l G to the car and getting inside.

They arrived at the Courtyard Marriott where the entire family was staying for the weekend. Pharrah got out of the car and walked through the lobby toward the elevator. "Hey, wait up a second. I need to get something before we go up," Li'l G called after her.

"Go ahead. I'll catch up with you later," she answered as she pushed the button for the elevator.

"No. I mean, don't go up without me. This will only take a second. I left my, uhm, my MP3 player by the pool and I need to get it from the manager," he said, walking over to the desk.

Pharrah did not notice him winking at the bellhop who then motioned for them to follow him. They walked down a short hallway to a large party room and the bellhop opened the door. Li'l G walked in, then turned around and urged her to follow.

"Surprise!" she heard in unison as soon as she stepped inside. Before she could catch her breath, a mountain of pink and green balloons fell from the ceiling, filling the entire room. She looked around at her family and many of her friends who'd graduated the year before, including Kelli. Their faces were lit up with huge smiles. On the wall near the back corner a banner hung, proclaiming "Congratulations Pharrah we love you!"

Her mother was the first to approach her and pull her out of her stunned daze. She hugged her tightly. "Congratulations, baby!" Phoebe said. Pharrah hugged her back, followed by a long line of everyone else in the room offering congratulations and bearing gifts. She could not remember ever being so happy in her whole life.

The rest of the evening was filled with music, dancing,

and lots of good food. Her family had arranged for an exquisite party, complete with a DJ, a soul food buffet, and lots of fun. Pharrah posed in her graduation gown for pictures with her cousins, her aunts and uncles, her friends, and even with a busboy and a waitress. Everyone had to get in on the festivities.

As the third hour of the party approached, Gary motioned for the DJ to turn off the music and he, Phoebe, Phylicia, Jarvis, and Wayne stepped onto the dance floor with a cordless microphone. Gary was the first to speak.

"Pharrah, I just wanted to offer you congratulations, and best wishes for the coming years as you begin medical school this coming fall. We are all going to miss you but we understand that Duke University is a pretty good school." The crowd chuckled and he paused for a moment. "Your real dad couldn't be here today, but I know that if he could, he'd be as proud of you as we are at this moment. I'm honored to be able to stand in for him today, and in your life." Gary suddenly handed the microphone to Wayne as he became overcome with emotion.

"Pharrah, today I'm a proud uncle. Over the years I've missed my baby brother so much, but when I look into your face I realize that he lives on. You are beautiful and talented, and as Gary said, we are all very proud of you today."

"You guys are getting too mushy," Mrs. Farmer suddenly said as she stepped onto the dance floor, taking the microphone away from Wayne. "And you men say we women are emotional," Mrs. Farmer joked as the crowd laughed loudly. "Anyway, Pharrah, what they are trying to say is we love you. So your uncles and I, along with Reverend Gary, Phylicia, and your mom, got together and bought you a graduation gift from your family." She held out her hands, offering Pharrah an envelope.

With her hands shaking, Pharrah opened it and pulled out the card, then read it aloud:

You are about to embark on one of life's greatest adventures and we wanted you to be able to travel in style. We love you. Your Family.

Confused, Pharrah searched the envelope for more, but it was empty.

"Follow me, baby," Phoebe said as she led her out of the side exit doors into the parking lot. Pharrah was flabbergasted to see a brand new canary yellow convertible sports car tied with a huge green bow. She jumped up and down, screaming as she ran toward it.

Hours later, Phoebe sat in a chair holding her daughter's diploma in her arms, snuggling it. "Phoebe, aren't you coming upstairs? The hotel staff wants to start cleaning up in here." Phylicia asked.

"I want to wait for Pharrah to come back. You go on up. I'll be fine."

"Are you sure? She loves that car. It might be hours before she decides to stop joy riding."

Phoebe looked up at her sister. "She did love it, didn't she? Thank you guys for helping me get it for her."

"No thanks needed. It was a great gift idea. Now she won't have to depend on public transportation while in medical school, and she'll have a way to get home if she wants to visit."

"I'm just glad I could finally do something special for her. She's worked hard for this day and she deserved for it to be perfect."

"It has been absolutely perfect, Mom." Phoebe and Phylicia looked up as Pharrah rushed breathlessly into the room, followed by Li'l G.

"That car is awesome! Hey, Mom, when can I get one?" Li'l G asked.

"You'll get one when you graduate college summa cum laude just like Pharrah, and not a moment sooner," Phylicia teased. "Now come on, it's late and we've got to drive back to Brown Bottom early tomorrow morning so we don't miss church service."

"All right, I'm coming. Good night, Aunt Phoebe; good night, Pharrah," he called as he followed his mother out.

Pharrah plopped down in a chair near her mother before noticing she was staring at her diploma. "What are you doing, Mom?" she asked.

"I can't stop looking at it. I'm just so proud of you. I know you've heard that a million times today, but it's true." Phoebe opened the cover of the diploma and began reading aloud. "Pharrah Lynn Carson, Bachelor of Science degree. It's unbelievable."

"You know what, Mom? I'm proud of you, too."

"Me? Whatever for? I barely got out of high school."

"No, I don't mean that. I mean everything. The change in you these past months has been amazing. You are the woman I remember when I was a little girl. The woman who picked me up in Florida and told me she would always love me. You don't know how scared and alone I felt when Mom Philomena died, but you came in and made me feel safe again. You told me I'd never have to feel alone again."

"I had to. You are my baby."

"I know, Mom, but after my illness last year, I felt scared and alone again. I know I had Dad Gary and Aunt Phylicia, but I missed you so much. I missed the woman you used to be. I needed you, but you weren't able to be there for me."

"Pharrah, I'm so sorry for all that."

"No, Mom, you don't need to apologize. I understand.

Thank you, Mom, thank you for today and for everything."

"Don't thank me. I was lost for so long."

"I know that, but I'm just so happy that you're back. Everything about you says you are a new woman. You've taken that awful weave out and your hair is gorgeous and healthy. You still dress beautifully, but now it doesn't seem like you are advertising. Aunt Phylicia is ecstatic at how helpful you've been at the church working with the women's ministry, and you've been so supportive of me through my recovery when the chemo made me barf and the exhausting physical therapy. Even when I had setbacks you wouldn't let me give up. You stood right by me. I know I could not have gotten through it without you."

Phoebe looked at her daughter and blushed. "Oh, stop it. I'm not all that," she laughed.

"Well, you are to me. Today has been absolutely wonderful. Seeing all of those faces cheering me on at graduation, this incredible party, and the new car just made it everything I'd always dreamed it could be. It was a perfect day, Mom. I love you." Pharrah leaned in and kissed her mother gently on the cheek.

"I love you too, Pharrah. Now, Phyllie's right, we have an early drive in the morning. You may have a new sports car, but we don't want you getting any tickets, now do we? Let's go upstairs." Phoebe answered as they gathered their things.

As they neared the door, Phoebe looked back into the room, then suddenly stopped. "Uhm, I forgot my purse. Go hold the elevator and I'll be right out."

"Sure, Mom."

As soon as Pharrah was gone, Phoebe walked over and smiled at him. "I haven't seen you in a while."

"I'm here to say good-bye, Phoebe," Tino answered.

"Good-bye?"

"Yes, graduation was beautiful, but it's time for me to go."

"But . . . I don't understand."

"I'll always be here, Phoebe, in your heart and in your mind. When you look into Pharrah's eyes, you'll see me there. But you're stronger now. You don't need me to push you. You've found your place with our daughter and with God. The prodigal daughter has finally come home."

He blew her a kiss, then Phoebe watched him fade away into the wallpaper as a busboy turned on all the lights and began clearing away the remnants of the party. She held her head high and walked out, joining Pharrah by the elevator.

"Is everything all right, Mom?"

"It's fine. Let's go," she answered.

THE END

Reader's Group Guide Questions

1. Did you feel the characters of Phoebe and Phylicia depicted a real relationship between sisters? If not, why? If so, why?

2. Were the problems the characters faced believable, in that they reminded you of yourself or someone that you know?

3. *Prodigal* has been described as a story of a "bad" twin and a "good" twin. Who would you describe as the good one or the bad one?

4. Was there any point in the book that your opinion changed regarding which one was the good or bad one?

5. What emotions did *Prodigal* stir in you as a reader? Did you laugh? Did you cry? Were you angry? Were you disappointed?

6. At what specific points in the book did you feel these emotions?

7. Which sister did you sympathize most with? Phylicia as her seemingly perfect life was shattered; or Phoebe who constantly coveted what her sister had?

8. *Prodigal* has a theme of forgiveness. Phoebe, Phylicia, Pharrah, and Gary had to forgive extreme hurts from a loved one. What was a time in your life when you struggled with forgiving someone?

9. Did reading *Prodigal* prompt you to search your heart for forgiveness of someone?

10. Mrs. Farmer met her husband through prison ministry. What are your views on prison ministry?

11. If your church has a prison ministry, have you been involved? What has been some of your experiences?

12. Does Mrs. Farmer's situation encourage you or discourage you regarding prison ministry?

13. What did you think of the relationship between Gary and Li'l G, in whom Gary confided twice?

14. Tino appears in Phoebe's head and Gary's dream. What did you think of this element of the story, using a deceased person to communicate with the living?

15. God speaks to us all in different ways. Was there a place in *Prodigal* that may have been a minor point that you felt God was speaking directly to you?

Biography

Zaria Garrison was born and raised in Greenville County, South Carolina. She began writing as a teenager. In 2005, her first novel, *Baring it All*, was published by Publish America under her birth name Gena L. Garrison.

However, as she continued writing she felt she could no longer write stories that involved explicit sex and violence. She could only write what God told her to write. God gave her stories of everyday people who have faults, struggles, and sometimes pain, but they continue to trust in God to get them through. With God's guidance, a new author was born. Following her transformation, as He did with Saul, God gave her a new name, "Zaria," which means new beginnings.

Zaria spends her free time with her son and their pet Pekingese in their home in Greer, South Carolina.

Urban Christian His Glory Book Club!

Established January 2007, **UC His Glory Book Club** is another way by which to introduce to the literary world, Urban Book's much-anticipated new imprint, **Urban Christian** and its authors. We are an online book club supporting Urban Christian authors by purchasing, reading and providing written reviews of the authors' books that are read. *UC His Glory* welcomes both men and women of the literary world who have a passion for reading Christian based fiction.

UC His Glory is the brainchild of Joylynn Jossel, Author and Executive Editor of Urban Christian and Kendra Norman-Bellamy, Copy Editor for Urban Christian. The book club will provide support, positive feedback, encouragement and a forum whereby members can openly discuss and review the literary works of Urban Christian authors. In the future, we anticipate broadening our spectrum of services to include: online author chats, author spotlights, interviews with your favorite Urban Christian author(s), special online groups for *UC His Glory Book Club* members, ability to post reviews on the website and amazon.com, membership ID cards, *UC His Glory* Yahoo Group and much more.

Even though there will be no membership fees attached to becoming a member of *UC His Glory Book Club*, we do expect our members to be active, committed and to follow the guidelines of the Book Club.

UC His Glory members pledge to:

- Follow the guidelines of *UC His Glory Book Club.*
- Provide input, opinions, and reviews that build up, rather than tear down.
- Commit to purchasing, reading and discussing featured book(s) of the month.
- Agree not to miss more than three consecutive online monthly meetings.
- Respect the Christian beliefs of *UC His Glory Book Club.*
- Believe that Jesus is the Christ, Son of the Living God

We look forward to the online fellowship.

Many Blessings to You!

Shelia E Lipsey
President
UC His Glory Book Club

**Visit the official Urban Christian Book Club website at *www.uchisglorybookclub.net*